BLOOD REVOLUTION

GOD WARS SERIES, BOOK THREE

CONNIE SUTTLE

Print Second Edition (2018)
Print ISBN: 1-63478-053-1
Print ISBN-13: 978-1-63478-053-7
eBook ISBN: 1-93975-903-X
eBook ISBN-13: 978-1-93975-903-0

Published by:
SubtleDemon Publishing, LLC
PO Box 95696
Oklahoma City, OK 73143

Cover art by Renée Barratt @ The Cover Counts

To Walter, Joe, Larry, Lee, Dianne, Sarah and Mark.
Thank you.

And for Kathy, Beth, Albert and Lisa F. You are always in my thoughts.

ACKNOWLEDGMENTS

As always, this book is the result of collaboration. If it weren't for the support of my editor, my cover artist and my beta readers, it would be less than it is. All mistakes, as usual, are mine and no other's.

About the Author:
Connie Suttle lives in Oklahoma with her husband and a conglomerate of cats. They have finally banded together to make their demands, which has proven disconcerting to all humans involved.

You may find Connie in the following ways:
Facebook: Connie Suttle Author
Twitter: @subtledemon
Website and Blog: subtledemon.com

High Demon Series:

Demon Lost

Demon Revealed

Demon's King

Demon's Quest

Demon's Revenge

Demon's Dream

God Wars Series:

Blood Double

Blood Trouble

Blood Revolution

Blood Love

Blood Finale

Saa Thalarr Series:

Hope and Vengeance

Wyvern and Company

Observe and Protect*

First Ordinance Series:

Finder

Keeper

BlackWing

SpellBreaker

WhiteWing

~

R-D Series:

Cloud Dust

Cloud Invasion

Cloud Rebel

~

Latter Day Demons Series:

Hot Demon in the City

A Demon's Work is Never Done

A Demon's Due

~

Seattle Elementals Series:

Your Money's Worth

Worth Your While*

~

BlackWing Pirates Series

MindSighted

MindMage

MindRogue

MindMaster*

~

Black Rose Sorceress Series

The Rose Mark

Rose and Thorn

Black Rose Queen

Queen of Thorns and Roses

Future Wars Series

Buffer Zone

Black Zone*

Other Titles from SubtleDemon Publishing:

Malefactor

Transgressor

Underhanded*

by Joe Scholes

*Forthcoming

CHAPTER 1

*L*issa's Journal

She's sleeping, now. I had to heal skull fractures. Karzac's mindspeech was relieved and grumpy at the same time. Only he might pull off those emotions in mindspeech and I wasn't sure what to make of that.

What happened? Who threw her against a wall?

I have no idea. I was hoping you'd know.

Belen is dancing around like he's drunk, though, I pointed out. He'd had some news and I was waiting for him to say what it was. He was doing the Nameless One version of a touchdown celebration in my study, and I was only waiting for Karzac to tell me my sister was all right before I demanded (as much as I could) that Belen tell me what he knew.

Your sister is fine for the moment, and as you have no idea how she was injured, I will have guards posted around her suite and outside her balcony, Karzac informed me. *Go. Do what you must. Ask Belen what you wish to know.*

Thanks, honey. I leaned forward and pulled Karzac's head down for a kiss. I had my sister back, things were looking up at the moment and I felt happy for the first time in months. Karzac's mouth settled over mine, with a promise that later, he'd be in my bed. I didn't mind that in the least.

≈

Gavin waited outside Breanne's room until he was sure she was alone before folding inside. Lissa and Karzac had left seconds earlier, while guards took their positions outside the door and on the balcony.

"I should have done this the first time," Gavin murmured, bending down and kissing Breanne on the cheek before lifting a slender arm and tucking a teddy bear beneath it. "You saved me. You saved Lissa, and you saved my son. I can never repay those things, but should you have need, all you have to do is ask."

Breanne moaned softly as a finger trailed down her cheek. "Hush, my pretty child. Sleep now. Sleep."

≈

"She destroyed the army?"

"Most of it, yes."

"But how?" I stared at Belen. His face was beaming so brightly I could barely look at it.

"I cannot explain it. I am the one lesser god allowed to know it. Only Breanne can recreate that event, should it become necessary, and the information will not be leaked to others. She will be hunted, now, actively."

"But you just said the army was dead."

"I did, and it is. A few individuals escaped. Most importantly, however, is that the majority of the army is gone. Their general, however, remains."

"General?" I gaped at Belen.

"Yes. That is how we describe him, but that does not adequately define what he is. Now that most of his minions have been destroyed, he will become more devious and far more dangerous."

"You're scaring me. I thought we had cause for celebration," I pointed out. I was ready to celebrate. Ready to be happy. Obviously, that wasn't to be.

"There is cause to celebrate, beloved. I feared that the army would be nearly impossible to defeat and take many lives and much of our time in a prolonged war. Your sister managed to defeat them. Now, we must turn our efforts to their commander."

"How strong is he?" I blinked at Belen.

"Even with only a few left in his command, he may still hold the power to destroy us all."

Breanne's Journal

I woke in my old bedroom on Le-Ath Veronis. My head hurt, and that wasn't a surprise. What was a surprise was that my skull was in one piece after it had come in forceful contact with one of Lissa's palace walls. A teddy bear lay in the crook of an arm, too, and I had no idea how it had gotten there.

The bear was a handsome one, and soft. I'd never had a bear. Ever. I hugged it to me and hoped the headache would disappear soon.

"Awake?" Karzac appeared from nothing beside my bed. "Don't worry, vampires have acute hearing," he grinned. "The guards outside heard you stirring and notified me."

"Why am I here?" I hugged my bear tighter.

"Because I had to heal skull fractures, that's why," Karzac's grin disappeared quickly.

"But why was I tossed back here?" I asked petulantly. Le-Ath Veronis was the last place I wanted to be. Too much pain had happened inside my sister's palace, yet that's where I'd been flung after the brief consideration of ending my corporeal self.

"Breanne, stop thinking about that fucking book." I jerked my head up at Karzac's words—and the profanity. He didn't employ it often—I knew that from past readings.

"I didn't know they took pictures," I sighed helplessly, burying my face against soft, faux fur.

"So many things should not have been," Karzac settled on the side of my bed. "So many blows should not have fallen. So many wounds cannot be healed completely."

He was right—there were scars on my spirit that would never disappear. Brief thoughts of Hank—and Jayson—crowded my mind and I hunched my shoulders against the pain of it.

Jayson likely knew about the book, and that was hard enough to swallow. Hank usually knew whatever Jayson knew, and that meant he'd been aware of the book, too. My heart squeezed in my chest and I hyperventilated. Karzac's fingers were against my forehead quickly, and I was unconscious.

"Terry's still keeping the house up for her. He has it cleaned every three months and makes sure the lawn service is paid," Jayson sighed.

Hank sat across from Jayson in a booth at Bogey's. "It's been over two years," he muttered.

"She's probably dead," Jayson wiped a hand over his face. "The old man just blusters and makes excuses every time somebody points out that Breanne's disappearance happened right after the book was released. Barry Stokes got hit hard, too, when a copy of that letter he sent out telling Breanne he didn't want her associated with Mercy Crossings anymore was published in a competitor's newspaper."

"Your mom and dad still split up?" Hank asked.

"Yeah. Mom won't talk to Dad. She's at the Tahoe house and refuses even to talk to Dad's assistant. She asked me the other day if I missed Bree. How do you respond to that?"

"With the truth?" Hank chewed on two drink straws.

"Hell, it squeezes my heart every time I think about her. Part of me feels responsible, when I had nothing to do with that. I talked to my lawyer, too, and he says it's a good thing Bree is missing. He says the release I bugged her to sign has enough documentation behind it to indicate it may have been coerced. He also pointed out that it could end up in a really ugly trial, since Bree had no indication that the book was in the works. We misrepresented ourselves when we asked her to sign the paper."

"Is that what's worrying you? A lawsuit?" Hank's eyes darkened. Jayson hated to see that—it meant Hank was dangerously angry.

"No. Fuck, no. I wish she'd come back so I could explain. You know I didn't know about any of that shit. Mom knows it, too. At least Mom's heart is healthy and she's exercising and taking better care of herself. Maybe I could ask her to explain things to Bree if she'd just come back to us. The statute of limitations should have run out on the lawsuit, too, but Terry filed papers to extend the time period. I understand it's to protect Bree's interest in all this, but it's damned inconvenient."

"So you are worried about a lawsuit?"

"Yeah. I guess I am." Jayson's gaze held worry as he blinked at Hank. "I want things to be like they were. Before that fucking book ruined everything. If we see her again, she won't talk to us. You know that, don't you?"

"I'll do my best to convince her otherwise. Where I'm concerned, at least. You'll have to fight your own battle on this one, Rome."

"It doesn't matter—she's dead. People have been looking for her for two years. People from the government. They stopped showing up at my house nine months ago. They know she's dead, too."

"I won't give her up unless I'm given evidence," Hank growled. "I'm going home." Hank rose from the booth and stalked out of Bogey's, leaving Jayson to pay the tab.

~

Breanne's Journal

"Breanne?" Lissa's voice woke me. Opening my eyes, I blinked at her. What was I supposed to say? What?

"Why are you here?" I blurted. Yeah, those probably weren't the smartest first words to say to your half-sister.

"I guess I should have expected that," she sighed. "Thank you," she added, settling on the side of my bed and blinking at me.

"For what?" Yes, my manners definitely needed work.

"For saving my life. And Gavin's. Rigo's, Tony's, Gavril's."

"My asshole nephew?" Yes, Gavril, whom everyone else knew as Teeg San Gerxon, would likely never be in my good graces.

"Look, we all made mistakes. Some of us bigger mistakes than others," Lissa turned her gaze away and stared at the door leading to my closet. It was empty, just as it had been before. I'd never owned anything I'd worn the whole time I'd posed as my sister. It troubled me, too, that only twelve weeks had passed on Le-Ath Veronis since I'd left it behind to go to Earth in the past. So much time had gone by for me, while little had happened in the future.

I also wanted to point out that Teeg had placed compulsion on Trevor, Stellan and Kooper. They didn't remember me and probably wouldn't ever. It didn't matter—all my relationships eventually disappeared, for one reason or another. I wasn't destined to have that. My sister, on the other hand, had a plethora of mates. So many, in fact, that she had trouble keeping up with all of them.

"How's Merrill?" I asked. Yes, I liked him. He was decent, as was my half-sire, Adam Chessman.

"Merrill is amazing. Adam wants to see you soon."

"I figured as much. Look, I realize you're Queen of the Vampires and all that, but I really have no desire to bow down to any sire, no matter how nice he is. I read that crap when Gavin handed a comp-vid to me and told me to read the rules. I think I'm past all that, now."

"I don't think Adam will be demanding," Lissa began.

"I don't want anybody telling me what to do. I talked to Graegar not long ago. He told me what I am. Are you going to argue with that?"

Lissa stared at me in shock. "No." She held up a hand. "No. I wasn't aware that you knew."

"I didn't for a while. I still don't think it's sunk in, and frankly, I really don't feel comfortable here, now."

"I know you don't—I've talked to everybody. Asked questions, too. I realize this isn't easy. What I can't figure out is how you ended up back here."

"I don't have an answer to that, either. I was slapped back here—that's all I know."

"Somebody slapped you back here?"

"Yeah. I was thinking about doing away with my corporeal self, so somebody somewhere kept me from doing that. I'm sure if I read you now, I'd see that you and every other vampire from Earth have read that stupid, fucking book."

"Breanne, look, we didn't know. Nobody did. Gavin just wanders around in a daze, now, and that's not good."

"Put Rigo in charge of the Palace Guard." I said what I'd wanted to say for a while.

"Gavin's okay for that. Tony, too. It's just that he had some sort of mind cloud and things turned out badly. For you. Besides, Rigo has his hands full with all his spies."

"I know." I wanted to turn over so I wouldn't have to look at Lissa. Why had things come to this? Would I ever be comfortable around my sister? Probably not.

"He may want to apologize," Lissa began.

"Not interested."

"Does this mean you won't come to dinner tonight?"

"I was never asked to come to dinner, as you put it. Gavin would have let me starve before he'd allow it. He tried that, actually."

"I know." Lissa rose and walked away from the bed. I struggled to sit up, eventually working two pillows behind my back to make that achievement more comfortable. "Look, I know that still hurts you. I know it doesn't mean much to say he was affected by a mind cloud. After seeing that book, I understand how you distrust everybody who has ever mistreated you."

I almost snorted at her statement. Distrust was such a tame word. We shared some things, my sister and I. We both knew what it was like to be beaten by an angry, crazed human bent on destroying what they perceived as the source of all their problems.

She'd had a mother who loved her, however. I'd never had parents. I wanted to shudder, too, at that thought—of my first meeting with Griffin—when he'd dismissed me as nothing. I'd trembled and worked not to gape as I'd stared at my father. Would I ever consider him a parent? No. My grandfather, too, had stood next to Griffin and dismissed me just as easily. I wanted to weep at the memory.

"I know my mother protected me from a lot of blows," Lissa said softly. She'd wandered to my window to stare at the constant darkness blanketing Lissia.

"I know that, too."

"Do you want to meet Griffin again? He knows he has another daughter, now. I'll allow him to visit if you'd like."

"I don't want to see him. Or Wylend, either."

"I understand." I watched Lissa's head nod as she continued to gaze out the window. "He's had so many chances, and he hasn't delivered on any of them."

"He's shut all that off," I sighed. "He was tortured before he came to the Saa Thalarr. Maybe he's afraid to feel, now. That doesn't make me want to see him, though."

"I think he feels for Amara."

"Perhaps."

"Do you think he knows you saw all those things in him? I can't read him and haven't ever been able." Lissa turned to look at me this time, her curiosity almost tangible.

"I doubt he has any idea," I snorted and flung covers back. At least my headache was gone—Karzac was a miracle worker in my opinion.

"There's something else," Lissa sighed.

"What's that?"

"Ashe wants to see you. He says you may be able to help him with something."

"Not interested."

"I understand your first meeting wasn't ideal," Lissa began.

I was ready to leave—too many uncomfortable subjects had been brought up and I didn't want to talk about any of them. "I guess I have to borrow clothes again," I muttered. "I don't own any, here."

"What?" Lissa blinked in shock.

"I had to wear your stuff last time. Rathik Erwin stole my money and Gavin certainly felt no guilt about not giving me anything."

"I'll take you shopping."

"No. I can do this myself." I did. Just as the Larentii could do. I collected atoms and clothed myself in jeans and a plain T. Canvas shoes covered my feet as my sister watched in alarm. "See—not your problem." I held out my arms. "I'm not coming to dinner. I can get my own." Snatching my bear from the bed, I disappeared as Lissa called my name in desperation.

CHAPTER 2

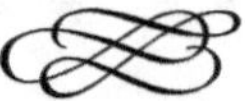

The General studied his lieutenant carefully. Considered killing his current body, too, for the grievous mistake he'd made, sending half a million rogue godlings after one of the Mighty. Somehow, the one they'd pursued managed to destroy the godlings completely, when he'd have said that feat was impossible. Still, he didn't know exactly how it had been accomplished, or whether, in truth, they'd actually been destroyed.

"Perhaps it will be as it was with you before," the General mused aloud. "You were confused for days after being in close proximity to one of our enemies. We may see them straggling in before long, with little recollection of what happened."

"That is my hope," the lieutenant nodded vigorously.

"If they do not," the General went on, "perhaps I shall find a way to punish you for your mistakes. You should have instructed many to follow cautiously. The most powerful, certainly, should have been held back. We have no way of knowing how much power the Mighty have gathered or how well they understand what they are. Until we know these things, they are more than dangerous."

More nodding followed the General's words, and the lieutenant swallowed nervously. He liked his current body. It suited him and he had no desire to lose it. "I have assignments for you and your remaining minions," the General added.

"Yes?" the lieutenant looked up eagerly. He'd certainly do better on this assignment so he'd be in the General's good graces again.

"I have a list prepared—of those who have influenced the timelines in favor of our enemies. Only a few, mind you, but the impact has been great. I desire that you devise a way to kill them discreetly, so the enemy won't suspect. For some, you will be required to traverse the timelines to accomplish your assignments. Employ the Sirenali we have stationed throughout, and any others under your control. Allow them to do as much as possible, to keep the Mighty away from us and our remaining army."

"It will be as you say," the lieutenant readily agreed.

Breanne's Journal

The house in San Rafael hadn't changed at all. I landed there two years after I'd disappeared from Earth. It was my house, after all, and the only real home I had. People had short memories, too, so I was hoping that they'd been distracted by something else and didn't remember much about that stupid book.

I wanted to shout at Jayson, still. He and his father had ruined everything for me. I'd never be able to face Hank again, thanks to Rome Enterprises. Whether Jayson knew about the book or not, his family had profited from it—I'd read that easily in Lissa's face.

The book had been a bestseller for months and netted Rome Enterprises nearly half a billion in profits. I guess Jayson could afford a few more cars at my expense—I wanted to weep from the callous betrayal. Hank (and everybody else on planet Earth) had seen photographs of my tortured, nude body. They'd bought the books by the truckload, and eagerly swallowed up the horror of my early life.

That wasn't the full extent of it, either. The book didn't cover the things Joyce Christian said while she'd beaten and tortured me—

nobody knew about that. She'd always sent the housekeeper away on an errand while the dirty work was accomplished.

Sighing, I shoved the memories away and attempted to rein in my emotions. There was one more place to go before I settled in and attempted to put myself back together. I misted toward Terry Johnston's office.

~

"Terry, I don't want to talk about it. I just need updated credit cards—the old ones are expired," I muttered as I sat in front of his desk.

"Breanne, I've already done that," Terry slid a thick, sealed envelope across the desk toward me. "There's a new phone in there, too; I bought a new one after your old one ended up in deep water."

"Please tell me somebody didn't go to the trouble of pulling it out of there," I mumbled, feeling embarrassed.

"Yep. Government agency, I heard. Somebody was worried about you, I know that much. Kept showing up here, asking if I'd heard anything. They finally stopped about nine months ago."

"I want to kick Rome ass," I muttered angrily.

"So do I. I think you have a viable lawsuit against them, if you decide to sue. I've tolled the statute of limitations, if that's what you want to do."

"Terry, what do you think that might do for me, besides telling everybody where I am again? I want nothing to do with that. I just want to be left alone."

I did—peace and quiet sounded really good to me. PTSD is a strange animal. When you think you have it beaten, something comes along and triggers it again. It's the way things seemed to happen for me.

I just hoped Jayson and Trina never noticed I'd come home—I had no desire to see anybody. After all, I'd just walked away from my sister, and she did want to see me. Wanted to know me, too, and I was too numb and upset to allow it.

"Miss Hayworth," Terry said sternly, his dark-brown eyes quite serious as he blinked at me. "You cannot let that ruin your life. Get help if you need it. I was hoping that's what you were doing while you were gone. I kept hoping you were alive, too, since no body was ever found, but I was beginning to worry."

"I know. I didn't mean to worry you. You've always been there for me, and I appreciate that."

"You pay me well for my services," Terry sighed. "But that's not all it is. I like you. I can't say the same thing about a lot of my clients."

"People are different," I shrugged.

"Your car may need a new battery—it hasn't been started or moved since you disappeared."

"I know. I'll look into that. I think it has less than a thousand miles on it."

"You don't drive much."

"Yeah."

"I've gotten payments from Hank Bell—the entire loan—with interest, has been paid and he's expanded the club. You still own half —he continues to refuse my offer to sell your half back to him."

"I don't care anymore. Send the money he paid to a good charity, Terry. I don't want any of it."

"You think he knew about the book, too?"

"Possibly. He and Jayson Rome are good friends. What one knows, the other generally does, too. That's the way things usually turn out for me." I rose and lifted the envelope off Terry's desk. "Thanks for this, Terry. Give yourself a raise." I walked out of his office.

The grocery store had remodeled, and I couldn't find anything. That meant grocery shopping took twice as long as it should have. That would teach me to jump forward two years in time, expecting everything to remain the same in the meantime. I took the liberty of disguising myself, too, while I shopped. I had no desire to be recognized by anyone.

Was I depressed? In truth, I was so depressed I could barely move.

It didn't matter—I'd worked under more difficult circumstances in the past. I pushed myself to do what needed to be done, whether I felt like it or not.

Lissa hadn't brought up the subject of what I'd done or where I'd been, either, and I was grateful. I was afraid I'd voice my fears aloud—that although I'd gotten rid of a large number of rogue gods, I felt I hadn't gotten all of them.

In addition to that fear, I worried that some of the remaining rogues were the worst of the lot. I had to work through my depression in a hurry, if I expected to have enough energy to deal with anything else that might come along. I wanted to shiver at the thought that I had absolutely no idea what form that might take or whether I'd survive it.

A cup of coffee was in order after I put groceries away, and I drank it on the back patio. Fog rolled in, obscuring San Rafael Bay below, and I watched as it enveloped the hill where my house lay. Was it wrong that I hadn't even glanced toward Jayson's house at the top? I felt no guilt over it.

~

Lissa's Journal

"I can't keep her here. What makes you think I can?" I blinked at Ashe in confusion. He and Trajan had both come. Trajan was prepared to go to wolf and growl for some reason, and I couldn't figure that out.

"What about Chessman? He might have convinced her to go to NorthStar at least," Ashe pointed out patiently.

"She said she didn't want a sire. She likes Adam, but she didn't want that. What was I supposed to say?" I shook my head at the Mighty Hand.

"I didn't even feel it when she pulled all those rogues into her wake," Ashe shook his head in disbelief.

"You know what happened to them?" I asked.

"Yeah. I know. It's not information I feel comfortable telling," he replied.

"Belen said the same thing. He said he couldn't say."

"Better that way. Much, much better," Ashe sighed. "Any idea where she went?"

"None. Never knew where she was before. Probably wouldn't go back there anyway. That would be crazy unless she wanted somebody to find her."

"True."

Breanne's Journal

A month passed. I read. Bought a computer and did research. Drank coffee and hot chocolate. Lost weight anyway. Took a chance at times and misted to Francie's for a veggie sandwich if I didn't feel like cooking. I always kept an eye open for Jayson and Hank. So far, I'd managed to avoid them.

I left the lights off at night, too, so Trina and Jayson wouldn't know I was at the house. As a vampire, I could see well enough at night without light of any kind. I'd only used them before because it was a comfort. Too many times, I'd been left chained in a very dark closet, in pain and suffering greatly, so I understood comfort more than most. Now, I lived without that tiny bit of reassurance.

The television barely saw any use, either, except during news times. I always watched the news when I ate or went to bed—after making sure the blinds were tightly closed.

"Three men were killed last night after leaving the Sub-Mariner, a club in the Castro District," the news anchor announced. "While there are no signs of struggle, each man died of a slashed throat. The bodies were discovered at a vacant rental property in Oakland. Police have determined that the men died elsewhere and were later dumped at the property across the Bay."

I watched as they showed images of a two-story rent house in Oakland, with yellow crime scene tape strung around the yard. Then the images jumped to an interview with a man identified as Dale Saylor, owner of the Sub-Mariner.

"I knew all of them, and this is horrifying," Dale Saylor said. I could tell easily that he really was upset. I toyed with the idea of reading him before dispensing with that notion. Several people stood behind Dale Saylor. I paid little attention to them until the camera moved slightly to catch someone standing nearby.

Hank Bell stood there, arms crossed over his chest in a familiar gesture. He looked angry. I blinked at him for a moment before turning back to Dale Saylor and reading everything I could from him. Dressing in record time, I folded space toward San Francisco.

Hank was doing very well. Dom Bell's now took up at least half the block as I watched the club's name blink in (much larger) green neon over a newly bricked façade. Looked like he'd bought the businesses on either side plus the accompanying apartments overhead, too. I didn't want to think what those apartments might be used for. Yeah, I used to live right over the original bar. He'd expanded, so business was obviously good.

As I stood across the street, watching a few people walk in and out, six who exited the building caught my attention. Three women were on leashes and a dark limo pulled up outside as they waited on the sidewalk. Yes, my stomach turned at the sight of three women who'd allowed themselves to be leashed like dogs. I shivered and recalled Hank's explanation—this was their way of gaining permission to do what they craved. They wanted to be controlled. I shivered again.

One of the men spoke to the driver in Russian before shoving the girl he held inside the back of the car. "Drive to the house in Sausalito," was the terse command. The words contained a threat—a promise of violence to come. I was about to see what that threat involved, and if it involved extreme physical harm against any of the women, well, compulsion might be placed and those three men might become docile chimps. Yeah, I wasn't in a charitable mood.

Misting inside the car, I hovered over the heads of the three women, all of whom were squeezed onto the limo's back seat, too obedient to look up at the men who'd convinced them to play. I lowered my shields and read all three men. I didn't bother with the driver—he was a flunky and only doing what he was told. If I'd had blood running through physical veins at the moment, it would have run like ice water. These men—all three of them, bore an obsession.

An obsession meant I couldn't read past it to find the intent of the one who'd placed it, but they'd been ordered to find three women at Hank's bar, and then drive them to a specific house in Sausalito, where all would be gruesomely murdered. It didn't take a genius to add two and two—looked like somebody had it out for Dale Saylor and Hank Bell, and this was a way to expose and ruin both.

Shoving those thoughts aside and hoping that the one who'd placed the obsession was waiting in Sausalito, I did my best to calm down while I took the forty-minute trip as mist, following the would-be murderers and their victims.

The house was on the southern edge of Sausalito. A much better home than the one I'd seen in Oakland, it was single story with a well-maintained lawn. Misting through the roof of the vehicle, I waited for the women to be pulled from the back seat of the limo and hauled inside the house.

Two of the men were short and square-built, with shaved heads. I seldom used my nose, but it told me these two were brothers. My reading also told me they'd been involved in petty crime for years. Perfect for an obsession—it didn't take much to convince them to increase their activities.

The third man—taller, heavier and Russian by birth, appeared to be in charge. He ordered the driver to park the car in the garage around the side before jerking his head at the other two, who now held all three leashes. I followed as the women were led inside the house.

Murder had already taken place inside—the smell of old blood was evident, although it had been cleaned up as much as possible. A square sitting room was located right off the front door and the women were ordered to kneel near a wide doorway leading into a rectangular dining room. No furniture was inside either room—I had the idea that the house, like the one in Oakland, had been rented hastily for the purpose of committing murder.

"Remain on your knees," the Russian ordered the women. "Do not look up." His accented English was low and vulgar to my ears. All three women lowered their eyes to the floor, just like the obedient submissives they were. I watched as the Russian pulled a thin, metal knife from his boot. Well, the obsession was activating and things were about to go down unless I acted now.

It only takes a bit of power to heat metal, and the long, thin blade the Russian held became hot so quickly he swore in Russian and dropped it immediately, howling in pain. His two American flunkies rushed forward, which made things ridiculously simple for me.

No, the one who'd placed the obsession wasn't there; I'd known that the moment I misted inside the house. Only the ones I'd followed were inside. Exerting more power, I released the particles of all three men. The three women, who hadn't even looked up when a knife clattered to the floor in front of them, never saw the sparks of the men fly away. I defied anyone to convict me of a crime with no evidence or witnesses.

The driver walked into the house as the last man's sparks winked out. I materialized before the women while the driver squeaked in fear. Turning to him, I placed compulsion. "You will not remember me. Drive these women to their homes," I commanded. His eyes went blank and he nodded. I hated placing compulsion—on anybody—no matter how deserving. This situation required it.

"Now, you three," I knelt to look the three women in the eyes. The men had been choosy, selecting a blonde, a redhead and a brunette deliberately. "You will tell that man your address," I said, "and you will go home and not go out again tonight. Do you hear me? You will forget me and the three who brought you here."

They stared and nodded fearfully at me. "You may speak," I told them.

"Who are you?" the redhead's voice wobbled.

"Somebody who doesn't appreciate injustice," I replied. "Go with the driver, now. He'll deliver you safely to your homes. I have things to do." I backed away and watched as the three women rose and followed the driver out the door. I left the door of the house open when I misted away, flying as fast as I could toward my house in San Rafael.

≈

"Charles!"

"Yes, Honored One?" Charles stood in Wlodek's study seconds later, an inquisitive expression on his face.

"Three murders occurred in San Francisco recently. I want you to track this, as all three died after their throats were cut. Should more murders transpire in the area from similar circumstances, I wish to be notified immediately." Wlodek pushed handwritten notes toward Charles, who reached out to take them from Wlodek's desk. "I received this call from one of ours in the area, and he is quite concerned about this."

"I understand," Charles nodded slightly. "I will research this right away. Anything else?"

"Bring me whatever you find. This troubles me."

"Of course, Honored One." Charles nodded respectfully and left Wlodek's office as quickly as he'd arrived.

≈

Breanne's Journal

It didn't matter that I'd saved three women. Two others died anyway. At least these were last seen at a third club. The news described the two as a couple who had teenaged children at home. I was so angry I could spit.

These two were dumped at a house in Daly City. It looked as if they were killed after I'd taken care of the thugs the night before, so either this was a copycat crime or there was more than one team at

19

work. More than one team wouldn't surprise me, with a Sirenali and an obsession on the loose.

Another house was shown, with more crime scene tape draped around it. With very little hesitation, I *Looked* to see where it was and turned to mist.

Scents came, which might help me find the killers. With an obsession clouding two murderers, I couldn't *Look* to get their location. I'd had to mist through the Daly City location, too, because it was still under investigation. A few investigators still wandered through the property, looking for anything they might have missed during their initial round of evidence collection. They had no idea I was there for the same reason.

While at the Daly City location, I found scents from the two murderers at the Oakland house, plus older scents from the three men I'd dispatched in Sausalito. Nobody was at the Oakland house, either, when I returned for a second time—they'd removed the crime scene tape already after gathering evidence.

I'd materialized inside the room where the bodies were found, and there was little blood. I wondered where they'd been killed, but with the clouded obsession blocking my way, I couldn't make a determination.

That meant one thing—I'd have to go looking for scents or other evidence around the clubs where these had disappeared. I knew what kind of clubs they were—the same kind Hank owned. Breathing a worried sigh, I misted home.

Here's the mail I thought you might want to see, the note read. It came in a large envelope sent by Terry. Inside were a few thank you cards from children who'd benefited from my charity. They had no idea who I was—my name wasn't attached to any of the funds, but they'd taken the time to write anyway. I wiped tears away after reading them.

At the bottom of the packet, I found another letter. This one had been addressed to me in care of Terry Johnston, Attorney at Law. Terry had opened it to read the contents, since I wasn't available for more than two years. The return address bore Mercy Crossings' logo. I pulled the letter out and began to read.

Dear Ms. Hayworth, it began. *Regarding recent events, i.e., the publication of* Torture in Texas (yes that's what they'd named the fucking book), *our legal department has advised us to terminate your association with the Mercy Crossings organization, as the book's impact could give our charity an unwelcome negative image.*

While we sympathize with you for any pain and suffering you may have experienced in your past, it is our hope that you will understand our position in this and accept it for what it is—an attempt to dissociate our organization from such deleterious social implications. Sincerely, Barry Stokes, Director.

Well, that spelled one thing to me—Barry didn't want to offend any contributors who might have been (or still were) Joyce Christian fans or supporters. I sighed and folded the letter before slipping it back inside the envelope.

While I had no plans to return to Mercy Crossings—too many people would stare and whisper and I certainly didn't want that—this was a blow I hadn't expected. He hadn't even bothered to thank me for the service I'd given to the charity—in fact, he'd glossed over it altogether. Well, maybe he was a Joyce Christian fan, too. If so, I didn't need him or Mercy Crossings. At least that's what I kept telling myself as I wiped tears away.

"Opal, I'm not sure we ought to close the files on Oscar Forde and Keir Arthur," Bill sighed. He leaned back in his leather armchair and lifted an eyebrow at Opal Tadewi. "Just because we haven't seen or heard anything from them and the college girl murders have stopped doesn't mean they're not still out there, waiting to do more damage."

"I know." Opal stared at her hands. She was dressed as she usually was—comfortably—in nice jeans and a pullover shirt. "I know you still miss her," she added. "I do, too."

There wasn't any need for them to say the name—Breanne had come to be a subject they approached carefully with each other. Bill had even sent Opal to San Francisco twice—looking for any sign of Bree. They'd found nothing. Bill figured that Breanne would approach Opal before anyone else, and he'd hoped that she'd turn up.

More than two years had passed instead, and there'd been no sign. He still had Bree's crumpled cell in his desk drawer—and the suitcase from her hotel room in his closet. Those things were all he had left of her, and he held onto them as if the mundane items were the most precious things on Earth.

"Is the Vampire Council still hunting those two?" Opal changed the subject.

"I believe they're on the wanted list, but they've had no sightings either, so these two are dead or far underground. Wlodek agreed to let us know if they were found and eliminated."

"I think they left Austin the minute Bree disappeared. I just can't figure out how the two things might be connected."

"It is strange, I agree," Bill nodded. "I'm just concerned that we still may have two outlaw vampires on the loose, waiting for who knows what to happen before they start killing again."

Breanne's Journal

I waited in line at the small deli a mile from my house. The salesclerk, brown-haired, blue-eyed, pretty enough and wearing a nametag proclaiming her *Janine*, moved slowly at best, and her disinterest tried my resolve not to read her. The only reason I came to this particular shop for lunch was for their freshly made potato and leek soup.

"I'd like four servings of the potato soup to go, please," I said when I finally made my way to the counter.

"I can't do that. We only have two servings left," Janine sniffed.

"Then I'll take what you have," I said as politely as I could. I intended to make several meals out of what I was getting.

"It may be only one-and-a-half," Janine lifted the lid from the soup warmer with a metallic clatter.

"I'll take that, then. Charge me for two servings anyway," I said. Honestly, I'd waited in line for twenty minutes and now Janine wanted to annoy me.

"All right, I'll charge you for two," Janine fiddled with keys at the register. I handed her a twenty, she handed me bills and coins back and went to dip the soup.

"Can we move a little faster?" the man behind me demanded.

"You want to come back here and help?" Janine snapped before knocking the container holding my soup off the counter and snarling angrily at the man.

I stared at the mess that was meant to be my lunch, which I'd already paid for. Well, it was the way my life was destined to be. Without a word, I turned and walked out of the deli while Janine and the man began a shouting match.

While I ate a peanut butter sandwich later, I switched on the news. A microphone was shoved in Hank's face and I blinked at him in shock. He was angry—extremely so—and not just with the reporter—I could tell by his words.

"Yes, my assistant manager didn't show up for work last night. I called the police because John is always on time and never misses a shift. I am only discovering now, through you, that his body was found near the wharf an hour ago."

"The police didn't call you?" The reporter—a young woman—feigned surprise.

"No. I assume they notified John's family first. How did you learn of the murder?"

"Through ah, well, the usual channels," she stuttered. I figured she'd gotten information through a source or listened in on police communications.

"You probably shouldn't mess with Hank right now," I spoke to the television screen. Too bad the reporter couldn't hear me.

"Are you involved in your assistant manager's disappearance?" Her question proved (to me, at least) that she had very little common sense.

"My whereabouts have already been disclosed to the police, who are in charge of this investigation, no matter how much you'd prefer to believe otherwise," Hank growled. "Where were you when my assistant manager disappeared?"

"What?" she squeaked.

"I can account for my time last night. Can you?" I almost laughed as she turned a bright pink. Yes, I dropped my shield and read her. She'd been in bed with her (married) producer. The station quickly cut to commercial while I snickered.

"Jayson, I need to hire another assistant manager. Trey can't handle everything by himself, and John's family is asking for help with the funeral as soon as the medical examiner releases the body," Hank sighed into his cell.

"I saw the ambush on television," Jayson replied. "I have no idea what that trollop thought she might accomplish by accusing you. How is John's family doing?"

"Not well. They knew where he worked and what he did, but that's about it. They didn't interfere with that, as far as I know."

"They need money?"

"Yeah—I'm planning to pay for the funeral, but John left instructions on what he wanted done with his brother, and quite a few from the community will be there."

"Will his family be able to deal with that?"

"I assume so, but this will be a private service, in case the media wants to show up."

"You know I can't come—I can't be seen there in case reporters are parked outside," Jayson pointed out.

"Yes. I'm well aware."

"Do you think somebody's targeting the community?" Jayson turned to a new topic.

"It looks that way, doesn't it? Sometime after the funeral, I want to check out that new club. I know it's been open for six months, now, but something about this bothers me."

"I've driven by a few times—it's certainly upscale. Has valet parking, even."

"For wannabees with money?"

"Possibly. You know the subject's gotten hot the past couple of years. Too many wanting to experiment, when they don't have a clue about safety or where to start."

"Yeah. Got a call from Paul the other day. He's still working as a paramedic, and says he's seen some interesting injuries lately."

"No surprise," Jayson snorted.

∾

"Well, he's handsome, but rude." Colbi Wayde muttered to her producer.

"Sweetheart, he shouldn't have said those things to you." Mitchell Graves, producer for the morning and afternoon local news segments, married with three children and having an affair with Colbi, muttered. "Come here. Sit on my lap." He patted his knee suggestively. "I'll tell you the best news you've heard in a long time if you do."

Mitchell, in his early forties, kept himself fit. He also felt protective of his wife—and his girlfriend.

"What did you find?" Colbi's sunny blue eyes narrowed as she sauntered toward Mitchell.

"I found," Mitchell began as he pulled Colbi onto his lap, "That Hank Bell has a co-owner for his club. It's a BDSM oriented business."

"Really? We can run with that," Colbi whispered, her eyes lighting with immediate interest. "We can drag him through the muck for being an asshole."

"Wait, you haven't heard the best part," Mitchell grinned before leaning in for a kiss. "You'll never guess who his business partner is."

"Who is it?" Colbi held her breath.

"Breanne Hayworth."

"*Torture in Texas* Breanne Hayworth? *Oh my God!*"

<h1 style="text-align:center">CHAPTER 3</h1>

I almost choked on my cereal when I saw the news the following morning. Three more deaths the night before—two men and one woman, all found in an alley of the Tenderloin. While crime in the Tenderloin might be a common occurrence, these three died from slashed throats, just like all the others, and the murders were already being attributed to the same killer or killers.

My guess was that all three victims were prostitutes, but I couldn't say for certain. Part of me was relieved that the Sirenali seemed to be branching out from Hank's community, but it wasn't any consolation for the families the victims might have left behind.

I hadn't considered it before, but it did look as if the killers were targeting people with—in Jayson's terms—non-vanilla lifestyles. Like Jack the Ripper, or something. That concerned me, because Hank and Jayson could still be targets. Hank's assistant manager had certainly been.

The local news stations were still going on about the murders, and frankly, the body count was growing. I knew a Sirenali was behind this, and worried that more vampires might be involved.

If it were the same Sirenali who'd orchestrated the college girl murders, then he or she was certainly branching out. Keir Arthur and Oscar Forde crossed my mind, too, but my research and *Looking* after arriving back on Earth told me they'd disappeared and the college girl murders had ceased after I left.

"This is so confusing," I muttered, shoving my half-eaten bowl of cereal away. All I had so far was three men I'd killed already, two scents belonging to humans unknown, a pile of bodies and a mystery the size of a small planet.

"This is so frustrating," Bill muttered. Ashe looked up from his ham and eggs as Bill dropped Kay's breakfast tray on the kitchen island. "She's in another world again today. I had to put the fork in her hand and tell her to eat a dozen times before she even focused on me."

"Bill, I'm sorry, but you and Franklin are the only two who can get through to her at all. I'd love to feed her, but she's terrified of me."

"Do you think Frank might come for a visit, then? I could use a break."

"I'll ask, but Trace may be able to persuade him better."

I'll talk to Trace, then," Bill nodded determinedly.

"I want Gavin on this," Wlodek muttered, shoving the file across his desk toward Charles.

"Honored One, Gavin is in Stockholm at the moment."

"Might he be finished there soon?" Wlodek's face held no emotion, but Charles knew the Head of the Vampire Council was quite irritated.

"He may be closing in on the rogue, according to his latest report."

"Tell him to move swiftly, then. I want him in San Francisco as soon as possible."

"Of course, Honored One."

~

"What are you planning to do?" Mitchell lifted an eyebrow at Colbi, who tapped notes on her computer. They were alone inside Colbi's small office, and the door was closed.

"I'm going to wait outside Dom Bell's until Hank Bell shows up tonight, ask him if he's involved in Breanne Hayworth's disappearance and then follow up with the question of whether his assistant manager's death is connected, somehow."

"I love how your devious mind works," Mitchell squeezed Colbi's shoulders affectionately. "I'll be watching the live feed from here. This'll be fun."

"Oh, yeah," Colbi brushed dyed-platinum hair over her shoulder. "I'm looking forward to this."

~

Breanne's Journal

John hadn't been murdered where his body was found—just like the others. That had been evident, not only to me but to the authorities investigating the murders as well. I misted past the crime scene tape, but there wasn't much left now for me to examine. One of the same human scents came to me—he'd come alone to dump the body.

It made me want to sniff around the body in question, to see what I could get from it, but the thought of misting into the coroner's office and getting close to a body that was likely cut open unnerved me. Yeah, my vampire mojo probably needed work.

Sighing, I misted toward the Lean Bean for a latte. Late afternoon fog rolled in as I materialized in a nearby alcove and walked half a block to the coffee shop. The difference in the service I received from the coffee shop barista and grumpy Janine was astounding. The young man was smiling, joking with his customers and serving them with cool efficiency. I had my vanilla latte in only a few minutes and found a small table near a window to enjoy it.

My thoughts turned to Bill and Opal as I sat there, drinking my latte and recalling breakfasts and coffee with both of them. For me, it had only been a month and a half since I'd seen them. To them, I'd been gone two years and four months. I could only imagine how upset they might be if I suddenly appeared again, with no prior word and no good excuse for my prolonged absence. Aside from the book and betrayal, that is, which neither of them had anything to do with.

Well, the coffee shop sold little racks of cards. I knew Bill's office address. Writing a note was the polite thing to do, and maybe he wouldn't be too mad at me. I walked to the counter, bought a handful of blank cards with envelopes and went back to my seat to sort out messages for Bill and Opal.

~

After delivering the cards, I misted through the alley behind Dom Bell's. I detected no scents there from any of the murders and I was grateful for that. The club wouldn't open until six, and it was four in the afternoon. I misted home and wondered what I might put together for an early dinner.

~

A spoonful of homemade minestrone was almost to my mouth when Colbi Wayde's image appeared on the news. There she was, dressed in a pale-blue suit, microphone in hand, a malicious gleam in her eye and Hank Bell cornered in the doorway of Dom Bell's.

"I hear you have a silent business partner," Colbi's voice indicated triumph as she spit the words in Hank's direction. My spoon clattered into my bowl, splashing minestrone on my T-shirt. I barely noticed as I stared at Hank and Colbi in shock. In my wildest dreams, I never imagined things might come to this

"Did you have something to do with Breanne Hayworth's disappearance, too?" Colbi asked with false sweetness.

"Fuck," I muttered before folding space.

~

"What the hell is this?" Bill stared at the envelopes left on his desk. One was addressed to him, the other to Opal. No last names.

"Sheila," Bill snapped, bringing his assistant into his office at a run. "Where the hell did these envelopes come from?" He still hadn't touched them—there was no return address and for all he knew, they might be dangerous.

"Director, I'm the only one who's been inside your office, and those envelopes weren't there when I arrived this morning."

"But where did they," Bill squinted at the writing. "Sheila, hold my calls for the next half hour, please."

"Would you like me to leave, Director?"

"Yes. Thank you, Sheila." Bill waited until his assistant closed his office door before lifting the envelope addressed to him.

Bill, the note began. *I'm so sorry I haven't contacted you sooner. I just couldn't. I'm still really upset and depressed, and I hope everybody who's read that stupid book has a short memory. I worry every time I walk into a store or restaurant, because I'm terrified somebody will recognize me and start asking questions. I hope you understand how painful that would be. Love, Breanne.*

Bill read the note six times before lifting his cell and dialing Opal's number. "Bill?" Opal answered right away.

"Opal, you have a note in my office from Breanne."

"I'll be there in half an hour."

~

Breanne's Journal

From my position on the inside of Dom Bell's door, I listened while Hank answered hostile questions from a bitchy reporter on the opposite side. Gulping air into my lungs, I worked to forced down the panic attack that threatened to reduce me to a shivering mass.

I was about to reveal myself to everyone on live television, and it was to save Hank from uncomfortable questions and a potential investigation. Yes, I was transferring his suffering onto my shoulders. It wasn't a fair trade, but I had no desire to see Hank bullied.

"You can do this," I mumbled, struggling to convince myself. "You can do this, you can do this, you can do this." I gripped the doorknob in my hand and pulled. Hank almost fell over the threshold; he'd been leaning against the door so hard.

"Hi, honey," I said brightly, once I got Hank fully upright and steady again. "Who are you?" I glared at Colbi Wayde accusingly.

"What, uh, what?" Colbi, at a momentary loss for words, jerked her head from me to the camera, and then back to me again. The very person she'd just accused Hank of doing away with stood before her, while her cameraman recorded the whole thing. I'd just taken the wind out of Colbi's sails and she floundered for a moment.

"I'm uh, Colbi Wayde, reporter for News Seventeen," Colbi attempted to regain her equilibrium. "You're Breanne Hayworth? *The* Breanne Hayworth, from *Torture in Texas?*" Colbi was breathless as her mind gripped just who (and what) she had in front of her—the only live interview anyone had gained from the one remaining victim of Joyce Christian's unholy inclinations.

"Yes," I grumped. "And no, I'm not giving an interview. That book has obviously ruined my life and any anonymity I might have, hasn't it?" My voice was cold and trembling. No, I couldn't keep the quaver out of my voice—it was a struggle to remain standing as it was. My skin shivered over every part of my body and my legs shook under me.

"I hear you weren't aware of the book. Do you have ill feelings toward Rome Enterprises? How do you feel about having those nude photographs on display? How much did you suffer? Have you been in therapy all this time? What did your doctors say? What's the diagnosis?"

"I said no interview, and how I feel about Rome Enterprises and my health is my business and not yours." My legs refused to hold me up any longer and I almost fell. Hank, who'd stared at me before blinking several times in confusion, caught me as I went down. His hand went to my forehead, too, just before I fainted.

~

"Everybody in the country saw Bree faint in your arms after that woman badgered her," Jayson huffed. "Every news outlet is out for blood and Colbi is hiding behind her producer at the studio. I hear the media wants to talk to Breanne—and to you or Colbi or anybody else involved. I told Stephanie to hold all my calls. How's Bree doing?"

"Still asleep, but that won't last much longer. She was shaking so bad, I don't know how she managed to stand up as long as she did." Hank lifted the blinds on the window inside his bedroom to check the street below. He'd bought a new condo six months earlier, and he was glad about that—Breanne would wake up in comfortable (if unfamiliar) surroundings.

He'd left the club in Trey's hands—he didn't want Bree to wake there or in his office, which lay over the club and inside her old apartment.

"PTSD," Jayson murmured.

"Yeah. Probably GAD too," Hank agreed. "I don't think she'd have shown up if I hadn't needed bailing out."

"I heard the coroner is releasing John's body," Jayson said.

"Yeah. His brother called just before I left for work. Funeral will be Friday at eleven."

"You think Bree will consent to talk to me?" Jayson asked.

"No idea. Let's take this slow, okay? I don't know what she'll say to me, even, when she wakes, or if she'll just disappear again." Hank's cell beeped. "Look, I have another call. I'll let you know how Bree is after she wakes."

"All right." Jayson terminated the call from his end.

"Hello?" Hank answered the other line.

"Hank Bell? I just saw Breanne on television. Is she still with you?"

"Director Jennings?" Hank said.

"Yes, it's Bill Jennings. Is Breanne there with you? Is she all right?"

"She's still out, but she's sleeping—her vitals finally came back to normal. That reporter bitch wouldn't have left her alone if she hadn't fainted."

"Have you known where she was all this time?" Bill demanded.

"No, Director. I'm just as shocked by this as you are. I believe Breanne knew I was in trouble, so she showed up to bail me out. I have no idea where she's been, and I don't want to grill her the minute she wakes up. She needs somebody to look after her."

"I can help with that."

"If you can, I'd appreciate it. She may not be happy to see me, and she sure as hell may not be happy to hear that I'm still friends with Jayson. He really didn't know about the book, and he's horrified by the information and the photographs. I realize his father had a vendetta against Joyce Christian, but Breanne has been victimized twice."

"I understand that," Bill sighed. "I've been terrified for more than two years, Bell. Terrified that she was dead—possibly by her own hand. My heart aches every time I think about it."

"Mine, too, brother. Mine, too."

~

Breanne's Journal

"Baby, are you gonna wake up for me?" A gentle hand brushed my forehead. I moaned, still mostly asleep. I had no idea what black velvet I'd fallen into, but it had given me rest and a dreamless sleep.

"Baby, wake up, now. I need to feed you and make sure you're okay." Fingers touched my wrist and I realized it was Hank, taking my pulse. It jumped and sped up.

"Bree, don't do that. Calm down and open your eyes for me, all right?" I moaned again before turning on my side and curling into a ball.

"Baby, I won't let anybody hurt you. I promise," Hank murmured before brushing my cheek with his lips. "Come on, wake up, now." He pulled me against his chest. My hand was cradled in one of his as he kissed the inside of my wrist. My pulse jumped again and my eyes flew open.

Grateful that the blinds were drawn and the bedside lamp muted, I blinked into Hank's dark, worried eyes. "There's my girl," he sighed before tucking my head beneath his chin. "Hank's here, baby," he crooned.

"I'm okay," I whispered. "Mostly. Did the bitch go home?"

"Yeah. With her tail between her legs. She's getting skewered by the other news outlets for bullying you."

"She's having an affair with her married producer," I mumbled against Hank's chest. "I don't have a problem with multiple mates, but his wife doesn't know. That's what I have a problem with."

"Yeah." Hank kissed the top of my head. "I missed you. So much."

"How's Jayson? Did he know about the book? How's his mother? I hope his dad and Ross Gideon rot in hell."

Hank chuckled into my hair. "Baby, Jayson really didn't know. He got blindsided by this, just like I did. Jayson's mother left his dad—they're separated but not divorced. Not yet, anyway. Kathleen won't speak to James Sr., I know that much. I want to talk to you someday about all this, too. Baby, if I'd known, I would have kept you as far away from the club as I could. Still, you need to deal with this—maybe a little immersion wouldn't be a bad thing."

"Hank," I moaned, huddling against him.

"No, shhhh, you'll be with me. You'll be safe with me. Nobody's gonna hurt my girl. Come on, now. Let's get you fed. I've listened to your stomach growl for the past hour."

I recalled that my bowl of minestrone was still on the island at the house in San Rafael. I'd never gotten to take a first bite of it. "Hank," I pulled away from him—stared at his beautiful face for a moment before reaching up to tentatively ruffle his black hair. He smiled at me. I let my fingers slide down his face. I'd never gotten to touch him like that before. He took my fingers in his and kissed them.

"Come on, shorty. We're going to the kitchen," he said and slid off the bed.

~

"How was I to know she'd show up?" Colbi wiped her eyes with a tissue. She'd spent the last two hours crying on Mitchell's shoulder.

"If you'd been a bit more tactful, we might have had the interview of the decade," Mitchell muttered.

"What?" Colbi turned hurt-filled blue eyes in Mitchell's direction.

"I'm saying it's okay to ambush a grown man. When you jumped all over the most widely-recognized victim in the country, you lost any sympathy you might ever get," Mitchell pointed out. "I've taken three calls from my boss, and both our jobs may be on the line over this."

"Why did she have to show up now?" Colbi wailed.

"Jayson, where is she? I want to send flowers—or something."

"Mom, calm down. She's with Hank right now, and I imagine he has his hands full. We need to approach carefully, I think. I sure don't want her to disappear again."

Kathleen Rome had dialed Jayson's private number the moment she saw Breanne on a national news program. "I want to talk to her, Jayson. Surely, she won't say no. I want her to know I've pulled all my support from Mercy Crossings after that stupid letter Barry Stokes wrote to her was published."

"Mom, we can't deny that the company made money off those books. While we may have donated to other charities since then, Dad hasn't let go of a single cent of that money."

"He knows he did wrong. Look at all the letters published by other newspapers."

"They're just angry because they didn't get there first. You won't fool Bree like that—she's too smart. It's been over two years since anybody's seen her, and the minute she shows up, she gets blindsided again."

"That poor girl. Jayson, please tell me you've never hurt anybody like that."

"There are big differences between what I am and what Joyce Christian obviously was. First, consent is the biggest factor, and I sure as hell know how far to take things. You don't do shit like that. That's not just abuse, that's torture. At least Dad got that part right. Don't ever put me in the same category as Joyce fucking Christian."

"Jayson, watch your language," Kathleen Rome snapped.

"Yeah. But it just gets me mad, whenever somebody thinks I might stoop to that," Jayson muttered angrily. "I give what's asked for."

"Honey, please calm down, I didn't mean it like that," Kathleen sighed. "It's just that I can't get those photographs out of my mind. They're horrible."

"Mom, I feel exactly the same, and it pisses me off that I feel so helpless about it. Why didn't somebody get her out of there? That idiot sheriff could have cut her loose and taken her to a hospital, yet all he did was stand there and take incriminating photographs. That stupid, evil bastard."

"I'll agree with your language there, hon. He was a stupid, evil bastard. But as bad as he was, Joyce was worse."

"I'll give you that. Bree said to me once that she'd met the devil. Now I know what she meant."

"Jayson," Kathleen sighed, "You didn't try to convince her to—you know. Did you?"

"No, Mom. I didn't. She made her feelings known after she found out about Hank."

"I don't know how she managed to stay friends with either of you."

"It wasn't easy. I just thought she was being unreasonable. Hank thought something else was there, but he couldn't figure it out. Everybody knows, now, don't they? Thanks to Dad and Ross. Why couldn't they hand what they had to the FBI or something, and let them handle it? Bree's name could have been kept out of it."

"Honey, you know your father. He wanted Joyce when she was alive, and he settled for her reputation after she was dead. She was always touting her religious beliefs, and belittling anybody who didn't think the way she did. The book may have opened a lot of eyes, but there are still some who refuse to believe any of this."

"I've read the stuff from the conspiracy theorists. Two websites are devoted to it. I have no idea what Breanne's appearance will mean to some of those people—they've been saying all along that Breanne doesn't exist and this is a government conspiracy to destroy religion and Joyce's image as a decent human being."

"Idiots," Kathleen huffed.

"Crazy idiots," Jayson agreed. "I think Bree might be in danger, if any of these crackpots learn where she is."

"Oh, honey, that's too horrible to consider."

Breanne's Journal

"I'll feed you better next time, but this is the best vegetarian I can do on short notice," Hank said.

"It's good." I bit into the grilled cheese sandwich and chewed. At least he'd bought vegetarian cheese slices. Yeah, some cheeses are vegetarian, some aren't. I'd always made sure to go to restaurants with vegetarian-friendly cheese on the menu. I was grateful in the beginning that Bogey's was one of those places.

"You're not going to hover, now, are you?" I blinked at Hank. "I have stuff to do."

"What stuff?" Hank asked. Briefly, I considered telling him about the three men who'd intended to kill the subs they'd picked up at his club. Telling Hank that I'd offed them might be a mistake, so I kept that to myself.

"I want to investigate John's murder. And the murders of those other people."

"Bree, that could be dangerous."

"Look, I was safer helping Director Bill than with the Rome family," I pointed out before taking another bite of my sandwich.

"Director Bill called me earlier, after he saw you on the news."

"Fuck," I tossed the sandwich onto the plate and rubbed my forehead. I hoped Bill had gotten my note before he saw the garbage on TV.

"Eat," Hank lifted the sandwich and placed it in my hand. "Drink your milk, too. Director Bill was worried about you, that's all. I told him you were okay."

"Thanks," I sighed and took another bite of my sandwich.

"Will you be all right alone if I call to check on the club from my study?" Hank asked after settling me onto a leather sofa in his living room. He'd moved up in the world—his new condo had two bedrooms, a nice kitchen, a study and a spacious living area, complete with a big screen television. "You won't go anywhere, will you?"

"I don't have any plans right now, but I ought to go home," I muttered.

"Bree, how long have you been back? Here, I mean?" Hank's dark eyes grazed my face, searching for a suitable answer.

"I've been home nearly two months," I dropped my eyes and stared at my hands.

"And no word," he growled.

"Look, I had no idea who knew about that fucking book beforehand. And that stupid release form Jayson badgered me to sign? I wasn't given the truth, the whole time. How do you think that makes me feel? That every person on the entire planet may have seen those photographs? My childhood was fucked up. Now, my adult life is just as fucked. Tell me that isn't so, Hank. Tell me I can go downstairs and walk on the sidewalk without somebody recognizing me. Tell me the news outlets aren't looking for my phone number right now. Tell me I won't get hounded until the end of time. I came home, hoping people would have forgotten about me. For a while, that worked. Sort of. Now you want to quibble about two months."

"Bree, my heart is squeezing in my chest. All I'm thinking about is lost time. I've lost more than two years with you. Baby, you scare the shit out of me when you disappear. We never really talked about that misting trick you do. Remember—you told me about that before you found out about the book. How am I supposed to react to this—that you can do that and I can't hold onto you? All I want to do is keep you safe."

I stared at him—his face had gone paler than I'd ever seen it, and he looked sad. Troubled. "Honey," I rubbed my forehead, "I can't tell you about this. Not only will you not believe me, you'll try to have me committed. Frankly, if somebody came up to me and said these things, I wouldn't believe it, either."

"Start with the least fantastic thing, then. Tell me something you can prove easily, so I can start to believe."

"Hank, I'll scare holy hell out of you if I do that."

"Baby, I've been in wars. I've seen scary shit. Try me."

"Hank, I'm warning you—you don't need to see any of this." I watched as he walked toward me. Blinked as he knelt beside the sofa and reached out to touch my face.

"Baby, just give me something, so I can try to believe."

My breath was uneven—almost a shudder as I gazed at Hank's beautiful face. "Hank, after you see this, be honest. If I scare you, tell me. I'll leave. You won't see me again if that's what you want."

"Bree, there's nothing you can show me that'll do that."

"You haven't seen it yet," I muttered before letting my vampire claws slide out. My eyes were red, too—they always were when my fangs dropped. I showed him that. All of it. Frankly, it was the least scary thing about me.

Hank stared in shock. Well, most people would, if they didn't faint in the floor. "I don't drink blood, it makes me ill to even think about it," I let my claws slide back in and retracted my fangs. "I can toss your safe into the bay from here, most likely. I was called to help with those investigations, because vampires were behind those murders," I informed Hank, who still stared at me, his dark eyes unblinking.

"I killed the vamps here and in D.C. Another vamp killed the one in Austin, but he and I were both chasing him when he died. Director Bill thinks I'm talented, but he doesn't know that I'm a vamp since I can walk in daylight and eat normally. You're one of three people on Earth who knows this, now."

"Bree, that's amazing," Hank whispered. "I was so worried about you."

"See, I really can take care of myself. Mostly. Vampirism is why I don't have those scars anymore," I added. "I was covered with them, and half my bones had healed crookedly before I was turned. I could barely walk, and I was in constant pain."

"Baby, come here." Hank pulled me into his arms. "I still want to protect you. I don't care that you can toss my safe into the water from here. You're my baby girl." He rubbed my back gently as he held me tightly against him. "Bree?" Hank eventually pulled away to look into my eyes.

"Huh?" I blinked at him. In the dim light of his condo, his eyes looked black.

"This," he said, and put his mouth on mine. I fainted from the intensity of the kiss.

<h1 style="text-align:center">CHAPTER 4</h1>

"You can have this suite," Jayson pointed Hank through a door. Hank carried Breanne's unconscious body in his arms. He'd driven her to Jayson's home in San Rafael not long after she'd fainted. "Is she all right?" Jayson followed Hank into the bedroom and touched Breanne's cheek gently. "If Mom finds out she's here, she'll fly down immediately."

"Give it some time, Rome. Bree's fragile."

"Yeah. I get that," Jayson raked a hand through thick, blond hair. "Will she fight me? I think I want to hold her."

"I hope not. I told her you didn't know about the book, but she's still upset that she was misled on the Mercy Crossings story."

"I didn't mislead her. The only reason I didn't run that story was because of Barry fucking Stokes. He called and had a fit. I didn't want to upset Breanne any more than she might be already, so I canceled the article."

"Barry Stokes can fuck himself," Hank muttered before placing Breanne on the California king-sized bed.

"Agreed. Are you staying here, too?"

"Planning on it, unless you don't think it's a good idea. I want to share Bree's suite, but we'll see how she feels about that when she wakes."

"What about clothes?"

"Can Trina buy for her? Does she know what Bree likes?"

"My mother might be better at it," Jayson sighed.

"Then ask her. We'll need shoes, too. I can give your mother sizes, if she'll go out tomorrow."

"She'll be here tomorrow, if I tell her."

"True. Call your mother, Rome. I guess it can't hurt."

"She loves Breanne, and I'll tell her she needs some space. Mom won't push."

"Good. How does your mother feel about polyamory?"

"I haven't approached that subject, yet."

"Well, she may see things she might not understand, then."

"I'll make sure it's okay."

～

"Mom?"

"Honey, I didn't expect to hear from you again so soon."

"Mom, Bree's here. At the house. Hank brought her. She's sleeping in one of my bedrooms. The media is camped around her house and she needs clothes."

"I'll be on a plane tomorrow," Kathleen said immediately.

"I already arranged to have the jet pick you up at nine. Pack a bag if you want to stay."

"Of course I do. I want to talk to that poor girl."

"Mom, Hank says she's fragile. Give her some space, okay?"

"I know not to push. If she wants to tell me, that's fine. I'm not going to grill her."

"Good. Just act normal. I think that might help more than anything."

"I'll do my best. I just can't help but think about those photographs, though."

"I know. I can close my eyes and still see all that. It's horrible."

~

"Do we have a phone number yet?" Opal sat across from Bill at a restaurant near his office.

"I don't, but I can contact Hank Bell again," Bill nodded. "I think she'll talk to us. At least I hope she will. She sent notes, anyway, so that's a start."

"How did she live with that?" Opal shook her head.

"I don't know how she survived, or how she came out of that halfway sane."

"I figure there are plenty of emotional scars left behind," Opal snorted. "Do you think we'll ever get to work with her again?"

"I don't know. I worried about her before. I think I'd be more worried now."

"She's the best partner I've ever had," Opal nodded to the waitress, who set a burger basket in front of her.

"Thanks," Bill said as their waitress set grilled chicken in front of him. He waited until the waitress walked away before saying anything else. "I just worry that this book will do permanent damage. Look what happened today. That idiot reporter jumps all over her and she faints. I'm just glad Bell was there with her."

"I get the idea if the reporter hadn't badgered Hank Bell, Bree wouldn't have been there to begin with."

"You may be right. Let's face it, I don't stand a chance against that," Bill muttered.

"Bill, she cares about you. The note proves that. Don't go down without a fight. I think Hank was the reason she wasn't sleeping before. If that's the case, you've got a really good shot at this."

"Maybe we should plan a trip to San Francisco," Bill lifted an eyebrow at Opal as he cut into his chicken.

"Yeah. I kinda like it there."

~

Breanne's Journal

A cellphone ringtone woke me. John Mayer's *Waiting for the World to Change* played somewhere nearby, and I was at a loss to explain that. I didn't have that ringtone. Actually, I'd never downloaded any of those cool things—I always had one of the standards that came with the phone.

"Baby, your face is all scrunched up," Hank nuzzled my neck. My eyes popped open. We were in bed. Together. When had that happened?

"What?" I croaked. Yeah, my voice isn't the best when I wake up, and my hair probably looked like birds had nested in it.

"Better," Hank rumbled against my shoulder. "It's nearly noon. Kathleen Rome is out buying clothes for you and Trina is making lunch."

"Huh?" I attempted to slide away from Hank. He nuzzled his way toward my breasts and held onto me tighter when I tried to get away. "Why is Trina making lunch? Where the hell are we?"

"At Jayson's. Your house is surrounded by the media, right now."

"But what about your condo?" My mind was fuzzy, and the last memory I had was of Hank's mouth on mine. He'd kissed me for the first time, and I'd been unconscious during most of it.

"This is safer. Much safer. Plus, Trina, Kathleen and Jayson can help me keep an eye on you."

"Hank, I don't want to be mothered or smothered," I grumped, still trying to get away from him.

"Shh," Hank lowered his head and gripped a nipple in his teeth. Yeah, that got my attention right away. One of his hands wandered between my legs. "Oh, yeah. Yes. Yes, yes, yes," he breathed as his fingers made their way inside.

"That T-shirt doesn't do anything for you." Those were Trina's first words to me when I appeared in Jayson's kitchen. I hugged her for them. There was no *where have you been, or how did you live through that*

or any other nonsense. It was just Trina, and I appreciated that more than I could say.

"I agree, olive green doesn't do a thing for me," I grinned at Trina after I hugged her. "It looks good on Hank, though."

"Hank would look good wearing burlap," Trina nodded. "Want lunch?"

"What do you have?" I lifted an eyebrow at Trina. She'd cut her hair since I'd seen her last, and added highlights. It looked good. I told her that as we put soup and sandwiches together.

"This soup is awesome," I muttered after my first bite. Trina had cooked vegetable soup for me, and it was exceptional.

We'd all settled around the kitchen island to eat—Hank beside me, Trina on the opposite side so we could talk. That's where Kathleen Rome and Dan, her driver/bodyguard, found us a few minutes later.

Trina and I got food set in front of Kathleen, who wanted to fuss about it but held back. Dan merely nodded his thanks and started eating. He'd carried a carload of bags into the house, so he was likely starving anyway.

"Breanne, we've missed you," Kathleen murmured after taking a few judicious sips of her soup. "Trina, this food is excellent, as always."

"My pleasure," Trina grinned at Kathleen.

"Bree, I bought everything I could think of. If any of it doesn't fit or you don't like it, we'll return it," Kathleen turned to me.

"I'm sure it'll be fine," I said, studying her face as she went back to her food. I thought about reading her, then quickly changed my mind. I didn't want to see horror, overwhelming sympathy or guilt there. It would make me uncomfortable. All I wanted was for things to be as they were—before that stupid book's release.

"We can wash what needs to be washed this afternoon," Trina said. "After you try it on." She lifted an eyebrow at me, tacitly telling me I *would* be trying on the clothes Kathleen bought.

"Fine," I said.

"It better be fine. Ms. Rome probably spent a fortune on you."

"You're right. Thank you, Kathleen. I have no manners, in addition to no brain cells, obviously." I offered Kathleen a wobbly smile.

"Don't even worry about it," Kathleen waved away my thanks, but her shoulders relaxed visibly.

Hank left in one of Jayson's many automobiles to check on the club after lunch, leaving me to try on clothes while Trina and Kathleen Rome passed judgment on the purchases. I was allowed to keep two-thirds of it. The rest was placed in a return pile, and Kathleen told me she'd already made arrangements with a sales associate at the high-end department store where she'd bought clothing and shoes for me.

"It won't be a problem—I told her they were gifts and that some of it would likely be returned. It happens often," Kathleen shrugged. "Dan will take it back tomorrow."

We washed clothing after that—what needed it, anyway. I wanted to hug Kathleen for thinking of jeans, socks, athletic shoes and pullovers, in addition to the dresses, slacks, blazers and heels. Trina washed jeans and pullovers for me, right after the underwear came out. I folded, Kathleen supervised and Trina kept a conversation going.

Yes, it might seem stereotypical that Trina worked as Jayson's housekeeper, but she appreciated the fact that she could call him an ass to his face—when he was being an ass—and he'd laugh and agree with her. Jayson was an interesting paradox at times, and I just shook my head at all of it as Trina told us funny stories while clean clothes went into my borrowed closet.

"He really didn't know," Trina blinked dark eyes at me as we settled around the kitchen island for a before-dinner drink. "He growled at everybody for six months after that. Bree, it made him sick. Really."

"Yeah." I hunched my shoulders.

"Look, I know you don't want to talk about that. If you did, I would have heard about it before. I get that. If you need anything to get you through how people are gonna treat you now, just let me know. We can go to movies, shop on the Internet or just plain get drunk."

"The drunk thing doesn't sound bad," I gulped the wine I'd poured for myself.

"You can stay with me in Tahoe, if you need to get away," Kathleen offered. She'd accepted a glass of red wine—said it was better for her heart.

"I can't believe you cook meat, since you're vegetarian," Trina said when I rose to baste the game hens roasting in the oven.

"I cooked for Joyce's twins. They weren't vegetarian. Rice, pasta and beans is always cheaper. That's what I ate," I said, shutting the oven door and lowering the temperature.

"Breanne, do you know how horrible that sounds?" Kathleen's eyes were troubled.

"It suits me now," I shrugged. "I could change it, if I wanted. I don't want to."

"What's going on?" Jayson walked into the kitchen, followed by Hank.

"Cooking dinner," Kathleen rose to give Jayson a kiss on the cheek. "Breanne is cooking game hens for us."

"Bree?" Jayson turned a frown in my direction.

"I can cook it—I just don't eat it," I sighed. "I'm having a salad with fake chicken chunks and mashed potatoes with veggie gravy," I said.

"Are you mad at me?"

"No. Hank and your mother both say you didn't know. I believe them."

"Would you have believed me if I said the same thing first?"

"I hope so," I stared at my wineglass. "Although I feel the need to be really drunk right now."

"Bree, you're with friends. You don't have to get drunk unless you want to," Jayson said.

"Baby, don't be uncomfortable. We don't want you to feel that way," Hank pulled me off my barstool and hugged me.

"Packed? I found this military jet going our way," Bill grinned at Opal.

"Yeah. Two cases."

"Good. Let's go."

"I'm glad Hank asked us to come before we started begging," Opal nodded.

"We have a ride set up when we get there," Bill said. "They'll take us to Jayson Rome's place. I'm putting some discreet guards in place, too. They'll be watching that hill while Breanne's there. I don't want those snakes to get anywhere near her."

"You read those stupid websites too, didn't you?" Opal flipped long black hair over a shoulder and blinked once at Bill.

"Yeah. The conspiracy theorists are not only calling this a staged event, some are threatening Bree's life. They say she's an imposter and they're going hunting. Honestly, I have no idea where some of these fucked-up assholes come from. The truth is staring them in the face and they still don't believe it."

~

"Rome, we need to make room for two more," Hank said. He and Jayson had gone into Jayson's study after dinner, leaving Breanne, Trina and Kathleen in the kitchen. All three women were talking while Bree and Trina cleared things away and cleaned the kitchen.

"Which two?" Jayson lifted an eyebrow at Hank.

"Bill Jennings and another agent. Breanne knows both, and will likely be glad to see them. With Jennings here, keeping Bree safe will be much easier. He can chase the media away if he wants."

"How much danger might she be in?"

"Jennings says that death threats are showing up on those conspiracy websites. We don't have a clue how serious any of these are, or who is behind them. Bill told me he had people on it, but it's a low priority at the moment. Breanne isn't connected to national security, and while the FBI would normally handle this, Jennings has a close working relationship with the FBI Director. He'll get additional resources if it becomes necessary."

"Joyce Christian is still torturing Breanne—even from the grave. Sometimes, I want to strangle the old man."

"You'll have to stand in line," Hank growled.

"Does she seem more timid?" Jayson blinked at Hank. "Bree, that is?"

"In some ways, yes. PTSD can do that. That book was a big trigger."

"You have more experience with that than I do," Jayson raked fingers through his hair. "How's the funeral planning going?"

"All right so far. I've had a few calls from the media, since John's family won't talk to any of them."

"This is so tough," Jayson sighed. "Even with all the notoriety lately, the lifestyle still has to be hidden. Too many don't have a clue."

"They get the wrong kind of clues, usually," Hank rumbled.

Breanne's Journal

My whole body ached. The day had been long—and stressful. I didn't feel as if I could just be me anymore. My past had been blown open for everybody to dissect, and it put me on edge, no matter how nice the people around me were. The tension and stress made my body ache.

I climbed into bed after a hot shower. I had no idea whether Hank would show up—he and Jayson were talking in Jayson's study. It was after eleven; I was tired and wanted to read in bed. Unless I misted to my house to get it, I didn't have my tablet to read the novel I'd started.

With my back against a padded headboard, I hugged a pillow and contemplated going after the item in question. If Hank discovered I was gone, he'd likely go nuts. If I told him what I wanted, he'd do his best to talk me out of it. There wasn't any way to win the argument and I knew it. While I was busy silently debating the whole thing, Hank and Jayson walked into my bedroom. Without knocking, I might add.

"I want to go get my e-reader," I said, while Hank announced, "We're coming to bed with you—to talk," at exactly the same moment

"What?" all three of us said in unison.

"Hank, no," I said. "No offense, Jayson, but that's just," I didn't finish.

"Uncomfortable?" Jayson lifted an eyebrow. Yes, he was eye candy, but when he stood next to Hank, well, there was no comparison. Not to me, anyway.

"We just want to keep an eye on you, that's all," Hank said. "And ask questions."

"Jayson," I flopped a hand down beside me. "We can talk some other time. I'm exhausted."

"Bree, we just want to take care of you. Make sure you're safe. That's all. Hank told me about your disappearing trick. And a couple of other things I'm having trouble believing."

"Hank?" I stared at Hank in hurt surprise. No, I hadn't told him not to say anything, and he'd blabbed to Jayson fucking Rome. "Get out. Both of you," I snapped. Sliding off the bed, I went looking for the expensive silk kimono robe Kathleen had purchased for me. I pulled it on angrily while Hank and Jayson watched.

"Breanne, you're overreacting. Jayson will keep that information to himself, I promise," Hank said.

"Really, Hank? Do you know what the Council will do if they figure out I not only exist, but wasn't officially made—at least in their eyes?"

"Breanne," Hank said, a dark eyebrow lifting in surprise.

"Bree, I know about vampires. And werewolves. Hank told me two years ago. Right after you disappeared. Showed me some, too. Don't worry, we kept our distance," Jayson explained.

"Hank, what the hell?" I stared at him in shock.

"Baby, I told you I've seen scary stuff. I was special ops in the military. I just happened to have medical training, too. Sometimes I went into difficult situations because of that training. Nobody suspected I was anything other than a medic."

"Uh-huh," I crossed arms over my chest and glared skeptically at Hank.

"Baby, we're not gonna hurt you. We've told you that often enough."

"Sure. And that entails both of you getting in bed with me —to talk?"

"If we feel like it," Jayson sat on the left side of the bed and patted the mattress. At least they were still dressed. If they'd shown up in underwear, I probably would have freaked.

"What about the way I feel about it?" I demanded.

"Bree, you'll sit between us. Jayson isn't a total pig. If he falls asleep, he snores less than I do."

"How do you know that?" I narrowed my eyes at Hank.

"Survival camps," Hank grinned. "We go twice a year."

"Are you kidding me?" I turned to stare at Jayson, who shrugged modestly.

"I taught Jayson how to shoot, too. We usually go to the shooting range on Saturday mornings."

"Guns, too?" I turned back to Hank.

"Baby, we're not gonna threaten you with those. What did that asshole sheriff do to you?"

I wanted to cry. Right then and there. I couldn't. Gus Fulton had threatened to kill me the last time I'd run away from Joyce, at age fourteen. He'd have done it, too, if I'd resisted—I'd read it in his face. After Joyce got done with me, dying from a bullet in my brain would have been preferable.

"I'm not talking about that." I stalked toward the bedroom door. I had no idea where I might go—I wasn't familiar with Jayson's house. All I'd seen was the kitchen, laundry, formal living, dining and my bedroom.

"No, don't go, let's talk about this," Hank said, gripping my arm. I'd had to walk past him to get to the door. I probably should have misted out instead.

"Hank, just let me go," I muttered.

"Come on, we won't force you to talk. Just let us hug on you for a while," Jayson had gotten off the bed and came to stand beside Hank, who pulled me against him. Jayson's breath was warm against my temple as he leaned in to kiss my cheek. I have no idea what might have happened next. No idea. Bill and Opal's images filled my vision; I screamed, grabbed Hank and Jayson and folded space.

~

A local agent had been waiting for Bill and Opal after a transfer flight from McClellan AFB. "Why are we going this direction?" Opal asked as they passed Daly City.

"Traffic," their driver replied, taking an exit off the highway. The car was surrounded the moment they stopped at the end of the exit.

"Get out," their driver turned a gun on his passengers. "This is where we end you."

~

Breanne's Journal

Hank and Jayson were dumped behind the car as I screamed compulsion. "Let them go," I shouted. Two men held Opal; another two held Bill while the driver took aim—his pistol was pointed toward Bill, first.

Four men took their hands away, but the driver turned in my direction. I gasped as I read him—he had an obsession, and I had no idea whether my compulsion might work against him. "Girlie, I'm gonna shoot you first," he grinned, pointing the gun at me. I didn't have time to register that my question was answered—I held out a hand and he dissolved into glittering sparks.

"Don't you ever, ever, threaten Bill and Opal," I hissed as the sparks winked out. "Now, the rest of you," I turned on them. Yeah, my eyes were red and fangs pricked my bottom lip. "You're going to tell us everything you know, aren't you?" I stalked angrily toward them.

"Breanne, let us handle this," Bill said softly. "We'll take them in. Come on, sweetheart, you've done enough."

"Bree," Hank gripped my elbows, pulling me against his chest. "Let it go, baby. Okay?" They thought I was crazy. Maybe, for a few seconds at least, I had been. If I hadn't stepped in, Bill and Opal would be dead. I wasn't willing to let that happen, and I sure didn't want to attract the attention of anybody else out there by *Changing What Was* again.

~

Jayson closed my hand around a cup of hot chocolate. I was shaking while waiting in a small room inside a ten-story building in San Francisco. Bill had made a call; we'd gotten a conventional ride back to the city and Bill and Opal were in another room while four men were questioned by local agents.

Hank, Jayson and I waited in a small room nearby while the questioning took place. Hank paced and Jayson sent confused looks my way occasionally, but the wait had been made mostly in silence.

At least Bill had seen the sense in placing compulsion on the four men before we were picked up—they didn't need to spill their knowledge of me—that they'd seen me separate particles while showing red eyes and fangs. Bill knew I was vampire, now, and I had no idea what he'd say or do about that. I hunched my shoulders and sipped hot chocolate.

Bill and Opal walked in and closed the door behind them. I was too afraid to look up. I didn't want to see fear or condemnation in Bill's eyes. It brought back too many memories—memories of people staring while their faces (and minds) registered the horror they felt after seeing my scarred and misshapen face and body.

"Breanne," Bill knelt on one knee beside me. "Look at me, sweetheart." I lifted my eyes to him. He smiled. "Thank you for saving us," he said, before leaning in to kiss me.

~

"What is that called—what you did?" We all sat around Jayson's kitchen island. Jayson and Hank had passed out drinks; there was no glass of wine, this time—Hank handed me a Scotch and ginger ale, and at least two-thirds of it was Scotch. Jayson asked the question while sipping Scotch and soda.

"It's called separating particles. The Larentii do it," I mumbled. Well, they may as well have me committed for telling the truth.

"Those tall, blue men?" Bill blinked at me.

"You've seen them?"

"I've seen one. He saved your sister."

Lowering my shields, I read the memory in Bill. He'd seen Pheligar. I sighed and stared at the ice in my drink—it reflected the light from pendant lamps over Jayson's island. "You don't ever want to get into an argument with the Larentii—they know too much," I said.

"And they can apparently separate your particles," Bill blinked at me. "In addition to saving lives with their healing skills."

"Larentii," Jayson shook his head. "I'm having a dream. A really, really, vivid dream."

"They don't interfere, as a rule," I said.

"The Council doesn't know you exist, do they?" Bill sipped his drink.

"No, honey. In their eyes, I would be a rogue."

"We'll keep you away from them," Bill sounded determined.

"What is this Council everybody keeps talking about?" Jayson asked.

"The Vampire Council," I said. "They have a stranglehold on any vampire made. If you're not registered at your turning, you're a rogue. They have assassins and enforcers. If they find out about me, they'll send somebody hunting," I said.

"It doesn't matter that you can count the number of female vampires on your fingers and one set of toes," Bill said. "They tried to kill Lissa, too."

"Lissa?" Jayson turned back to me.

"My sister. Half-sister," I amended. "She and I have the same father. Different mothers, obviously."

"The vamps don't remember Lissa. Only the werewolves and a few humans do," Bill sighed. "It's tragic."

"A sister?" Hank blinked at me.

"Long story. Don't really want to talk about it," I said.

"Your father?" Bill asked.

"Still alive," I nodded. "Didn't have a clue he'd fathered me. Don't care if I never see him again."

"Breanne looks exhausted," Opal spoke for the first time. "Can we finish this discussion later?"

~

"Bree, do you want to go to the funeral with me?" Hank stroked hair away from my face. I don't know where he'd spent the night, but it hadn't been with me. Hank was waking me Friday morning with a question.

"Huh?" I raised my head and blinked into his dark eyes.

"John's funeral. Do you want to go? I think we can disguise you well enough."

"I can disguise myself," I mumbled. "Do you want me to go?"

"It doesn't matter," Hank began.

"Wait—they didn't cremate him, did they?"

"No—why?"

"I want to sniff around the body. See if I can tell anything from it."

"Are you kidding? It'll probably smell like embalming fluid or something."

"Well, I want to try," I sat up in bed with Hank's help and pushed hair away from my face.

"Then come eat breakfast. We need to leave by nine to get there on time."

By the time I walked out of my en suite bathroom, I looked like a distant cousin instead of myself. I'd kept my dark hair, but my eyes were also darker and my face looked quite different. No, I wasn't ugly —I'd spent too much of my life being ugly after facial fractures.

Hank took a long look at me and sighed when I walked into the kitchen. "I like the real Bree better," he muttered, lifting a coffee cup off the island and draining it.

"I like the real me better, too, but I figured it would freak Bill out if I disguised myself as my sister."

"What might freak me out?" Bill walked in dressed in workout clothes, Jayson close behind. Jayson apparently had a weight room in his behemoth of a house.

"Disguising myself as Lissa," I sighed.

"Yeah. And a few werewolves would be camped out on Rome's door if they caught sight of you," Bill took my chin in his hand and turned my face this way and that. "I like the real you better."

"We just had that conversation," I pointed toward Hank.

"Director Jennings might give you some competition in Krav Maga," Jayson informed Hank. "He handed my ass to me. On a plate."

"You're not bad, Rome," Bill settled on a barstool at the island. "The Department might hire you, if you weren't filthy rich and notorious," Bill grinned.

"I'm notorious?" Jayson tapped his chest with a finger. "I do my best to fly under the radar."

"You do, for the most part," Bill chuckled. "You can't hide from me, though."

"You had me investigated anyway?" Jayson sounded hurt.

"I have to make sure Breanne is safe. As much as I can, anyway. Hank has been a big help, and completely honest with us from the beginning. I like that."

I watched the conversation as if I were watching a boxing match. At the moment, Bill had gotten in several quick punches. Jayson was taking it on the chin, and he didn't like it. At all.

"Bill, can we talk after the funeral?" I asked. He already knew I was going with Hank. Yeah, I needed to tell him about the three I'd killed from Hank's club—I knew their names and I knew all three were on Bill's radar. He needed to know they were dead. I also needed to explain about the Sirenali, and that wasn't going to be easy.

"Sweetheart, I think Opal and I will come with you. I'm almost afraid to let you out of my sight." Bill's eyes had gone honey-brown as he blinked at me. Yes, he loved me. Adored me. I had no idea why, but it made me feel good. I still had no idea how Hank really felt about me, other than possessive. I still kept myself from reading him, but more and more, I was too afraid it might be painful if I did.

"Thanks, Bill." I put my arms around him and squeezed. His arms moved around me and large, warm hands rubbed my back carefully.

"It's okay, baby," Hank's fingers were stroking my hair as Bill held me. "Bill understands, now."

"Huh?" I pulled away from Bill and blinked at Hank.

"Polyamory," Hank nodded. "We talked for a while after you went to bed last night."

"This is confusing," I stepped back from both of them.

"That's not what we intended to happen. Just let this go, Bree. Do what you want. We're okay with that," Jayson interjected.

"Aren't we going to be late if Bill doesn't get in the shower?" I said, intentionally changing the subject. We'd just gone into uncharted territory and it frightened me.

"I'll get in the shower," Bill accepted a cup of coffee from Jayson, who'd gone to the coffeepot and poured two cups. "I'll be out in fifteen. Opal should be ready about then."

"Miss Thang, is your bed made up?" Trina walked in with a basket of laundry.

"Miss Trina, my bed is all made up," I nodded. "And the bathroom counter is wiped off, too. Towels in the hamper."

"You're just too neat for your own good," Trina set the basket on the island and grinned at me.

"You're too hyper, did you know that?" I grinned right back.

"I have to be, to pick up after Mr. Messy Rome," Trina said.

"Mr. Messy Rome is right here," Jayson pointed out.

"Did you hear anything?" Trina pulled a towel from the basket to fold. Jayson laughed.

"Are they really?" Opal was right behind me as Hank and Bill walked into the funeral home as if they owned the place.

"Yeah." A knot of people stood just inside the door, most of them dressed in leather. Three of the women wore everyday collars—made to look like necklaces, but bearing a large locket with a pronounced keyhole at the center.

Opal had whispered her question, and I knew what she was asking. These were John's friends—from the leather community.

"How do they do that?" Opal muttered.

They want it. Hank says they go looking for it. If they're happy, I'm happy. I sent mindspeech as we walked past the people in question.

"I'll admit, I was a little worried when Hank dressed as he did," Opal murmured as we were led to a pew in the chapel. Hank was dressed in leather, too—pants, boots and a jacket over a long-sleeved black shirt. Hank and Bill left me with Opal while they went to speak with John's family.

"Baby, come with us, the family says you can see the body before they bring it in," Hank was back with Bill.

"Thanks," I said, rising from my seat. Opal followed, too—I think she was afraid to let me out of her sight.

Hank was right—the body did smell like embalming fluid—to me, anyway. That didn't stop me from getting information, though. John's spirit stood right next to the polished black coffin.

CHAPTER 5

reanne's Journal

Bill drew in a breath while Hank and Opal went completely silent. I'd linked with them and allowed them to see the vision of John's spirit through my eyes. They could hear him, too—through me. John's brother, Chris, stood nearby, and since I didn't want to alarm him, I left him next to the coffin and unaware.

"I don't know the names," John said. "All I saw were faces."

Visualize the images, I silently requested. Images filtered into my mind. Opal gasped softly. She recognized Oscar Forde just as easily as Bill and I did. The two humans I didn't recognize, but with an obsession and without a scent, I couldn't identify them, either. I figured one of them had dumped the body, and at least we had faces to connect to the crimes.

"Do you have any message for your family?" I asked aloud. "Give me something only your brother might know, so he'll believe," I added.

"Tell him we set the grass on fire behind the garage after we stole the old man's cigarettes to smoke," John said. "Nobody ever found out about that."

"All right. What do you want me to say after that?"

"That I love him. That this isn't the end. We'll see each other again."

"I'll tell him," I nodded.

"Thanks." John faded away.

"Chris," I turned to John's brother, who looked very much like John except he didn't shave his head, "John says to tell you he loves you, and that this isn't the end. You'll see each other again. And just to make sure you believe that he said those things, he also said to tell you that he remembers stealing cigarettes from your father, smoking and setting the grass on fire behind the garage."

"What?" Chris gaped at me. "How did you know that?"

"He told me," I said, shrugging. "He really does love you, but he's made the walk to the other side, now. That doesn't mean he won't check in now and then, because he probably will."

"To the other side?" Chris wiped away tears.

"Honey, he needs the rest and support he'll get there. Let him leave all this behind for a little while, okay?"

"I don't know what to do," Chris wept. My heart broke for him, and then I did something I hadn't done since I was tiny. I sent *Love* to Chris. He wrapped me in his arms, sobbed once and then pulled away, staring at me through his tears.

"Oh, my gosh," he whispered reverently. "Thank you."

"You're welcome. Just remember, John will always be a part of you. If you need anything, let Hank know. He'll pass the message to me and I'll do what I can."

"Thank you. You just made this day bearable."

"We'll get through this," I squeezed his fingers in mine.

"Yeah."

"What was that you did—was that a ghost?" Opal blinked at me as she, Bill and I sat at a table in The Lean Bean.

"I guess you could call it a ghost. It was John's spirit." I knew this conversation might come, and I didn't want to upset or frighten Opal or Bill. More than I had already, anyway. And I wanted to explain about the Sirenali, too.

Hank had gone with John's family to the cemetery in Oakland. Bill and Opal took charge of me and we ended up at my favorite coffee shop. Bill wanted to discuss Oscar Forde's involvement in John's death, and he and Opal both wanted to know about ghosts.

"I've seen some strange things, and figured I'd seen ghosts a few times, but I could never prove anything," Opal shook her head.

"I've only seen a few—most of them head to the other side as soon as the way is cleared. Some wait a while. Some refuse to go at all."

"Weird," Opal sighed.

"Yeah."

"Is that the only information on Oscar Forde?" Bill asked, lifting his cappuccino to drink.

"I haven't gotten any prior news about him being in the area, so yeah. It is," I watched Bill's face as he digested the news.

"I figure Keir Arthur isn't far away," Opal said. "At least that's the idea I got when we were in Austin—that they usually stayed close."

"There's something else you need to know," I said, toying with my cup. I should have been proud of myself—my hands were only shaking a little.

"What's that?" Bill set his cup down and studied me carefully.

"What's behind all this to begin with," I said. "Beginning with the college girl murders."

"What's behind this? It's not just crazy rogue vamps?" Opal shrugged out of her jacket as she whispered the words. The Lean Bean was busy and nobody was likely to overhear, but there was no need to take chances.

"It's someone belonging to a race called the Sirenali," I said. "You don't want to meet this person—he, she or whatever. It would be best if I track it, because it's just too dangerous."

"But what does this have to do with the rogues we're chasing?" Bill asked. "What can these creatures do that's so dangerous?"

"The Sirenali can place obsessions. Not compulsion, like the vamps can—these are obsessions. Once placed, only the Sirenali who placed it can remove it, or the one obsessed dies. If a Sirenali asks you to kill, you'll become quite inventive on how and when you kill, in an effort to please your Sirenali master. The other problem with them is this— normally I can use mental ability to find somebody. I can't find the Sirenali or anybody they've obsessed. Something blocks the power used, and I can't explain that."

"You're saying that Oscar Forde and Keir Arthur are obsessed by one of those things?" Opal stared at me in alarm.

"And Tanner Johns and the other two vamps involved in those murders," I nodded. "All of them had an obsession. Bill, your driver had an obsession, too. That's why I had to kill him the way I did. We couldn't arrest him—he'd never lose the desire to kill you and Opal. It was the only way."

"Breanne, that's the most frightening thing I've heard in a long time." Bill's eyes had gone dark with worry. "I don't have a body to give to the driver's family, either. This is far too complicated."

"You ought to know this, too," I went on. "Sirenali look human— actually they use power to appear human. They're not, obviously. If they drop the disguise, you see what they really are—scaled amphibians with a mostly humanoid shape. They have sharp teeth and prefer seafood of some kind when they eat. I believe Sirenali may be behind all the Earth myths about Sirens, only they don't sing—not to my knowledge, anyway. They just place obsession, and most people have no way to resist."

"So they could use their talent to instruct a ship's crew to wreck on sharp rocks," Opal observed.

"Yep. Or any number of other, nasty things. Since I don't know how long this Sirenali has been here, I can't say if this is a recent arrival or somebody who's been around for a really long time, and just decided to conspire with the enemy." I realized my mistake the moment the last few words left my mouth.

"Conspiring with the enemy?" Bill was immediately alert and more than curious.

"Bill, that one's not your fight. It's somebody else's," I said. "Even with all the firepower on Earth, you wouldn't have enough to engage in that battle. What we have to do is concentrate on this particular Sirenali—at least I'm hoping it's only one—and take it out."

"Have you fought any of these before?" Opal's eyes narrowed in speculation.

"Yeah. Their obsession doesn't work on me, for some reason. The last one I killed was a piece of work. Nasty, too."

"Let's get back to the more immediate problem—Oscar Forde and the two human men we saw through Breanne," Bill said. "If we track any of them, perhaps we'll find the Sirenali at the end of that trail."

"I was hoping for that too. Bill, there's something else," I said.

"There's more? Breanne, I'll have to get my heart checked as it is," Bill placed a hand over his heart.

"Honey, you're not feeling bad, are you?" I was about to come out of my seat. I'd already had one close call when Kathleen Rome had a heart attack. I didn't need Bill to fall, too.

"No, sweetheart, sit back down," Bill motioned with a hand. "I'm fine, it's just that this is almost too much for we mere mortals."

"Well, here it is, then," I said. "I followed three men who took three women from Hank's club one night. One was Russian—Igor Karyavin was his name, and the other two were Americans. Brothers, too. Jack and Caleb Stafford."

"We've been tracking Karyavin for a while. I had no idea he was in the country," Bill said. "Do you know where he is now? Karyavin can cause more trouble than anybody might imagine."

"Dead," I said. "Along with the other two. They all bore an obsession, and they were going to kill those women. I stopped them and sent the women home."

"You killed them the same way you did the driver?" Opal asked. "Damn, I knew I liked you for a reason."

"Opal, it only sounds impressive," I sighed. "It's a necessity when I do it, because there isn't any other way to protect the innocent."

"Breanne, I realize it's a necessity," Bill said. "I'm just glad we have you here to explain this. If you weren't, we'd still be in D.C. and fumbling in the dark, thinking this was just another crazy serial killer that the locals should deal with."

"I've been sneaking around, doing my own investigation, but this is such a confusing mess," I said. "Hank doesn't want me out of his sight, and how can I explain any of this to him and Jayson, anyway? I haven't told him that he was almost in the same situation as Dale Saylor—having customers taken from his club and murdered. He still ended up in the spotlight when John was killed. Three dead women would have made things a whole lot worse."

"Breanne, I don't know what to say about this. You continually terrify me," Bill huffed. "It's not that I think you're helpless—far from it. I'm just afraid of losing you. I don't think my heart will take that much punishment again. Hank probably feels the same way—he doesn't want to lose you, either."

"Bill," my shoulders drooped. "I don't want to upset either of you, but who else do you have to track a Sirenali? Do you know how dangerous these obsessions really are? How many girls died because of it? How many have died in San Francisco, recently? All it takes is obsessing vampires, werewolves or anything else that's stronger than humans and things get bad in a hurry."

"This isn't good," Opal placed a hand on Bill's arm. "If this thing can order vampires around, we really don't have any defense against it. Bill, we don't have a choice except to put Bree in the middle of this."

"Breanne, I worry about your emotional health, not just your physical well-being," Bill shook his head. "I don't want you out there on your own, chasing these things down. You need somebody at your back. Opal will be here with you, if I can't be. I have meetings scheduled in D.C., but I can fly back and forth when necessary. Hank's ex-special ops, so he can help out whenever he's available. I have his records—Hank's a badass when he needs to be."

"I worry about you—I know you think you're protecting me, but really," I began.

"That's not up for debate," Hank settled in the seat beside me.

"Huh?" I stared at him. He was still dressed completely in leather—except for the shirt he wore under the vest.

"Breanne Hayworth, listen to me," Hank took my chin in his hands. "Bill and I love you. Opal loves you. Jayson, Kathleen and Trina love you. You're not going anywhere without somebody with you. I have a license to carry a gun. Jayson does, too. Opal can carry whatever the hell she feels like carrying, as can Bill. I don't want more of your disappearing for two years. That's bullshit."

"Hank," I attempted to pull away from him. He held onto my chin and leaned in to kiss me. Hard. "I just buried a friend," Hank murmured against my mouth before kissing me again. "That was hard enough. If we lose you, the world might fly apart."

He pulled back, his dark eyes locked on mine. "Understand me? You don't go anywhere alone. Somebody goes with you, and that somebody better be packing."

"Breanne, it's not just the ones you're hunting," Bill said.

"Huh?" I turned my gaze from Hank to Bill.

"You're getting death threats on those fucking websites," Opal jumped in. "All those Joyce Christian supporters. They've claimed the whole time you were gone that you were fictitious and a front for the plot to bring down Joyce's shiny reputation. Now that you've conveniently shown up and your face has been televised all over, threats against your life are being made on those conspiracy websites. We're trying to track them, but we have limited resources to put on it and frankly, those may just be the crackpots. Those who are serious are probably loaded up and actively hunting you, since they know where you were last seen."

"Are you kidding?" I stared at Bill in alarm.

"These people aren't known for patience and rational thinking," Hank turned my face toward him again. "They have weapons and they're crazy enough to use them."

"Hank, this is insane," I quavered.

"Baby, we need to guard your back while you're doing what needs doing. Okay? Come on, now, let's go back to Jayson's and work up a plan of action."

~

"We've got three we're tracking, but they're not in California," Bill pointed out. "I got that information this morning. This one," he showed us a photograph on a tablet, "we're concerned about him. We think he's been involved in other things, but we can't prove any of it."

I stared at Vernon Clark's face and blinked. "Bill, he was directly involved in the murder of two border agents," I said.

"Fuck. Bree, are you sure?" Bill came to stand behind me as I stared at Vernon's face.

"Yeah. He was there and ordered two others to shoot," I said. "After driving them across the border into Mexico," I added.

"We found the bodies, but couldn't figure out how they got there," Bill said.

"Are you doing that trick again?" Opal lifted a dark eyebrow at me.

"Yeah. I guess I am," I replied. "Usually I keep a shield up, so I won't see everything, but in a case like this, I drop the shield so I can see what's there."

"You read people?" Jayson had been invited to the planning session, and he thought he was in heaven. Aside from his kinky tendencies, he was no mild-mannered magazine mogul. Jayson wanted to get into it; his excitement was easy to see.

"Yeah. I can read most people, but there are a few I can't read. Sadly, you're one of them."

"Thank goodness," Jayson leaned back in his chair, relieved. We sat around Jayson's poker table in his game room—Trina and Kathleen were the only ones not with us. Bill still stood behind me and squeezed my shoulders gently.

"That's probably a good thing—that you can't read Jayson," Hank said. "Have you read me?"

"Hank, I haven't tried. I was afraid to, after a while."

"Try now," he insisted.

"But," I whined. I had no desire to read everything there was to know about Henry Hank Bell—it frightened me.

"Come on. Let's do this," Hank ordered.

"Fine," I grumped and lowered my shield. I shouldn't have been surprised. I couldn't read him, either.

"I can't read you," I said.

"Did you try?"

"Yes, Hank. It's not something that has to be forced. If I can't read you, I know right away."

"How many people have you not been able to read?" Bill asked.

Ashe. Trajan. Trevor. Kooper. Stellan. Fes. Kalenegar. All their images flew through my mind before I answered. "Counting Hank and Jayson, nine," I said. "I can sort of read the Sirenali, but their obsessions are obscured for some reason."

My admission forced me to explain about the Sirenali to Jayson and Hank, who'd missed the previous conversation.

"I'm living in a science-fiction novel," Jayson tossed up a hand.

"Just because you've never seen it doesn't mean it can't exist," I pointed out. "You just haven't been in the right place or time before."

"Being in the right place and time with Sirenali sounds crazy and scary as hell," Jayson breathed. "Why can't it be some of those short, friendly guys?"

"There are short, friendly guys, but they don't have any desire to invade somebody else's planet," I said, thinking of the Amterean Dwarves. The only thing they might want to invade was Earth's libraries and information systems. Information was more valuable than precious metals on Amterea.

"We're screwed," Jayson muttered. Opal stifled a snicker.

"We'll be checking out that new club Monday night," Hank poured more wine in my glass at dinner. I didn't want to go, but there was no other way. KingDom's was the new club in town and had been in operation roughly six months. I'd seen photographs, and it was certainly upscale, there was no doubt.

Bill checked on the ownership, but it was listed under a corporate name. He was still trying to get individual names for us, since Hank and Jayson thought there might be connections between it and the deaths in San Francisco. If that were true, then Oscar Forde had to be involved in some way.

"We can't just walk into the place and start asking questions," Bill noticed my pout. "We need those tricks you have, Bree. I realize this might be hard for you, but you'll be with Hank and Jayson. I'd send Opal in, but she wouldn't be as effective."

"Baby, I'll punch anybody who bothers you," Hank said. "We have to appear as if we belong, or they'll know something's up."

"Plenty of people there may recognize Hank and me, but you," Jayson accepted the wine bottle from Hank and filled his glass.

"Yeah, yeah," I grumped. They intended to dress me as someone they might bring into the club and that terrified me.

"Just do that reading trick long enough to tell if anybody's involved," Hank said, pushing my wineglass toward me. "There's no need to be afraid."

"Says you," I lifted my wineglass and pointed it toward him accusingly. I didn't want to have a meltdown in a dungeon where most people had gone for a good time, just because I didn't view what they were doing as a good time.

"What about that mind communication trick?" Jayson asked. "I know you can communicate with us, but what if we want to communicate back?"

"Jayson," I muttered helplessly before letting my forehead fall onto the island.

"Baby, don't do that," Hank pulled me up and rubbed my forehead with gentle fingers.

"It would make things so much easier if we could all do that," Opal sighed.

"Huh?" I blinked at Opal. Well, was I who I was or not? Lissa had given mindspeech (and a few other nice gifts) to Norian Keef and several others.

"Fine," I muttered before doing what my sister had done. I gifted Hank, Jayson, Bill and Opal with mindspeech. I couldn't help but glow softly while I did it. They didn't feel a thing, and Opal was still gazing at me expectantly when I was done.

"Go ahead, think something in my direction," I told Opal.

Are you sleeping with Hank? Opal sent.

What the hell? What kind of question is that? I sputtered mentally.

You heard me? She sounded very surprised.

I heard you.

Are you gonna say it's none of my business? She smiled at me from her seat across the island.

It isn't, but the answer is yes. No funny stuff, though.

Gotcha.

"What's going on?" Bill had gone from staring at Opal to staring at me.

You have mindspeech now, honey, I sent. *Opal and I were having a private conversation.*

"I have mindspeech?" Bill sputtered.

"You, Hank, Opal and even Jayson has it," I grumped.

I can call you vanilla like this? Jayson sent.

Jayson, I could have predicted you'd insult me right away, I sent back. Jayson scooted his barstool back and stared. I was grateful that Kathleen and Trina had eaten earlier while we'd had our meeting. Both had gone to bed while the rest of us had a late supper afterward.

"Holy fucking cow," Jayson whispered reverently.

"You won't be able to communicate with anybody else who doesn't have the talent, but you can send to Hank, Bill, Opal or me anytime," I said.

Oh, baby, I want to fuck you until you scream, Hank's voice filtered into my head.

You know, I predicted Jayson's insult and your reaction, too, I sent right back, ducking my head so the others wouldn't see the way my cheeks heated.

We're going on a little errand tomorrow, too, Hank added. The jerk didn't even have the grace to look guilty about embarrassing me.

What errand? I refused to look at him.

We'll take care of your bush. You'll need that when we go to the club, and I prefer to keep that out of my mouth, he said.

"That's it, I'm done," I scooted my barstool back and tossed my napkin onto the island.

It's not an insult, love. It's just the way things are. Look, if it'll make you feel better, I'll get mine done at the same time.

Yours is bare, I pointed out.

It's a little prickly. It's almost time anyway. Waxing the first time might not be comfortable, but I'll get you through it.

Unbelievable. I marched right out of Jayson's kitchen and walked the maze leading to my bedroom.

❧

"Zen, do you think I'll ever be allowed to leave Nrath?" Perdil seemed mired in melancholy, for some reason.

"No idea. Perhaps you should ask Lord Kifirin. It has been quite some time since we were brought here," Zendeval turned away from the book he studied to stare at the Liffelithi Dwarf. "Surely your penance has been served," Zendeval added.

"Not likely. I made the mistake of loving the wrong woman," Perdil muttered.

"Then find another to love," Zendeval sighed and went back to the book.

"I cannot. She still visits my dreams, at times. No other will do for me."

"I cannot help you, then. When you focus your affections on the Dark Lord's mate, you can only expect woe to come of it."

"I will retain my hope that I will be allowed to go to her, although it is a trial to do so," Perdil muttered and walked away.

❧

Breanne's Journal

"Bree, waxing isn't a big deal," Jayson said. He and Hank had gone for their usual target practice earlier Saturday morning. Bill and Opal had gone with them. I had no desire to watch or listen, so I stayed home.

I didn't tell Hank, but I misted to my house to get my e-reader while they were gone. Only two news vans were still parked outside, and that made me feel a tiny bit better. I'd read a book until Hank and the others got back.

"Bree, you owe me for going after that idiotic tablet of yours," Hank lifted a dark eyebrow. Yeah, he was considering my punishment, and it involved hot wax and discomfort.

"I told you I wanted it." I only whined a little, and honestly, he should have been satisfied with that.

"I would have gotten a new one for you, if you'd just asked," Jayson broke in.

"I don't want a new one. I want mine," I whined a little more. "It has all my stuff on it already."

"Breanne, I told you not to go anywhere without someone with you," Hank frowned.

"I misted the whole time. You think I wasn't careful?" I glared at Hank.

"Come on, we're going to the salon. You can whine on the way," Hank gripped my arm and steered me toward the door.

Did I realize I'd be meeting Jayson's big-chested playmate at the salon? No. I almost breathed a visible sigh of relief to learn she was the receptionist and not the one who'd perform the hair pulling.

"Belinda, this is Breanne," Jayson introduced me when I walked in between him and Hank. She was around five-eight, had a chest anyone would be proud of and tattoos showing under a laced-up bustier and white peasant blouse over a dark skirt. Her hair was blonde with shocking pink highlights. On her, it didn't look bad.

Did you intend to embarrass me? I flung at Jayson. *A little warning might have been nice.*

"Jayson adores you," Belinda crooned at me.

"Jayson adores Jayson," popped out of my mouth before I thought.

"He said you were feisty," Belinda grinned. Okay, I might like her. I sure didn't want to read her, though. No way I wanted to read what kinky stuff she and Jayson might get up to.

We followed her to a room behind a beaded curtain. Three tables were inside. "We had to bring in another table, but it wasn't a big deal," Belinda grinned at me.

"Jayson Rome," I turned on him, then.

"Hey, I'm due. They'll do all of us together, and if you scream, Hank and I can laugh."

"Really?" Yes, sarcasm seemed appropriate at the moment.

Belinda left us after asking us to undress and wear the robes provided. Hank and Jayson dropped their clothes while I hid behind the changing screen.

"I don't want to do this," I complained when Hank herded me toward the center table.

"You don't have a choice," he lifted me and deposited me on the table. "Look at me, Breanne," he growled. I blinked at him. "Tell me now that you won't go anywhere without someone else with you," he said.

"Hank, we should discuss this some other time," I said.

"Then we'll discuss it another time. Soon." He moved away, sat on his table and lay back to stare at the ceiling, hands behind his head. I sighed and forced myself to stop watching him.

"I'm never doing that again," I hissed as I limped toward Jayson's SUV. My lady parts felt as if they were on fire, and I wanted nothing more than to find an ice pack, slap it on the affected area and moan out my misery.

Hank and Jayson seemed to be fine, the assholes. Well, they were used to having hair ripped out of tender parts. I wasn't. They weren't talking either, and that was probably a good thing—I wanted to kill both of them, just on general principal.

I squirmed in the back seat during the trip home, and misted from Jayson's vehicle straight to the kitchen.

"Ice pack?" I begged while Trina stared in alarm. Without a word, she opened the freezer and pulled one out. "Thanks," I whimpered and ran toward the hallway leading to my borrowed bedroom.

Misting out of my clothes, I flopped onto the bed and placed the ice pack over myself as gently as I could. It still hurt and tears threatened. I wished for ibuprofen, but I didn't want to move to get it. I only wanted the misery to go away.

"Bree?" Hank knocked on my bedroom door.

"Go away," I snapped. "I'm in the middle of a serious ice pack session." I was. I was naked as I lay on my bed, doing my best to will the ache away. The door creaked. "Do you ever do what anybody says?" I yelled when Hank came in anyway. I was grabbing for the blanket lying across the foot of the bed, but it wasn't cooperating.

"Baby, I have this." Hank was dangling a bottle of lotion in his hands. "This is made to treat freshly-waxed skin. It has aloe, vitamin e and other stuff that'll help."

"I want to kill you right now." I still held the ice pack to my (now puffy) privates, and I'd given up on the blanket.

"I figure you do." He settled on the edge of the bed and reached for the ice pack I awkwardly held against me.

"Don't touch anything," I refused to let the ice pack go.

"Baby, it'll go away. We'll put this on and things will be fine."

"Easy for you to say."

"Come on." He touched the ice pack with gentle fingers. His voice had gone soft, as if he were coaxing a feral kitten to his hand.

"I'll do it myself." I held my hand out for the bottle of lotion.

"No. I caused this, I'll fix it." He pulled my ice pack away. I slapped a hand over my face. When had things come to this? Did I have no shame?

"I'm a shameless hussy," I muttered as Hank dribbled lotion over the tender parts.

"Baby, don't ever say that again," He said softly as his fingers rubbed lotion over me in soothing strokes.

"But I am. All you had to do was crook a finger that first time and there I was, faster than a whore whose rent was due. Wax my pussy for you? Sure thing," I moaned.

"Shhh," Hank crooned. "My baby hurts. Let me fix it." His fingers rubbed more lotion into my skin. At least he wasn't heavy handed—I might have come off the bed if he were. "I'll find ibuprofen," he laid the ice pack over me again before rising from the bed and walking into my bathroom.

He was back in record time with three tablets and a glass of water. Lifting me gently against him after taking a seat on the bed again, Hank watched as I swallowed the pills and drank the water. "Try to sleep, okay?" He pulled the blanket up and settled it over me. "You'll feel better after a while, I promise. I'll wake you later for dinner."

"Not hungry." I wanted to roll over on my side, but the situation prevented it.

"Come on, baby, close your eyes," careful fingers stroked hair back from my forehead. "Hank loves his baby. So much. Go to sleep, love. Sleep." I fell into darkness.

CHAPTER 6

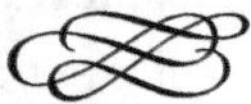

I had all day Sunday to get over Saturday. Hank woke me for dinner the night before as promised, but I only nibbled at a sandwich before going back to bed. At least I wanted breakfast when I woke at six-thirty.

The kitchen was deserted when I wandered in and made a cup of coffee for myself before searching for eggs in the fridge.

"Breakfast?" Bill walked in, freshly showered and dressed.

"Hey, Director Bill," I managed a smile for him.

"I like it better when you call me honey," he moved to the coffeepot and poured a cup for himself.

"Honey, are you hungry?" I asked.

"I sure am. What's on the menu?"

"I think I can throw biscuits together, and there's ham and bacon in the fridge to go with eggs," I said.

"That sounds good. Need help?"

"Can you make the bacon?"

"I've been frying bacon since I was ten," he grinned.

"Honey, you're just way too self-sufficient," I stood on tiptoe to kiss him. Bill blinked for a moment before wrapping his arms around me. That's how Opal found us—me wearing Bill as an overcoat.

"Breakfast *and* entertainment," Opal poured herself a cup of coffee while Bill and I sheepishly broke apart.

"For that, you get to make eggs," Bill informed her. "Bree's making biscuits."

"If somebody's willing to make biscuits for me, I'll do eggs anytime," Opal agreed.

We were gathering around the island to eat when Kathleen walked in. "Sit down, I'll fix a plate for you," Bill put a hand on my shoulder to keep me from rising.

"I don't believe I've ever had the Director of a government agency serve me breakfast," Kathleen laughed as Bill set a plate of food in front of her.

"It may never happen again, so enjoy it," Bill grinned.

"There's breakfast? That I didn't have to make?" Trina wandered in with a yawn.

"Yeah. Sit your tush down, I'll get it," I said.

"Tell me about Somalia," Kathleen said. I watched as she lifted a strip of bacon and bit into it.

"That," I hunched my shoulders. Well, Barry Stokes had fired me. Was I still obligated not to talk about that? Besides, Bill could talk about it just as easily as I could. I cut my eyes in his direction.

Breanne, I can't ever say I was there. You can talk about the sandstorm—I think that's what she's curious about, Bill sent. *Hank and Jayson told her and Trina about you and your peculiar talents,* he added. *They're okay with all of it.*

"It was awful," I said uncomfortably. "And it wasn't anything natural, either," I said. "I knew Mercy Crossings' tents would get blown away, and there were sick and injured kids inside. I did the only thing I could—I gathered everybody in the tents into my mist and got the hell out of there. I didn't realize at the time that the people I left behind in the city would die. They all died. Nobody lived over that."

"Where did you take them?" Bill asked. He knew, he just pretended he didn't.

"We had a ship in international waters off the coast. I took them there. I found out then that all the people died behind us, and those kids were orphans. It didn't make me feel good at all."

"Breanne, are we discussing Somalia now?" Hank walked in and dropped a hand on my shoulder.

"I don't owe Barry Stokes anything anymore," I muttered. "And I'm not talking about anything that concerns him or Mercy Crossings anyway. I got his volunteers out, plus eighteen kids. If he has a problem with that, then he can complain to my face."

"So you saw the letter he wrote. Did you read it in a newspaper?" Kathleen asked.

"No. I saw the actual letter after Terry mailed it to me six weeks ago," I sighed. "It was already open when I got it, so I think Terry's the one who leaked it to the press. I don't mind—Barry needed to be smacked around a little."

"He needs more than that," Trina grumped. "He needs to lose his job over it."

"That won't happen," I shook my head. "I wish I could say it doesn't bother me, but it does. He didn't even say thanks for my service, and let me tell you, he owed me that—in a bigger way than he might imagine."

"It's behind us," Hank leaned in to kiss my cheek. "Let it go. Stokes is an asshole and not worth our worry."

"Stokes *is* an asshole," Jayson agreed. He shuffled toward the island, his hair still damp from a shower. "Is there food? I'm starving." He and Hank served themselves and sat down to eat.

"These are really good," Jayson lifted another biscuit from the pan and spread butter on it. I'd made a huge pan of biscuits and they were nearly gone.

"Then I might make them for you again," I said, sipping a second cup of coffee. Usually my second cup was decaf, because caffeine left me feeling wired if I had too much.

"I wasn't aware that you could cook this well," Jayson spread jam on his biscuit and bit into it.

"I can cook," I hugged myself. "I just don't do a lot of it, nowadays." I'd spent too many years making three meals a day, with no breaks or days off. It was nice just to go to a restaurant if I wanted, or throw a veggie sandwich together.

"Tell me about Joyce's twins," Jayson said.

"They're beautiful," I muttered. "Completely innocent. They just need somebody to take care of them."

"And you did that—made sure they were cared for." Kathleen toyed with her coffee cup.

"Nobody else would," I said. "Look, this isn't comfortable for me."

"Someday, you have to talk about this," Hank said.

"Not today," I scooted my chair back. "It helps if I don't think about it. No, I don't blame myself for any of this, either, so a shrink doesn't have to worry about that part of the equation."

"Who do you blame, sweetheart?" Bill reached for my hand.

"Who can you blame? My father for not knowing I existed? My mother who was sent to prison for manufacturing drugs and giving me away? The orphanage? A deranged politician with too much power? Fate? Religion?" I shook my head. "I can't even cry about it. Not when somebody else is around. You know what happens if I do?" Yeah, I was about to out myself.

"What happens, baby?" Hank said gently.

"If you touch my tears, you see everything I can see in anybody else. Everything. Imagine reading your husband and seeing how many times he'd cheated on you. Or what your parents or kids really thought of you. Or your boss. It can drive people nuts."

"How long does that last?" Jayson asked.

"For a day or so. By the end of that time, most people will have lost any sanity they had. It's a curse."

"Does this happen all the time with you?" Kathleen sounded uncomfortable.

"I can put up a shield, now. I wasn't always able to do that. I block everybody, nowadays, unless it's absolutely necessary to read them," I said. Kathleen relaxed with a tiny sigh.

"So you can't cry at all?" Opal turned her unblinking gaze on me.

"Oh, I can, but it has to be when I'm alone. If you get any moisture at all, you'll wish you'd never met me. It's better to hold it back."

"That sounds painful," Hank said flatly.

"If that's the worst pain I'd ever had, I'd be in much better shape," I pointed out. "I think I want to be alone, now." I misted away from all of them.

~

Jayson, like his parents, had an indoor pool and spa. It just wasn't in a separate building; it was in a room at the back of his house. I slipped into my bathing suit quickly and misted straight to the spa. I felt cold and hot water might warm me up and relax aching muscles. At least the waxing dilemma seemed better and didn't burn when I took a seat in frothing water.

"So this is where you ended up." Jayson, dressed in a T and loose trousers, sat cross-legged on the edge of the spa and blinked at me. "Everybody is looking for you. I just sent mindspeech, telling them I found you. That's quite handy, as it turns out."

"Don't make me sorry I gave it to you," I muttered.

"Want me to get in with you?"

"I came here to be alone," I said.

"Haven't you had too much of that?" Jayson asked.

"Not today."

"Bree, you really ought to stop scaring us," Hank walked in, followed by Bill, Opal, Trina and Kathleen.

"How? I said I wanted to be alone. You automatically assumed I'd left the house. Didn't you?"

"What am I supposed to think? Your track record stands against you, and I don't want to wait another two years to see you again."

"See, you're thinking of yourself, here," I said.

"Yeah. I'm thinking of myself. I admit that. I'm thinking of you, too, whether you believe that or not. Is it wrong to worry that you might be hurt or need somebody and there isn't a damn thing I can do about it?" Hank pulled his T-shirt over his head and unbuckled his belt.

"Anybody not wanting to see this better leave now," he dropped his pants. Well, he'd gone commando, which was easy enough to see as he stepped into the water and sat beside me.

"Hell, I'm getting in," Jayson announced and started stripping. Trina and Kathleen left quickly after Jayson's announcement. Opal shucked her clothes and Bill wasn't far behind. I covered my eyes with a shaking hand as all of them climbed into Jayson's overly large spa.

"Well, what are we planning to discuss now?" Opal said brightly.

"Are you cold, sweetheart? Is that why you came here?" Bill asked. I dropped my hand and nodded at him.

"Fuck," Hank sighed.

"What's your plan if you do find Oscar Forde and/or Keir Arthur tomorrow night?" Opal asked. That gave me something else to think about, rather than the violation of my privacy.

"It depends on where I find them," I said. "You know I'll want to take them out, but it doesn't need to happen in front of others."

"We can't shoot them?" Jayson sounded disappointed.

"My sister once said you don't take a gun to a vampire fight," I pointed out. "You'll be dead before you can pull the trigger." The only gun that might be useful against a vampire was a Ranos pistol or rifle, and that technology didn't need to fall into human hands.

"They move that fast?" Jayson was skeptical.

"I thought you showed him vampires and werewolves," I turned to Hank.

"From a safe distance, and they were walking down the street," Hank defended himself.

"They looked human, just like you," Jayson said. Opal snickered.

"So these don't impress you at all?" I pulled a hand from the water and let my claws slide out.

"Don't touch them," Opal warned as Jayson reached out a hand. "You'll lose your fingers and be left wondering how it happened."

"I've seen them slice metal," Bill agreed. "Lissa did that."

"You can slice metal?" Jayson pulled his hand back.

"I haven't tried metal, yet, but yeah, I could."

"What have you cut, then?" Jayson asked.

"I've lopped off a couple of vampire heads," I said. "Bill knows about that already," I added.

"The one here and the one in D.C." Bill agreed amiably. "And she had a hand in taking one down in Austin, but I don't have the whole story on that one."

"I caught him in the midsection, he flipped into the air and Radomir beheaded him on the way back down."

"What about you?" Opal asked.

"I was knocked flat on my back and couldn't breathe for a while," I replied.

"Unbelievable," Hank muttered.

"You weren't there," I said, studying his face. He looked as if he wanted to argue with my tactics. Well, they may not have been thoroughly considered, but it was the best I could do with the limited amount of time I had.

"No, I wasn't," he said and put his arms around me. "It just scares the hell out of me. I'll have to work on that."

"Hank, I do the best I can. While it may not be up to your special ops standards, so far I've come out of it alive."

"Breanne," Hank gripped my jaw in a hand and forced me to look him in the eye. "Coming out of it alive is only half the equation. The other half is who'd be destroyed if you went down."

I blinked at him and struggled to keep my fear from showing. Yes, everything could fall if I died. There would be no second chances for those left behind. Hank was speaking from a personal level, but he didn't know how true his words actually were.

"We're going to take you to the Sub-Mariner tonight, to get you used to what you'll see tomorrow," Hank's voice—and his grip on my jaw—softened. "I've already talked with Dale Saylor and he knows the score. He says he'll help in any way he can."

"Hank," I shivered, even sitting in hot, bubbling water.

"Bree, we don't need you to freak tomorrow. We need to find John's killers." I blinked into his dark eyes while my stomach tied itself in knots and threatened to dislodge breakfast.

"I feel sick," I pulled away from Hank's hand.

"No, sweetheart," Bill stood and waded toward me. "Opal and I are coming with Hank and Jayson tonight, so you'll have plenty of friends and support around you."

"Opal?" I turned to her. I needed support and a lifeline. I didn't want to see what I was likely to see—it terrified me in ways I couldn't begin to describe.

"Bree, I swear we'll punch anybody who upsets you," Opal said. "If I understand correctly, people go to these places to have a good time. They're having a good time, okay?"

"No," I moaned, closing my eyes and moving away from Hank. I was feeling sicker by the minute, until I was forced to fold to my bathroom. I think I lost everything I'd eaten in the last three days.

"Here, now," Jayson washed my face while Hank held me and Bill fretted nearby. They'd found me dry heaving into the toilet.

"We'll take care of you," Hank murmured against my ear. "There's nothing to be afraid of."

Say that when your past is the same as mine, I snapped mentally. *Nothing to be afraid of? Most people don't know when to be afraid.*

"That's very true, they don't," Hank soothed. "We have to get you past some of this, so you'll be prepared instead of curling into a ball and shaking if you come across it in the outside world."

"That's frightening," I mumbled.

"Bree, things happen all the time. What if you ended up in a place where somebody needed your help, and they were being beaten? What would you do? Can you predict your actions, or could it go either way?"

"I can't predict my actions," I admitted reluctantly and lowered my eyes. "Either I'd freak and go catatonic, as you so kindly describe it, or freak in the other direction and make the person doing the beating dead—slowly, most likely—by cutting him into one-inch strips. While he screamed."

"Baby, quick death. Always give a quick death. It's merciful, and makes you stronger and better than the one you killed," Hank whispered.

"I pretty much have so far." I stared at my hands. The Sirenali I'd killed on Bexari, well, I'd removed limbs, but there'd been no other option unless I wanted to kill innocents. The moment he removed his obsessions, he'd died painlessly.

"But you didn't witness abuse when you killed. Did you?" Bill knelt in front of me and took my face in his hands. Jayson moved aside to give Bill more room.

"No. You're right, I'd probably freak."

"So we'll expose you to what you think of as abuse, even though it's not, in a controlled environment," Hank said. "We'll be around you, and we'll take care of you and get you used to this. You need your mind in good working order if you're faced with something like this someday, and it'll make me feel better if I can help you get through this without breaking down."

"I don't want to," I whined.

"Sweetheart," Bill stood and lifted me to my feet. "You don't know what you'll see, and let's face it, if Oscar Forde is involved with this new club in town, you may see things you didn't expect. Isn't that right?" My face was in his hands again, and brown eyes gazed steadily into mine.

"Yeah." My voice wobbled, and that embarrassed me. Were they right? That if I didn't do something about it, I could fold up like a wet cardboard box if I came across something that disturbed me? That could get me killed. Even worse—I could completely lose control and go berserk. I didn't want to join the ranks of torturers—that was repugnant to me.

"Jayson and I can go through some of the basics this afternoon," Hank rose to stand beside me. "We have some research materials, so you can prepare yourself."

"This is horrible," I muttered and pulled away from Bill to hug myself.

~

"Boss, I just heard from Trace. He says Ace saw the same car go past our gate three times. Windows too dark to get a good look at the driver."

William Winkler looked up from his laptop. He'd been tapping out emails at the breakfast table while he ate scrambled eggs and ham. His dark eyes studied his Second for a few moments while he chewed and swallowed a mouthful of food.

"Get a tag number?" Winkler asked.

Trajan Gibson, at nearly seven feet, shook his head in exasperation. "Boss, I know we look dumb, but most of the time we actually know what to do. Here." He passed a slip of paper to the Dallas Werewolf Packmaster. "Trace ran the plates. Car's from Oklahoma. Sold yesterday. No info on the buyer, yet. Paper tag removed, for some reason."

"That doesn't raise suspicions or anything," Winkler sipped coffee. "If it comes by again, have it followed. Discreetly. And call Director Bill. Let him know."

"Will do, Boss." Trajan left the kitchen.

~

Breanne's Journal

"There are several types of piercings. These," Jayson pushed a book with photographs toward me, "use long, thin pins to pierce the skin. Sometimes cord is laced around the pins afterward, for a more intense sensation."

I cringed at the photograph. A woman's labia had been pierced by several pins, which went through both sides. Another photograph depicted a woman's belly pierced similarly, with silk cord laced around the pins.

"You do this?" I stared at Jayson.

"No. I don't do piercings. People have specialties—things they like and are comfortable doing. I learned to go solo on fire play about a year ago," he stated proudly.

"Unbelievable," I shook my head. "Please tell me you haven't set anybody on fire."

"I haven't." He sounded offended that I'd mentioned it. "I saw what can happen, remember? I make sure the sub has clean, scrubbed skin and their hair is tied back and kept away from the areas in question. They ask me for this, Bree. Maybe once or twice a month I get asked. Their dom or master is there with them, just as they should be."

"Have you burned yourself, then?" I asked.

"I've been singed, and I don't have any hair left on my fingers," Jayson snickered.

"Pyromaniac," I accused. Jayson laughed.

"These next photographs," Hank pulled the book away and flipped forward a few pages, "are the ones I worry about," he said. The first one made me want to vomit again, and it wasn't the worst of the lot. A woman was lying on her belly, hog-tied. I freaked.

"Bill, this is Trajan Gibson," Trajan spoke over the phone. Bill, working on his laptop in a borrowed bedroom, had answered Trajan's call immediately.

"Trajan? Something up?" Bill asked.

"Maybe. We've had a suspicious car driving past the front gate all day. Paper tag missing, old tag registered in Oklahoma and sold yesterday. No info on the buyer."

"That doesn't raise suspicions," Bill observed dryly. "Have you tried tailing it? You think somebody caught wind of the update Winkler's working on for the software?"

"No idea, but that's the logical conclusion," Trajan agreed. "Had one of ours tail it after the last drive-by, and contacted the Grand Master, too. Since this is probably a human, there's not a lot he can do at the moment."

"Understood. Look, I'll see if there's anybody in the Dallas office I can put on this, and have them contact you. I'm in the San Francisco area at the moment, so if this turns out to be more serious, let me know. I can get a flight pretty quick."

"Will do, and thanks for the help," Trajan said.

"No problem. Keep me informed," Bill said before ending the call.

❧

Breanne's Journal

"They really like it—being tied up," Hank stroked my forehead. I was on the floor, flat on my back, staring at the ceiling and gulping shaky breaths. "It's exciting to them to feel that helpless vulnerability," he said softly. "They trust the person tying them up," he continued. "Generally, unless it's some idiot who's experimenting without knowing what he or she is doing, the one doing the tying knows how tight and how long. Some even do intricate patterns and knots, as an art form."

"Not helping," I struggled to draw enough breath to speak.

"Breanne, both parties love this," Jayson settled on the floor on my other side. "Just like some people prefer to dress in period clothing, or corsets and fishnet stockings with stiletto heels. Some like scenes or scenarios—such as getting questioned by others posing as foreign police for a crime they didn't commit. They're handcuffed or tied to a chair. The costumes look authentic. It feels authentic. It's still a fantasy, so sex may figure into it, but at the end, it's all play. A good dominant or master is going to make it feel real by taking things in a direction the sub doesn't expect. Lots of people love that."

"They wouldn't love it if it *were* real," I huffed out. "They wouldn't love it if their lives really were on the line. If the torture was real. If death weren't so close it was grinning in their face."

"Bree, few people have gone through what you have and survived. Most don't come out of that without serious mental and physical issues. Mostly you're able to deal with this, but your circumstances and abilities are going to leave you in vulnerable positions. We have to desensitize you, so you can at least carry on without falling apart."

Hank turned his head and looked away. At that moment, I wished I knew what he was thinking. Regretted—just for an instant—that I couldn't read those things in him. A trembling sigh escaped and I closed my eyes. His hand covered my face carefully. *Bree, baby, do this. For me. Okay? You can do this. I love you. Bill loves you. Even Jayson loves you, and he's not used to that. Block it out when you see it, and any or all of us will let you fall apart in our arms later. Cry all over us. If we see those things like you say we will when we touch your tears, we'll wear sunglasses or a blindfold until it passes.*

I didn't know at first that Hank included Jayson in his mindspeech, but he did. Jayson lifted one of my hands and kissed it before stroking my fingers. Hank removed his hand and I blinked at both of them—their faces wavered in my vision as I accustomed my eyes to the light again.

"Feel better?" Jayson asked.

"Not really," I said.

"You're going to see a lot of bondage tonight, so we need to go back to looking at photographs," Hank grabbed a hand and pulled me to a sitting position. "You'll sit between Jayson and me, and we'll talk you through this."

"You may get some looks for dressing like this, but it's okay for tonight," Hank rubbed the back of my neck as I slid my feet into turquoise ballet slippers. I wore jeans with a turquoise tank top, and a denim jacket over that. Not the normal costume for visiting a dungeon, I guess. I still didn't know how he planned to dress me for KingDom's, and didn't really want to ask.

The other thing I'd learned after Hank and Jayson forced me to stare at photographs, was that Bill signed both of them up as Special Agents, working part-time for the Department. Their first priority, it seemed, was to keep me safe. The second was to help track Oscar Forde and associates.

Everybody (except me) would be carrying concealed weapons. If you counted my claws and a few other talents, I guess I was armed as well.

$\sim$

"You will address me as sir," the receptionist pointed at me when I walked up to the front desk at the Sub-Mariner with Hank.

"Have you been knighted by the Queen?" I asked, blinking at him in disbelief.

"No. Why?" his voice was surly.

"Then you haven't earned that title from me," I replied evenly.

"Where's your leather?" The man eyed me speculatively before poking at me again.

"I'm vegetarian," I poked back. "The cow is still wearing my leather."

"Don't," Hank held up a hand as the guy seemed ready to backhand me into a wall. He nodded and stayed quiet as Dale Saylor walked up to us.

"Dale, this is Breanne Hayworth," Hank introduced me to the man I'd only seen on the news before.

"Breanne," Dale Saylor used my first name and nodded to me. I read him again briefly. He was bisexual; I knew that already from reading him during the news broadcast. He also considered me Hank's property and wouldn't touch unless Hank gave permission. I wanted to slap my forehead. I muttered pleasantries instead. Dale had read the book, just like anybody else might. The thing in his favor was that he found my torture repugnant, so I was polite.

"We don't allow breath play, knife play, branding or mutilations," Dale explained as we walked out of his office later and down a corridor. So far, I'd only seen the reception area and Dale's office. When I caught the first sounds of leather slapping on flesh, I jerked.

Opal's shifter hearing was sharp, although not as good as mine, so she didn't catch the sounds until moments later. My breaths were already ragged. "Bree, they're having a good time," she said softly.

"Huh?" Jayson turned to us—he and Hank were walking ahead of us, Bill behind.

"She has better hearing than a dog," Opal muttered angrily. "Just because she can't see anything right now doesn't mean she can't hear it."

"Fuck," Jayson mumbled.

"Bree," Hank turned to stand in front of me before pulling something from his pocket. "Do you want these?" He held out a small, plastic bag with foam earplugs inside. My lower lip trembled as I blinked at him.

"What if I need my ears for something else?" I hunched my shoulders and dropped my eyes to the floor. Hank wore polished, black leather boots with the black leather pants he wore. I studied the boots for a moment, attempting to even my breathing.

If Hank wanted, he could ride off on a motorcycle after we were done visiting the Sub-Mariner. It brought up memories of Kalenegar. That Larentii's reaction to my discomfort would be a mind blast and not earplugs, if he still harbored his previous disregard for me.

"I'll get through this," I whispered, lifting my head again. Hank gave me a short, half-nod and stuffed the earplugs back in his pocket. Bill's hand went to the back of my neck and rubbed it gently before we continued our journey.

Time. So much of mine had been spent enduring unpleasant things. The trick, I think, is just to keep walking. Life is putting one foot in front of the other, no matter how frightened you are or how hard your legs shake as a result.

I witnessed all sorts of things inside the Sub-Mariner that night. Spankings. Bondage. Flogging. Piercing. Flesh hook suspension. Sex. The list was long. Even with the people around me reassuring me with mindspeech at every turn, I was still shaking when we were ready to leave.

No, I didn't notice at first, because my head was lowered as I fought a battle with my inner demons. Her scent finally caught my attention. I jerked my head up. Janine—the same Janine from the deli who'd dumped my soup in the floor the last time I'd seen her, stood in front of me. Would it have helped if I'd read her before? Things would certainly be different, I know that much.

Janine was dressed for the Sub-Mariner in a leather corset, stockings and a thong; it registered on my brain without any explanation. I dropped my shield automatically to see why that was. The images that swam through my mind nauseated me.

Hank had never said who his last fuck buddy was. I was learning, through my reading, that it had been Janine. Yes, it might have been ironic that I was standing in front of his ex, because I was seeing the plot of nearly every romance novel I'd ever read race through my memory. *Girl meets boy. Girl meets boy's ex. The plot thickens.*

There was a twist here, though. I not only read how Janine had kept tabs on me before; she'd recognized me in the deli—after more than two years. I also saw exactly how she and Hank had kinky fun—I was too stunned to slam the shield back up at first. No, he hadn't had anything to do with her for more than four years, but she still wanted him.

"You bitch," Janine hissed at me. Hank stood there, his head swiveling from her to me and then back to her.

"Is that the best you have? Calling me a bitch?" Suddenly, my anger was white-hot. Yes, she liked being dominated by Hank. Loved getting flogged by Hank, along with many other specialties he seemed to have. Another woman? Different story. Her claws were coming out. Well, she probably should have stepped back, because mine were longer and infinitely more dangerous.

"I called you a bitch, bitch," Janine sneered.

"I can call you the same thing—in any language you choose," I said. "If Hank still wants you, you're welcome to him," I snapped before stalking past her. No, I could never, ever compete with what she'd done for—and with—Hank. Well, they were welcome to each other. It was time for me to leave.

"Breanne," Bill and Opal were right behind me. I didn't stop until I reached the sidewalk outside the Sub-Mariner.

"Bill, I need a hotel room." I walked—stiff-legged and angry—down the street.

"Bree, what happened? Who was that woman?" Opal gripped my arm and gently stopped me from walking farther away from Hank and Jayson.

"That was Hank's ex," I said. "I didn't read her until now. I wish I hadn't. She was hoping I really was dead, like everybody thought."

"You've seen her before?" Bill asked.

"Yeah. She works at the deli not far from my house. The last time I saw her, she dumped the soup I ordered on the floor. I didn't read her then and figured it wasn't worth the argument, so I left. She's been stalking Hank—and me before I disappeared. Now I'm on her radar again. I'm not going back to Jayson's. He and Hank can do whatever they want from now on. I'm out."

"Breanne, I don't think Janine matters to Hank," Opal said quietly.

"Opal, that's not it. I saw what they liked to do together. I'm never going to do those things." I started walking again.

"This is why you call it a curse, isn't it?" Bill said softly, keeping pace with me.

"Part of it, yes," I swallowed with difficulty. Tears were threatening now, and Opal and Bill didn't need to be anywhere near them. "I just need a hotel room somewhere," I said before the sobs came. I misted away to keep Bill and Opal safe.

CHAPTER 7

My cell vibrated while I handed a credit card to the desk clerk. I'd refused to answer mindspeech, so they were trying their second option. This time, I hadn't put the stalker app on my phone and made sure nobody else could do it, either. That might not keep Bill from tracking me, but Hank and Jayson could go fuck themselves. Or fuck Janine. I didn't care.

"You're on the fourth floor," the desk clerk handed a key card to me while the phone continued to vibrate in my pocket.

"Thanks." I got my credit card back and walked unsteadily toward the elevator.

"She can't read you, but she read Janine," Opal, her arms crossed angrily over her chest, glared at Hank. "Whatever she saw made her feel inadequate, and there is no way in hell that woman should feel inferior to anybody else. I don't care if good old Janine can fuck you upside down while playing *Yankee Doodle Dandy* on the accordion."

"Janine is nothing to me," Hank raked fingers through his hair in frustration. "You say Janine's been keeping tabs on Bree?"

"And on you."

"I knew she kept showing up," Hank shook his head. "But every time she walked into the club, she always left with somebody else."

"Trying to make you jealous, no doubt," Opal snorted.

Jayson sat behind his desk, watching the exchange. He'd taken the others to his downtown office to discuss what to do about Breanne's disappearance. Bill sat on the sofa nearby, staring at his hands.

"What worries me," Bill broke the ensuing silence, "is that Janine might place Breanne in danger. Let's face it—if she's approached by the nut jobs from those websites, she can point them in the proper direction. Can't she?" Bill lifted his eyes and studied Hank's face.

"Yeah," Hank turned away. "Of all the things to happen," he sighed.

"Janine's what they call a Velcro collar, and a SAM," Jayson offered. "She jumps from one dom to the next, and SAM means smart-ass masochist. She's always had a smart mouth, but while she was with Hank, that's the most subdued I've ever seen her."

"So she wants more of that," Opal snapped. "Maybe you two deserve each other," she hissed in Hank's direction.

"I informed Janine of the rules at the beginning," Hank began.

"Really? Fucking men and their fucking rules," Opal tossed up a hand. "A woman is always more involved and way more invested in any relationship, and men are just too stupid to see it. Did you try the same shit with Breanne? No wonder she always looked as if she hadn't slept for a week whenever we worked together."

Bill's cell buzzed while Opal and Hank glared at one another.

I'm at the Christopher Hotel, the text read. *I don't want company tonight.*

"She's at the Christopher." Bill turned his phone around so the others could see.

~

Breanne's Journal

I'm sorry you saw that, Hank's text read. *Janine was a mistake, but I took her on because she needed a firm hand. I guess you know that, too. I wish I could take those images away. Now I understand better what you've been suffering through all this time.*

Bree, Jayson's text read, *come home to us. We'll make this better, I promise.*

Breanne, I love you. Please don't let this upset you. I know this is difficult, but will you still go through KingDom's tomorrow night? I desperately need the information, sweetheart. I sighed as I read Bill's text.

Bree, men are assholes most of the time. I wanted to laugh at Opal's message. I brushed tears away instead.

Opal, bring Bill to the Lean Bean at nine tomorrow morning, I replied to Opal's text. *We'll talk about KingDom's there.*

Okay, her reply was immediate. *We'll be there.*

∾

"You didn't sleep, did you?"

Hank and Jayson had come to the Lean Bean with Opal and Bill. Hank's dark eyes narrowed as he assessed my appearance. I ignored his words. I hadn't invited him. Or Jayson. They'd come anyway.

"I thought Trina was going to hit me with a skillet this morning, and Mom won't speak to me," Jayson said as he slid into the seat across from me. I'd chosen the back booth by the window so the spotty sunlight might warm away some of the chill. I was cold again, and even the latte I'd bought wasn't helping.

Bill scooted in close to me, while Opal squeezed in on the outside. Hank took the spot next to Jayson with a heavy sigh.

"Bree, you don't look like you feel good," Bill began. He was right—I didn't. Images of Janine, strapped to a Saint Andrew's cross kept popping into my head while Hank—I shuddered and forced the images away for perhaps the fortieth time.

"You keep seeing it, don't you?" Hank said.

I turned away from Hank, but that didn't mean his words weren't true—all those things I'd read in Janine the night before played like a loop through my memory. I had no idea how to shut it off. I'd spent half the night sitting atop Morro Rock after discovering that sleep was impossible.

Yeah, I'd folded to Morro Bay and sat at the top of that dome of rock, like Lissa would in the future, and stared at an endlessly moving body of water. The Pacific's waters were the same as my thoughts—none of them calm or still at the moment.

Bree, I don't love Janine. I do love you, Hank's voice filtered into my mind.

You remember what I told you at the beginning? That there's no place we can meet in the middle? You are what you are. I'm this. I stared out the window. *Eventually you'll want those other things again,* I went on. *Find somebody to make you happy. I'm not that girl.*

Breanne, I don't know what to do to convince you that you're wrong. Someday, I hope you understand that. For now, give me a chance. We really need to protect you—Bill, Jayson and I. Opal, too. I thought she was going to take my head off over Janine.

You need to impress upon Janine that she has to stop stalking you. And me. She wants to murder me, Hank. If you don't do something about that, I will.

You don't intend to kill her, do you?

Hell, no. What do you think I am? I'll just hand her a bit of vampire compulsion and send her ass on its way. I don't want to be constantly looking over my shoulder for the ex-girlfriend, in addition to all the others who'd like to destroy me.

She's not my ex-girlfriend. That wasn't our agreement. She signed up for six months of training. I was glad to get rid of her afterward.

Unbelievable.

Baby, stop obsessing about this. I don't know how to get that crap out of your head, but if you have any suggestions, I'll be happy to work on that.

I have no idea what might work, short of a lobotomy.

Let's get this KingDom's mess settled; you need to come with me today. I want to hold my girl.

Hank, no, I whimpered mentally.

Baby, I've never asked you out. I'm asking now. I should have done that from the beginning, instead of what I did.

And where are we going?

Down the coast. Lunch. I don't think I've ever bought you anything except a sandwich.

Fine. I moved my shoulders uncomfortably.

"Are you done having a private conversation?" Jayson asked. "Some of us have jobs to do." A grimace crossed his face—he didn't like being left out of the conversation.

"Rome, shut up," Hank said amiably. "Bill, you have the floor." He nodded toward Bill, a slight smile pulling at the corner of his mouth. Well, he'd just gotten what he wanted and I was left sitting there, wondering why I didn't seem to have a spine where Hank was concerned.

"Breanne, are we still on for tonight?" Bill asked.

"I guess," I went back to staring out the window.

"What will you do if that woman appears again?" Opal asked. I turned around to blink at her in confusion, but the question wasn't aimed at me. She was asking Hank what he intended to do.

"I will send her on her way, after telling her a restraining order is never attractive on her record. I'll be happy to file one, and I'll make sure Breanne does as well," Hank replied with a frown.

"Breanne doesn't have to. I've already taken care of that this morning," Bill held up his cell. "Talked to the DA and a judge. I don't have names for those assholes on the Internet yet, but I do have Janine Webster's information. Maybe you ought to impress upon her that the Joint NSA and Homeland Security Department is watching her carefully from now on."

"Thank you," I said.

Bill smiled gently at me and said, "Sweetheart, I'd do just about anything for you."

"Same here," I nodded. Right then, I was glad I wasn't forced to choose between him and Hank. I might lose my mind if I were. *Are you sure you don't mind—this multiple mate thing?* I asked mentally.

Sweetheart, it doesn't make any difference to me, as long as I know you care.

I love you, I said simply.

"I love you, too," he said aloud and leaned in to kiss me.

"Hey, where's mine?" Jayson complained.

"Do you deserve one?" I said when Bill pulled back with a satisfied smile.

"No idea. I want one anyway," Jayson shrugged.

"Suffer," I said.

"Always the way," Jayson grumped.

"You poor thing," Opal snickered unsympathetically.

"Eight tonight?" Hank asked. "So I can get Breanne back in time to dress her appropriately."

"Sounds good. We'll wire you and Jayson, and you're authorized to carry weapons through the Department. Don't hesitate to send mindspeech if you need me. I'll have a few people on standby, including Opal."

"You're really worried about this, aren't you?" I watched Bill's face closely. I didn't want to read him—he needed that space between us.

"I've gotten some intel, and let's just say the financing behind that club is murky. That means the money may have come from criminal activity. We're still tracking information on individuals associated with the ownership, and that hasn't been easy. I want some answers. And, if things are like Hank and Jayson suspect and there's a connection to the club and the murders, then we really need to shut this down fast. It may only be an attempt to get rid of the competition. It could be something deeper and much worse."

"This doesn't sound good," I rubbed my forehead.

"Baby, you can sleep while I drive down the coast," Hank offered. "Come on. Bring your coffee and I'll buy an egg and cheese biscuit for you on the way."

"That sounds good," I said. "I didn't eat anything this morning."

"Not surprised," Hank muttered. "Bill, if you'd like to come with us," he added.

"I'd like to, but I have work," Bill said. "We'll get together another day."

We walked out of the Lean Bean together, and I found myself

surrounded by all of them. Jayson's SUV was parked nearby, and Bill and Opal climbed in with him, leaving me with Hank.

"I asked Trey to park a car near the club," Hank leaned in to whisper in my ear before kissing it carefully. "It's borrowed, so Janine or anyone else won't recognize it."

"Hank," I hugged myself.

"Come on," he pulled me against his side. "Don't let this upset you. This is our day, remember?"

"Hank, it's Monday."

"It is," he grinned.

"Where are we going?"

"It's a surprise."

"I know they were in that coffee shop, but I never saw them come out," Wildrif whined. He couldn't understand how Bill Jennings kept appearing and then disappearing from his visions, either.

"Where's that thing you have—that foresight?" Zachariah Tanner demanded. "Obediah told me you were something amazing, but I haven't seen much of it yet," he fumed.

"I am formidable," Wildrif defended himself.

"You are an idiot," Zachariah spat. "I asked you to watch Bill Jennings, and you let him get away."

Wildrif's wispy, pale hair lifted in the breeze while mismatched eyes surveyed the youngest of the Tanner brothers. Wildrif knew quite well the Tanners were werewolves. He'd also seen, through his gift of foresight, that Obediah would lend him to Zachariah for this assignment.

Zach was Obediah's lead assassin, and when the offer came to Obediah for Bill Jennings' death, Obediah had demanded (and received) the promise of ten million dollars upon delivery of proof.

Obediah had then instructed Zach to bring back Jennings' head, with or without accompanying agents' heads. Obediah never quibbled over numbers. His only concerns were results and covered tracks.

The trouble was, Zach found it difficult to track Jennings. As a werewolf, he had a keen sense of smell, but Jennings' scent baffled him. That's why Obediah had agreed to lend Wildrif to his brother. Wildrif, with his talent, could generally locate anyone. Bill Jennings was turning into a problem—for werewolf and seer.

~

Breanne's Journal

"Baby, we're here."

Hank's words woke me from a sound sleep. I hadn't even realized the SUV had stopped.

"I was more tired than I thought," I straightened up in the passenger seat, attempting—with the limited space available—to stretch the kinks out of arms and legs.

"If you'd been in bed with me last night, I'd have made sure you got some sleep," Hank's eyes darkened as he unbuckled my seat belt. "After a while," he added, leaning in to give me a quick peck. Well, at least I was getting kisses, now. Janine never got that from Hank. I shut off that train of thought immediately.

"I don't want to talk about it," I opened my door and slipped out of the vehicle.

"I get that," Hank climbed out of the driver's seat and shut his door. "I just want you to know that you can talk to me anytime about what bothers you, even if what bothers you is me."

"Sure," I said, turning to see that we were in a restaurant parking lot. It looked busy.

"Does that mean you're blowing me off or agreeing to talk to me about those things?" Hank's hand settled at the small of my back and gently pushed me toward the restaurant's door.

"Hank, I don't feel comfortable with that," I hung my head and watched my feet as they matched his stride.

"So you're blowing me off."

"I didn't say that," I lifted my head and blinked at him. "I wish you'd try to understand. I've never talked to anybody about anything that bothered me."

"Because there wasn't anyone to offer before," Hank pointed out.

"It scares me," I said and lowered my chin. I couldn't look at his beautiful face any longer, and I wanted so badly at that moment to know what he was thinking. I needed to know what he really thought about all this—about me—Janine, everything.

"I know it does, love. It doesn't have to happen all at once. A little at a time is okay."

"Hank, I don't think I can talk about most of it."

"Not even nasty Janine? Tell me what you saw that bothers you the most. I have a good idea, but tell me anyway. That way we can sort through it, and I can explain what was happening."

"I thought this was our day," I tried to move away from Hank when he reached out to open the restaurant's door. "Yet Janine keeps cropping up." Hank wouldn't let me get away; gripping my arm carefully, he pulled me inside with him.

"Two for lunch, please, under the name Hank."

"I have that reservation," the hostess nodded at Hank. Like most women, she couldn't take her eyes off him for several seconds. "Follow me, please." She lifted two menus and led us toward the back of the restaurant.

We were seated at a table next to tall windows overlooking Monterey Bay. The water was deep blue under a noonday sun and long strands of kelp moved with the waves.

"Amazing, isn't it?" Hank opened his menu. "Jayson and I have been here a few times. He talks about buying property here, but hasn't found the view he wants, yet."

"You mean Jayson can't just order people out of their homes?" I opened my menu and stared at lists of items without really seeing them.

"Not so far," Hank shook his head and continued to study the menu. "There are a couple of places he'd bid on if they came up for sale, though."

"No doubt." I shut my menu with a sigh.

"What are you having?" Hank looked up and studied me.

"Not hungry," I said, turning to stare out the window.

"I'll order for you if you don't pick something."

"Isn't that what you guys do anyway? Don't you assert your dominance by telling your sub what to do and when and how to do it?"

"Now it comes out," Hank breathed. "You saw that, too. It's part of the training. All of it was agreed to at the beginning. She knew what was happening, what was expected of her and why she would get punished if she didn't do as she was told."

"Punishment." I shuddered and my arms wrapped around my waist involuntarily.

"It's a part of it," Hank said softly. "Don't you think we know the differences in people? Some, all you have to do is say a word or two and that's harsher punishment than a dozen blows. Others keep making the same mistakes, when they know the correction is coming."

"That still places all the power with you. Like you know everything and the other person knows nothing."

"That's what it's about. It's a power exchange. They want to give it to the doms and masters. It's all part of the culture and lifestyle. We're not perfect, Bree. We know that. At least the best of us do. When we make a mistake, the best thing to do is to admit it. Right the wrong, if a wrong has been committed."

"So who flogs you, Henry Hank Bell, when you fuck up?" I stood abruptly, my chair making a harsh, scraping sound on wood flooring as I shoved it back.

"Bree, sit," Hank commanded.

"Fuck you," I snapped and folded space.

At least all the media had left my house. No news vans cluttered my driveway or the street in front of the house. It didn't matter—I would have gone elsewhere if they'd still been there. I wanted to cry. I wanted to scream. I wanted to be anyone except who I was. Grabbing a bottle of water from the fridge, I stalked through the back door and flopped onto a patio chair. My phone was in my hand shortly after, and I sent an angry text to Hank.

Fuckyoufuckyoufuckoff, I tapped before hitting send.

My next text wasn't quite as angry, but it certainly displayed my rebellion. *Bill,* appeared on my screen as I pushed letters on my phone, *I'll be going to KingDom's alone tonight. Tell Hank and Jayson to screw themselves. I don't need them.*

~

"What the hell did you do?" Bill wanted to yell at Hank, but he was at FBI headquarters in San Francisco and couldn't.

"Tried to get her to talk. Pushed a little too hard. That's what I did."

"I thought you were taking that trip to calm her down, not send her into harm's way."

"What are you talking about?" Hank's voice betrayed his worry.

"She sent a text telling me she planned to go to KingDom's alone tonight. I've tried to get triangulation on her phone, but it keeps breaking up. I don't know where she is."

"Jayson and I will go in as planned tonight. Have your people ready in case there are problems," Hank terminated the call.

~

"Did Gavin arrive safely?" Wlodek asked.

"Yes. He sent an email, telling me he arrived at the safe house," Charles set a folder in front of Wlodek. "These need your signature, Honored One."

"Thank you, Charles. That will be all." Charles turned to go. "If you hear anything else from Gavin, be sure to let me know," Wlodek added.

"I will." Charles walked out of Wlodek's study.

~

Lissa's Journal

"I don't know why I feel so unsettled," I rubbed my arms and paced at the foot of my bed. I was dressed in a sleeveless tank and pajama bottoms, but if Winkler had his way, I wouldn't be wearing them for long.

"I might be able to distract you for a while," Winkler lounged on the bed, grinning at me.

"You think you can, huh?" I wrinkled my nose at him.

"I know I can. Come here." My werewolf mate patted the bed beside him. Of course he was naked—werewolves are born without modesty. At least Winkler was.

"Are there any modest werewolves?" I lifted an eyebrow.

"Stop teasing me and undress," Winkler's grin widened.

"Stop playing with your dangly bits, it's distracting," I pulled my top over my head.

"Mmmm, boobies," Winkler chuckled appreciatively.

"Are you twelve?" I huffed, shucking my pajama bottoms and stepping out of them.

"I'm a grown werewolf. There's a difference. And these are not dangling at the moment." He cupped himself.

"Everybody's a comedian," I slapped a hand over my eyes.

"Come on. Come to bed." Winkler folded to me, pulled my body against his and ran his hands over my breasts.

"Do you remember when we first met?" I blinked up at him.

"Yeah. You made my junk stiff every time I looked at you."

"Is that all?" I asked innocently.

"Enough of that," his arm went beneath my bottom to lift me against him. I wrapped my legs around his waist.

"This is nice," Winkler nibbled my ear. "How does against a wall sound, instead of the bed?"

"You're driving," I pointed out.

"Yeah. I guess I am. Now, what was it you were worrying about?"

"Nothing." I buried my hands in his hair as he growled against my shoulder.

~

Breanne's Journal

Yeah, having a drink in a bar before going into KingDom's probably wasn't a good idea, but I only intended to have one. I'd found a bar across the street from the upscale dungeon, and I was fortifying my courage. At least that's what I kept telling myself.

Probably the best decision I'd made after walking into the bar was choosing a back table so I could watch everybody who came in. Had I ever thought it a possibility? The breath was stolen from my body when the door opened again.

Making sure I kept my shield tight around me, I watched as Gavin Montegue, *the* Gavin Montegue from the past, strolled to the bar and casually placed compulsion on the bartender to answer questions about the deaths of persons active in the BDSM community.

~

"Nine-millimeter Beretta. Nice," Hank examined the gun carefully. Bill's Department was arming Hank and Jayson for the evening.

"Be careful, and approach Breanne cautiously if you see her," Bill instructed.

"Yeah. I hear that," Hank nodded before shoving the gun in the waistband of his leather pants. "I'll get her out of there as soon as it's possible, too."

"I've already sent three texts, Bell, begging her to reconsider. If she won't listen to me, I'm not sure she'll listen to you, either."

"If she were human, I'd pull her out of there kicking and screaming if I had to," Jayson muttered before stuffing his borrowed gun into the waistband of his jeans.

"But she's not, and you will do nothing of the kind," Bill barked. "Breanne is fragile, by your own admission, Bell, and you pushed her too hard today, also by your own admission. Whose fault is this?" Hank almost took a step back from Bill's anger. He'd misjudged the man, just as so many others before him had. Bill hadn't achieved his rank by being meek.

"You're right," Hank nodded, his eyes meeting Bill's. "We'll approach cautiously. I'll try to convince her to come to you if things get bad."

"This is a fact-finding mission," Bill growled. "Don't forget that. The guns are for your protection only, not for aggressive acts. Hear me?"

"I hear you," Jayson mumbled.

"Yeah," Hank agreed.

"Then go. Find out what you can. Find Breanne if you can. If you care for her at all, you'll get down on your knees and beg if you have to, to get her back to us."

~

"I don't know if I've ever had my ass handed to me like that," Hank muttered as he and Jayson crossed the street to KingDom's.

~

Breanne's Journal

Who needs to walk anywhere when you can mist through? Especially when the place in question is filled with little rooms where people are binding, gagging, flogging, piercing, fucking, crawling and kneeling. At least my anger at Hank kept my mind clear and separate from what was happening all around me.

Bill would be shocked, too, to hear that all the employees at KingDom's were obsessed. *Every one of them.* That was more than frightening. A few I read had committed murder. So far, they'd managed to get away with it.

The dungeon monitors on duty were doing little more than observing, even when things seemed to be getting out of hand. Why was that happening? Was there a purpose behind it? Since I couldn't read the obsession—past the recognition that the employees had one, I had no idea.

My mind raced through possibilities, and I discarded them almost as soon as they popped into my brain. That's when I saw them. Hank and Jayson, as promised. Well, they could go fuck themselves.

I hadn't found evidence of a Sirenali, either, so I had no idea where it might be. The only places I hadn't checked were the administrative offices, on the top floor of the three-story building. I misted in that direction.

Should I have suspected it, since all the windows were covered in thick, dark film? Keir Arthur and Oscar Forde were drinking from two women when I found them inside the main office. These women weren't willing participants in the bloodletting, either. Both were visitors to KingDom's, and both had compulsion laid to keep them compliant.

While I hovered overhead, waiting for the vampires to finish their meal and let the women go, the last thing I expected to happen did, and it sent me screaming into action.

CHAPTER 8

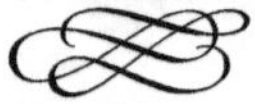

Gavin burst into the office as if he knew what was happening inside. With claws and fangs out and a growl I recognized easily, Gavin rounded on Keir Arthur.

"Stand back or they get it," Oscar Forde hissed. Both women were held against his chest with one arm, while the other hand, equipped with long claws, lay across their throats.

That's when I pulled the women away in my mist and flung them toward the door before appearing in front of Oscar, my claws and fangs ready for battle.

"Just handle yours, this one's mine," I hissed at Gavin, who stared at me in shock. No, he didn't recognize me. This Gavin hadn't ever met me. What he did recognize, however, was my scent—I'd dropped my shields when I became corporeal.

At least Gavin quickly focused on Keir again—after Keir punched him in the jaw. That's always an attention-getter.

"Well, well, well, a female vampire," Oscar laughed as he took in my scent. "What do you think you might do against me?"

"Want to find out?" I wiggled my long claws at him. Oscar lunged. I went to mist. He slammed into the wall at my back.

"Are my eyes deceiving me?" Oscar said when I came back to myself. "Do we have a mister, here?" He eyed me speculatively as we squared off again. "I thought it took much longer for a vampire to turn to mist."

Deep-red eyes studied me while Gavin and Keir fought across the room. A lamp broke and the light dimmed while glass sprinkled against opaque windows. I realized I didn't have time to pay attention to Gavin's battle; I had to keep my guard up with Oscar.

"Maybe you're just hallucinating," I said as Keir thumped into a wall. Gavin was efficient when he fought, there was no denying that, and Keir was beginning to show signs of wear. Gavin, on the other hand, appeared almost fresh and untouched, except for the bit of blood on his chin where Keir's ring had clipped him.

"You're just a baby," Oscar tossed a barb my way. "Baby want a bottle?" he laughed. Well, he shouldn't have done that. I misted forward and allowed claws only to form. His head rolled across the floor only a blink later. Quick death, just as Hank said.

If I'd known what killing Oscar would trigger, I might have done things differently. No, I hadn't bothered to read him, and it was a little late for that, now. The administrative offices took up the entire top floor and vampires boiled in from surrounding rooms seconds after Oscar's death. Was I prepared to take on all of them, with only Gavin Montegue as backup? No way.

~

"Something's happening," Bill shouted into his cell. "Get the hell out of there!"

"We don't have Breanne." Hank's reply was terse.

~

Breanne's Journal

Why does time slow down at critical moments? I saw Gavin go down under a mob of vampires as I went to mist. If Gavin died, so much of the future would change or die with him. Yes, I should have been paying attention, but as someone pointed out to me before; I wasn't the Mighty Mind.

How many deaths would change the future? Who might be targeted? Gavin had become a target—that was obvious. The enemy, just as I suspected, was still alive in some way. Yes, I may have killed his slaves or servants, but he was still out there, determined to destroy what he could.

I couldn't *Change What Was* without making myself a target again. Expending power similar to a Larentii? That seemed to have no negative impact.

Diving into a pile of seething vampires, I pulled a semiconscious Gavin into my mist and flew through the roof. Then, while hovering over the building, I considered what to do next.

I'm sorry, Bill, I sent, before extending power identical to a Larentii's and filtering the obsessed from those not obsessed. Hank and Jayson, too, I lifted away with the others who held no obsession. After dumping the innocent on the sidewalk across the street, I imploded the building beneath me. The boom shook the buildings nearby, but no harm was done to them. Nobody inside KingDom's survived, though, and that included thirty-seven vampires.

"What the hell just happened?" Thurman Bray, San Francisco's Chief of Police demanded.

"Thurman, there's no need to shout. I lost someone inside that building," Bill said. "If I knew what happened, I'd tell you."

"There's proof that the management was connected to those college girl murders two years ago," Jayson handed a flash drive to Bill. "Hank and I managed to get that before we uh, got out."

"Did you have anything to do with that pile of rubble out there?" Thurman tossed out a hand in disbelief.

"My agent here had nothing to do with that," Bill snarled. "And unless you can determine how a nine millimeter could cause that kind of destruction—because that's how he was armed—then shut the hell up."

"You think the management did that—you think they knew they were caught?" Thurman attempted to calm Bill down.

"That's my guess—that they had this in the plans in case we came snooping. We came snooping tonight. Now we're left with a missing agent, who knows how many dead and a big pile of rubble." Bill shook his head.

They'd taken over a back room at the bar across the street as a makeshift command post while officers, agents and medical personnel examined the remains of a three-story building. So far, only crushed bodies had been removed.

"Never figured you for an undercover agent, Rome," Thurman mumbled to Jayson before walking away.

"Keep that to yourself," Bill barked.

"Got it," Thurman tossed up a hand and kept walking.

"Jayson, where's Hank?" Bill covered his face with shaking hands.

"Said he had something to do." Jayson pulled out a chair and sat adjacent to Bill. Bill lowered his hands and stared at Jayson.

The bar's back room was reserved for parties and special occasions, with tables scattered throughout. Bill had chosen a table against the back wall to set up, and that's where he'd been for the last two hours, working the investigation with Thurman and the Fire Chief. The whole time, he'd been terrified for Breanne.

The Fire Chief hadn't stayed long—there was no fire to put out. He'd found that puzzling but didn't argue. He did leave his paramedics behind, however, to help those wandering about. Some of those affected were naked or nearly so; others were dressed in unusual ways. All of them seemed confused and unaware of how they'd gotten out of the building.

"Is he looking for her?" Bill asked Jayson.

"I don't know," Jayson sighed. "Hell, I'd like to look for her, but I have no idea where to start."

"Opal's trying to track her, but there are no signs or scents to track," Bill said, pulling his cell from a pocket and scrolling through messages. "No word since the last time I checked," he pocketed the phone.

"I don't believe this." Jayson raked fingers through smudged blond hair. He and the others who'd survived had been coated with a fine dusting of pulverized concrete when the building went down.

"You don't believe it? I have to explain it—to the President," Bill said.

~

"Hanlekidus?" he approached cautiously. He knew what his instructions had cost the one before him.

Hanlekidus Frebell, known to those on Earth as Hank Bell and as Li'Neruh Rath elsewhere, raised angry, dark eyes to the Mighty Mind. Hank sat at a booth at Bogey's Bar & Grill, located just outside the Castro District and not far from the club he owned.

"Wisdom," Hank snarled the name.

"I know you're upset," Wisdom, gray eyes expressing concern, took a seat across from Hank. "I understand that completely, and I'm sorry it's costing you like this."

"You understand nothing," Hank growled. "She thinks I'm nothing but an abusive asshole, now."

"She needed to be angry. It gave her enough energy to do what was necessary."

"I don't disagree with the result, just the method," Hank snapped. "And don't give me any patronizing shit about making it up to her later."

"You really have gone native, haven't you?"

"Wasn't that the point?"

"I have no idea what the point was. I didn't witness your conversation with a Shining One."

"It was The Ear," Hank rumbled.

"Ah. So everything said went straight to the One, then."

"Yes."

"Interesting, but irrelevant," Wisdom mused.

"What about Breanne?"

"She'll be away from you for a few days," Wisdom said.

"That's not acceptable."

"You'll have to accept it. I realize this is painful, but it is necessary, I assure you."

"Will she be protected?" Hank's words were a plea.

"I can't guarantee that, any more than I can guarantee my own safety. You know why. I do have a way of tracking her, now, and that in itself is highly irregular."

"Irregular? I didn't think there was any way to track the Vhanaraszh that she is."

"That is true for all others. I recently came across information that enables me to find her."

"What is that?" Hank leaned back and studied Wisdom for a moment. He knew this was Wisdom's true appearance—gray eyes, dark hair, slightly taller than Hank, too. "In case there's an emergency and I need to find her," he added.

"I cannot release that information—it could place her in danger. More than she's in already," Wisdom replied. "If you have need, contact me. I'll determine whether your reasons are sound enough to attempt to find her."

"And this thing—whatever it is—won't harm her?"

"I didn't say it was a thing, because it's not," Wisdom said. "And yes, there is potential for harm from that source, so I have taken steps to minimize that possibility."

"So it's a who."

"I didn't say that."

"You're not denying it."

"True," Wisdom grinned. Hank lifted an eyebrow.

"Sheriff Trevor?" Corent cautiously stepped inside Trevor's Casino City office.

"Corent?" Trevor blinked at the half-fae in surprise, although he kept a tight rein on any further display of emotion. Trevor knew who Corent was, but Lissa's Chief Gardener had never sought him out before.

"I came to ask a question," Corent nodded his thanks when Trevor indicated a chair in front of his desk. Corent sat down uncomfortably.

"What's that? Having problems with apple thieves?"

"Not recently," Corent shook his head. "That's not the kind of question I have."

"What's the question, then?" Trevor toyed with the comp-vid lying on his desk.

"Do you remember Breanne?"

"Breanne?"

"You know, the one Skel Hawer almost killed," Corent rolled his shoulders, as if they were tight with tension. Corent's hair, too, seemed to have a mind of its own as it transformed from pale to deep blue and back again.

"Oh. Her. No—don't remember much about her or that case. You might talk to Lissa or Norian, though. They'll know more. Why do you ask?"

"Because I think something's wrong," Corent replied. "I know this is forward of me to say, but you should know more than you do about that case, Sheriff. Much, much more."

~

Breanne's Journal

Larentii are amazing healers. I employed their skills to bring Gavin back to normal. His body, attuned to the night, breathed beneath my hand. I sat, cross-legged, next to my vampire sire's prone body. I'd transported him to the roof of a building near the Presidio after imploding KingDom's, so I could tend his wounds. It had been close; several claws had pierced his body before I could get to him, and at least one vampire had almost reached Gavin's throat before I could pull him away.

Was I comfortable, staring down at the face of my (at best)

indifferent and (at worst) abusive sire? No. I was decidedly *un*comfortable. I'd done a reading, however, while employing a Larentii's healing skills to Gavin's wounded body, and I knew if I didn't stay close to him in the following weeks, he'd die. I kept seeing his death repeatedly, until it was burned on my brain.

I couldn't let that happen. Not only would Lissa's life be affected, the Campiaan Alliance wouldn't exist. As much as I despised Teeg San Gerxon, he'd served a useful purpose and without Gavin, Teeg wouldn't be. I couldn't deny that, even if I wanted to do so.

Gavin groaned and moved. I watched as his eyes popped open. "Feel better?" I asked as kindly as I could. I knew this Gavin didn't know me from any other vampire, so I was willing to cut him a little slack. Until his true colors came to the fore, that is.

"You're a mister," his speech was rough.

"Not the first words I expected from you," I said, "but you're right. I am a mister. And I have mindspeech. I have some Elemaiyan blood. I know you know what that means."

"That you're more likely to have those gifts, although I can't recall both in the same vampire." He sat up and leaned on an elbow, studying me. "You're Breanne Hayworth, from the book."

"Yeah. I'm Breanne Hayworth, all right," I muttered.

"Who turned you?"

"I can't say," I said. Well, it was true. If I said *he* did—in the future—how much trouble might that cause?

"You were instructed not to tell," Gavin straightened and raked fingers through short, dark-brown hair.

"I guess," I shrugged.

Gavin softly cursed the compulsion of my sire. I wanted to laugh, because he was cursing himself.

"Everyone was looking for you," Gavin observed. At that moment, how glad was I that my recent, short stint on television, courtesy of Colbi Wayde, reporter, had been after sunset?

"Yeah."

"How long have you been vampire?"

"I can't say."

"Do you know if your sire was a rogue?"

"It was my understanding that he wasn't," I replied.

"Did he teach you the vampire laws?"

"I can recite all the vampire laws. I can even do them backward, if you'd like."

"What is the first law?"

"Never kill your donor."

I watched as Gavin stood and looked about him, taking stock of our surroundings. "Come quietly," he laid compulsion and held out a hand to pull me up. Was I about to tell him (again) that compulsion didn't work? Not on your life.

Silently I followed Gavin as he strode determinedly toward the edge of the building. Then he turned to me. "I will not harm you," he said before gripping my upper arms in his hands. I almost snorted at his statement before gasping in surprise—he stepped off the edge of the building and floated us to the street below.

We then began a swift trek toward the block where KingDom's had stood. Eventually, I realized we were heading toward a vehicle. Gavin had parked several blocks away, and I was grateful I wouldn't come in contact with anyone who might recognize me. I thought, too, about sending mindspeech to Bill again, but held back. I'd let him know eventually where I was, and why. Probably.

Without a word, I climbed into Gavin's luxury rental car—there would be no economy class vehicle for this vampire. I jerked as his hands pulled the seatbelt around me and fastened it.

"There is no need to be afraid," Gavin soothed. Did I stare at him in shock? Oh, yes.

~

"Bill, there's somebody outside who says he has information for you," Opal said. *He's werewolf,* she added silently to Bill and Jayson. *I don't trust him.*

"Then bring him in," Bill said. *Keep your weapons handy,* he sent.

Opal never blinked as Zach Tanner shouldered his way past her with a growl. He recognized the scent of a shapeshifter easily enough.

"Your name?" Bill asked, leaning back on his chair to study the newcomer.

"Zach Tanner," Zach grinned before firing the weapon that appeared suddenly in his hand. Zach was dead before Bill slammed against the wall behind him. Jayson stared at the nine millimeter in his hand with surprise.

∼

Breanne's Journal

"Climb down ahead of me," Gavin ordered. The trap door was narrow and located inside a closet of the elegant, frame house in San Francisco. I put my foot on the first step, testing the wooden rung. It felt solid enough. I made my way downward carefully, Gavin right behind me.

"Sit there," Gavin ordered, nodding toward a chair behind a tiny kitchen table. We stood in a small living area located across from a bathroom, which divided the two underground bedrooms. "I have a call to make," Gavin continued. "You will remain silent."

I watched as he punched a number on his cell. The call was picked up quickly. "Gavin?" the voice asked. *Wlodek.* Oh, Lord.

∼

"I always wear a vest when I'm on a project like this," Bill rubbed his chest where the bullet had slammed into him.

"I'm just glad it worked," Hank examined the bruise forming over Bill's ribs. Hank had arrived seconds after Jayson killed Zach Tanner. They'd had to move to another corner of the room—agents were collecting evidence around the body.

"I'll live," Bill reached for his shirt.

"You'll be sore for a while. We can get you to a hospital, if you want."

"I don't have time for that," Bill grumped. "Anything new on Breanne?"

"No," Hank sighed. "I was hoping you'd heard something."

"All I heard was *sorry, Bill*, before the building went down and a hundred people started wandering the street in a daze. Thanks, Jayson, by the way. You're pretty handy to have around," Bill complimented Jayson.

"I'm still trying to come to terms with this," Jayson flopped onto a chair and blinked at Hank.

"First time is always the hardest," Bill grunted as Hank searched ribs for any fractures. "Werewolves are tough to kill. Going for the head was a good idea."

"What are you planning to do with the body after they collect evidence?" Opal asked. She'd gone through Zach's pockets initially, but found no identification. All he'd carried was a gun.

"I'll contact the Grand Master in a minute, when Hank stops torturing me. Weldon may be able to confirm whether this really is Zach Tanner, or whether he was using an alias." Bill hissed as Hank poked another rib. "Either way, local wolves will come for the body."

"May have a crack there," Hank pulled back. "Sure you don't want to see a doctor?"

"Just wrap me up, I've had worse," Bill ordered.

"You're the boss," Hank reached for an elastic bandage he'd filched from paramedics outside.

Breanne's Journal

"Is the investigation complete?" Wlodek asked immediately.

"It appears so, Honored One," Gavin replied. I watched as Gavin moved about the small living area, placing folders and a laptop inside a case and zipping it up. "Keir Arthur and Oscar Forde are both dead, as are other vampires who attacked me."

"Good. I will expect a full report upon your return."

"I didn't accomplish this on my own," Gavin began.

"How was it accomplished, then, and who assisted you?"

"I have an apparent rogue vampire here with me now. I was attacked by more than thirty rogues, and this one was the only one who stepped in to help me. Honored One, this one is more than talented. This one has mindspeech and misting ability."

"Do you have him under compulsion? Will he willingly cooperate with us or shall the Council decide his future?" Wlodek's voice was matter-of-fact as he considered my fate.

"Honored One, *she* saved my life earlier. I would not have survived without her misting talent. Somehow, she managed to gather me inside her mist and transport me to safety. I believe the establishment was wired against intrusion, and it exploded behind us. You may be able to see images and human reports if you search the news outlets."

"A female vampire." I heard tapping as Wlodek considered this new twist. "Unexpected," Wlodek went on. "Bring her to me. I will assess her talents and willingness to cooperate."

"Of course, Honored One. If we move swiftly, we might make Chicago or New York tonight."

"Do so," Wlodek instructed. "I look forward to seeing this one."

"Come," Gavin ordered after terminating the call with the Head of the Vampire Council. He was already pulling a suitcase behind him and heading for the stairs.

"Are you hungry? You may speak," Gavin said half an hour after the plane was in the air.

"Yes." I hunched my shoulders. I was thirsty, actually, but Gavin would know something wasn't right if I asked for water. I knew bagged blood was coming, and I did my best to quell the resulting gag reflex.

Gavin rose from his seat opposite mine and went to the back of the jet. A bag of blood was in his hands when he returned. I reluctantly accepted it and twisted off the tubing at the top. Yes, I made a face as I drank about a third of my first dose of real blood.

"You don't like it?" Gavin asked, accepting the bag.

"I was a vegetarian," I shuddered, the salty taste of the blood still in my mouth.

"Have you ever taken from a donor? Tell the truth," Gavin placed additional compulsion. I worried my lip in shock at the question.

"No." I hung my head. "It was always that sort," I nodded toward the bag dangling from his fingers. I'd only drank blood substitute, but what else was I supposed to say? Blood substitute, where and when I was, hadn't been invented.

Gavin softly cursed my sire again—in Italian.

That night, in a safe house in New York, I slept in one of Gavin's shirts while my clothes went through the laundry. At least he didn't do heavy starch.

"Why are you here?" Ashe studied the one before him. He'd been commanded by a Shining One to take this one in and make sure he didn't leave until instructed to do so.

"Because I hold sensitive information," Thurlow hung his head.

Lissa's Journal

"Raona?" Corent stood in the doorway of my private study.

"Corent?" This was a first—he never came to me, I always sought him out.

"I wanted to speak with you about your sister."

"You met her?" I held a hand toward a guest chair, silently inviting Corent to sit. Here was more information—at least I hoped there was more.

"Yes. We talked on several occasions. I bought ice cream for her in Casino City."

"Thank goodness somebody was nice to her," I muttered, staring at the top of my desk. "What can I do for you? You never ask for anything," I lifted my eyes to my half-fae gardener again. He seemed troubled.

"Before your return, Trevor and Kooper Griff knew Breanne quite well. She even worked with them for a time. They worried about her. Until they didn't."

"What do you mean, until they didn't?" I blinked at Corent. His words didn't make any sense.

"One day they remembered her perfectly, and cared about her. The next they did not. I went to see Trevor earlier. He has no recollection that he investigated Skel Hawer after he nearly killed Breanne."

"Why do you think this is?" Fear—and concern—stole their way into my brain.

"Why would anyone forget anything on a planet filled with vampires?" Corent asked softly.

"It would have to be an old vampire to place compulsion on Trevor," I snorted.

"Or a King Vampire."

"I only know of four and they," I stopped.

"Yes. I believe we have come to the same conclusion," Corent nodded. "And you may wish to ask how well Gavril's Karathian warlocks recall your sister as well." Corent rose to leave.

"Why are you coming to me with this?" I asked.

"Because I love your sister," he said simply and disappeared. Until that moment, I had no idea that Corent could fold space. Something had changed, and I suspected I could determine the cause easily if I just took a few moments to do so.

Instead, I stood and sent mindspeech to Gavin.

"Cara?" he appeared in my study almost immediately.

"When did our son place compulsion on Trevor, Kooper and who knows who else, to make them forget Breanne?" I demanded.

~

"Colbi? Miss Wayde?"

Colbi Wayde looked up as a woman in her late twenties

approached her desk. "The guard let me in," the woman added. "I'm Janine Webster," she introduced herself. "I think we're sort of in the same boat, so I wanted to see if maybe we could work together a little."

"On what?" Colbi's voice held a bit of frost as she considered giving the guard at the reception area a piece of her mind. He knew better than to allow a stranger to walk into her office.

"On Hank Bell and Breanne Hayworth," Janine set a folded paper on Colbi's desk.

"What's this?" Colbi tapped the paper with a well-manicured nail.

"A restraining order," Janine said. "They say I've been stalking Hank and Breanne. That's a lie. That doesn't mean I don't know a few things about them," Janine whispered.

"Really? You have information, yet you haven't been watching them?" One of Colbi's shapely eyebrows rose in speculation.

"I said I didn't stalk them. I did watch them," Janine sniffed.

"Right. What information do you have that might interest me?" Colbi snapped.

"I saw Hank go into that building, just before it exploded," Janine said breathlessly. "I've seen Hank since then, but not *her*. She's disappeared."

"Really? Hank Bell was there?"

"With Jayson Rome," Janine nodded slowly.

"What does Jayson Rome have to do with this?" Colbi's interest was growing.

"Hank and Jayson have been friends for a long time. Jayson is supposed to have been Breanne Hayworth's fiancé before that book came out."

"That can't be true," Colbi pulled a legal pad to her and began scribbling notes. "How do you know this?" Colbi asked, studying Janine's frown. "Wait, never mind," Colbi waved a hand. "Give me what you have."

～

"Your brother is dead," Wildrif wept. "I tried to warn him," he sniffled into his cell. "Zachariah shot Jennings, just as you ordered, but someone else shot your brother. Jennings was wearing a vest and is still alive."

Wildrif listened carefully while Obediah Tanner began destroying everything within reach.

~

"Grand Master, I have a dead werewolf here," Bill informed Weldon Harper. "Likely a rogue, as he attempted to murder me before one of my agents killed him."

"Do you have a name?"

"We found no identification on the body, and the name he gave may not be his real identity."

"Send a photograph, and I'll see if I can ID from this end."

"Sending now," Bill forwarded a photograph he'd taken with his phone.

"Zach Tanner," Weldon growled when the photo eventually came through. "Might have known."

"You know him?" Bill was surprised the werewolf hadn't used an alias.

"Not personally. Usually if anybody got close enough to ID that bastard, they ended up dead. Surprised you lived over it," Weldon observed.

"Had a shifter with me and an agent quick with a shot. Wore a vest, too, or I'd be dead, just like you say," Bill explained.

"Tanner was usually more careful than that," Weldon mused. "Doesn't matter—he's dead now. I'll send some of mine to your location, and they'll ship the body my way. We'll handle this."

"I was hoping you would," Bill agreed. "Thanks for the help."

~

"Grand Master?" Winkler answered the call from Weldon immediately.

"Zach Tanner just got killed in San Francisco. Tried to take Bill Jennings out, it seems, and one of Bill's agents killed Zach."

"Obediah's gonna be pissed," Winkler pointed out.

"That's why I'm calling you. To watch out for that bastard," Weldon said.

"Weldon, you know Obediah's like a ghost. We haven't ever been able to pin anything on him."

"Just the same, I'd have said Zach wouldn't have gone down, either, but that's not the case."

"This doesn't make much sense. Do you know what happened?"

"I only have sketchy information, and didn't want to ask too many questions."

"Understood. I'll have my sources keep an eye on things in New Mexico."

"Sounds good. Keep me informed," Weldon said. "Anything new on that investigation? Has the car been seen lately?"

"Nope. Haven't seen it since Ace tried to tail it," Winkler said.

"Lying low until you turn your attention elsewhere, maybe?" Weldon said.

"Possibly. We're not going to let down our guard that easy, and now that Obediah might be on the rampage, we'll increase security."

"Good. We don't need another incident like the one a few years back. Lissa isn't here to cover our asses this time."

"No," Winkler sighed with regret. "We don't have Lissa this time."

Breanne's Journal

The trip from New York to London took six hours. Gavin had prodded me onto the plane as quickly after sundown as we could make it to the airport. We were cutting it close, I knew, with the time difference. Gavin didn't comment when I closed my eyes and slept, although I kept a tight shield up to keep him from hearing my heartbeat.

~

May in London wasn't bad, although I knew daylight was coming quickly when we touched down. I think we broke a few rules and regulations getting the jet's door open and down the steps to a waiting limo equipped with dark windows.

The driver was human and under compulsion to get us to a safe place. London traffic could be brutal, and there was no guarantee we'd make our destination without frying if we weren't in a car that might protect vampires from sunlight.

"Drive," Gavin barked the moment we were in the vehicle with the doors closed. The poor man might have broken a few laws on the way, but we pulled into a circle drive set in front of a large manor house ten minutes before sunrise.

Gavin pulled me from the back seat before I could squeal in surprise and ran me toward the front door. A very tall vampire waited there for us, and I read him briefly before being rushed past and into the house.

Poor Rolfe had seen similar behavior too many times to make a comment, and I wanted to weep for his fate in the future. I couldn't do that—I had no idea what effect my tears might have on vampires and had no desire to experiment.

I was flung into a bedroom with metal coverings over windows on the second floor and ordered to go to bed and sleep by a swiftly moving Gavin. I then watched as he slammed the door in my face. *Welcome to the UK,* I sighed and let my shoulders droop.

CHAPTER 9

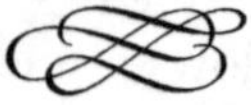

reanne's Journal

The first person I saw when I woke at sundown was Charles. I blinked stupidly at him, I know. He was kneeling beside my bed, arms crossed and leaning on crisp, white sheets with his face resting on his arms.

"Awake?" he grinned. Charles isn't bad looking, by any stretch. He has light-brown hair, hazel eyes and a wonderful smile. I held back from reading him.

"Yeah," I shoved hair away from my face.

"If you'll get dressed, I'll drive you into London for a new wardrobe," Charles offered, standing quickly. "After Gavin places compulsion to mind your manners," he added.

"It's really not necessary," I sat up in bed. I'd worn the same shirt Gavin lent me the night before to sleep in—he'd allowed me to use it as a sweater during the plane ride.

"One should never argue with Gavin or the Honored One," Charles chided. "When you're presentable later, the Honored One wishes to see you."

"Yeah. I suppose he does." I slid legs over the side of the bed and stood. "Do I have time for a shower?"

"If you hurry. I'll grab a bag of blood for you while you clean up. Soap and towels are laid out already," he added.

"Thanks," I said. "Which way?" I asked. I hadn't bothered to find the bathroom the night before; I'd just flopped onto the bed and stared at the ceiling for several hours instead, before getting undressed for sleep.

"Through that door," Charles pointed to the left. The room I'd been given had been used by Lissa—I knew that. It had sky-blue walls and white trim. Only the comforter, pillows and curtains had been updated, because the room was seldom used.

"I'll be out in five," I said.

"That should work," Charles whisked out of the room.

"I really hate this stuff," I eyed the bag of blood with distaste bordering on revulsion.

"Gavin said you did," Charles studied me as I worked up the courage to drink. "Does it bother you that much?"

"Yeah." I held my breath and drank as quickly as I could. Yes, it would sustain me, but I wanted spaghetti marinara. I think I'd even dreamt about it before waking to find Charles staring at me.

"Only half?" Charles took the unfinished portion from me.

"It's all I can handle," I mumbled, doing my best not to gag. "I have to brush my teeth," I said and fled to the bathroom again.

"Better?" Charles asked when I made my way out again.

"Yeah," I lied.

Charles likes to drive—fast. I considered (with longing) my TinyCar stuck in a garage in San Francisco, which felt far safer than the one I found myself in while Charles wove through London traffic like a racecar driver. In the dim interior of a very expensive car, I watched as Charles shifted gears almost absent-mindedly. Did I lower my shields to see what he was thinking?

Yes.

Could I read him?

No.

"Where are we going?" I asked, leaning back in my seat with a troubled sigh.

"We have an arrangement with the management of an exclusive shop in London," Charles replied. He kept his eyes on the road as we swerved around a van driving only a little above the speed limit. "It's vampire-owned," he added. "The other shops are closed, but they're keeping this one open after hours for us, since sunset is so late this time of year."

"It was nice of them to do that," I said, watching traffic blur around us.

"Wlodek ordered it, so there was very little nice involved."

"Oh."

"I read that book."

"You and millions of others." I turned my head to gaze out the window. With one sentence, he'd managed to send me into the land of *I don't care if I die in the next five seconds.*

"Wlodek will give you another name."

"Can he give me new memories, too?"

"Why did she do that?"

I knew whom he meant—Joyce Christian. "She was mentally ill. She chose children whose parents were criminals. She said she was beating the devil out of us." I snorted softly and kept my gaze pointed out the window. I had no desire to see any form of emotion travel across Charles's features.

"They finally found the other two bodies."

"Yeah."

"Did you know them—the ones who died?"

"No. She only took one child at a time. The first one was dead before the second came along, and he was dead before she got her hands on me."

"Why did she choose you? Did you beg her to take you away from that orphanage?"

Memories crowded my mind, then. Memories I'd shoved aside for a very long time. "She didn't choose me," I muttered. "Her twins did. She brought them with her, and they managed to locate me—I'd hidden behind a tree on the grounds."

"You knew to hide from her?"

"I knew something was wrong, so I hid. It didn't do any good, as it turned out." Vampire hearing is extremely sharp. I listened while Charles's fingers gripped the steering wheel tighter and the vehicle sped up.

~

The pile of clothing was staggering. There wasn't any way Charles could carry that in his car. The shoes—boxes of them, were stacked nearly to my waist and six deep. The underwear? I was embarrassed that a man helped me pick out underwear. It didn't seem to faze Charles at all, but he did grin now and then.

"It'll be delivered, except for these." Charles indicated a smaller pile of bags and two shoeboxes. "We'll take those with us and you can change when you get home."

I lifted an eyebrow at Charles. He was telling me, subtly, that I wasn't dressed well enough to be presented to Wlodek. I guess the Head of the Vampire Council wasn't into jeans, trainers and T-shirts.

"Come on, we have things to do," Charles reached for the bags destined to travel with us and pulled me toward the door.

~

"Miss Hayworth, Honored One." Charles ushered me into Wlodek's office. A huge Monet painting of water lilies graced one wall, and on the opposite hung a David portrait of Napoleon.

Wlodek, with dark hair and nearly-black eyes, expressed no emotion as Charles led me to a seat before Wlodek's desk. Gavin stood nearby, waiting. Charles took a chair next to mine and switched on the tablet he carried, preparing to take notes.

Wlodek's gaze might be described as severe as he studied me for several seconds. "You may keep your first name, but your surname will be changed," he spoke eventually. "Charles will have new identification for you soon."

I nodded at Wlodek's words—I mean, what can you say to someone you've met in the future, who is very different from the vampire who sits before you? This Wlodek wouldn't hesitate to kill me, and could order my death without blinking. The Wlodek in the future would attempt to protect me—as much as he could. It was the difference love might make, and Fox had certainly created a difference in her vampire mate's heart.

"Now," Wlodek continued, "there is the question of your continued education. Gavin says you can recite the vampire laws perfectly, and that you have never killed your donor. Both of those weigh in your favor, young woman. Had things been otherwise, you would be judged before the Council. Regardless, we must assign a surrogate sire to teach you. I believe Casimir might be suitable for this task. Gavin what do you think?" Wlodek turned to Gavin, who'd remained silent.

"I would like to teach her—between assignments, Honored One," Gavin nodded respectfully to Wlodek. My breath caught in my throat at Gavin's words. Why in the name of the Dark Realm would he offer? He didn't want a vampire child in the future. Why would he want one now? Briefly I dropped my shields and read him again. What I saw surprised me—on several levels.

"Anthony is ready to go out on his own—you know this," Gavin added. "He will remain in the house until he finds something for himself, but his teaching is nearly complete."

"But what about the times you go on assignment? Granted, Breanne might go with you at times, as you tell me her talents could enhance any Enforcer or Assassin's abilities to bring down rogues, but there will be times when she remains behind."

"Honored One, please allow me to work with her whenever Gavin is absent," Charles spoke up. "I would like to act as a surrogate sire—in case I wish to become a sire in the future."

"You, Charles?" Wlodek allowed one eyebrow to rise. "You've never expressed this desire to me before."

"But I would like this, Honored One."

"Honored One, I was contemplating what to do about the drinking lesson anyway," Gavin said. "Charles could take from her, then we could both choose her target for the rest of the lesson."

"Charles?" Wlodek turned back to his assistant. "Will this interfere with your work?"

"Not at all, Honored One. With Gavin's help, I think this might turn out very well. Besides, I understand Breanne can keep records and do many of the things I do easily. She can help me get things sorted for you."

"Very well, just make sure she has compulsion laid not to reveal sensitive information."

"I will deal with that," Gavin murmured.

"Very well. Breanne, do you have a preference as to what your surname should be? If you do not, Charles and I will assign one."

I wanted to sigh. I didn't. I had a legitimate last name—one I'd never used. It didn't matter if I chose to use it now. "Arden," I said. "May I use Arden as my last name?"

"I see no problem with that." Wlodek pulled a paper to him and wrote on it with a gold pen. "Charles, prepare the new documents, and have them ready should Breanne be assigned to go with any of my Enforcers or Assassins. Meanwhile, take care of the bite lesson while Gavin is here." He extended the document toward Charles.

"I will, Honored One." Charles rose and took the paper from Wlodek's hand.

"Miss Arden," Wlodek gazed sternly at me, "I am being generous in your treatment, as Gavin has described how obedient and helpful you have been with him. I have read the book and understand your background. That means I will not lock you away or restrain you. However, if you step out of line, I will sign for your termination. Is that clear?"

"Yes, sir," I nodded. What else could I do? I'd read Gavin's death in his face again, and so many things depended upon his survival.

"How shall we explain her existence to the Council?" Gavin asked.

"Do you recall Lawrence Oldham?" Wlodek asked.

"Yes. He was killed three months ago by a rogue," Gavin said.

"Lawrence will be entered as Breanne's sire, and the records will indicate that Breanne's turning occurred two years ago, after a botched suicide attempt on her part. The records will also reflect that her turning was kept secret, due to her notoriety. It is only after Lawrence's death that she was made my ward, and that I have made the decision as to who will take up her instruction. There will be no discussion concerning Miss Arden's legitimacy."

"But what about her presentation to the Aristocracy?" Charles asked.

"Because of Miss Arden's past, I will not entertain unsolicited offers until the five-year training period is over. This is a delicate matter, and they should understand. If they fail to do so, their lack of cooperation will be duly noted and subsequent offers made by them at the appropriate time will not be considered."

"That takes care of those offers, but what about her presentation to the Council?" Charles asked.

"That may be accomplished two nights from now. There are no executions on the schedule," Wlodek checked a tablet on the corner of his desk. "How are you with introductions to strangers, Breanne?" Wlodek's dark eyes leveled on me.

"I've learned to hide any discomfort," I dropped my gaze to my hands.

"Good. Very good. Charles, you will see that she is attired appropriately for the Council meeting, and the introduction will be made after business is concluded. I will also tell them that she has misting and mindspeech abilities, and will be trained to assist the Enforcers and Assassins."

That was Wlodek's dismissal from his presence, so I was ushered out the door quickly by Charles, with Gavin close behind.

"Charles, I will be taking her home with me," Gavin said as we walked down a narrow, back staircase to the lower level.

"Then with your permission, I will move some of my things there, and stay whenever Breanne is in residence. It isn't a long drive, and I can make it easily," Charles said.

"There is more than enough room, and Breanne's suite will be between ours. Anthony has his rooms in the other wing, so there will be no problems."

"Thank you," Charles inclined his head in Gavin's direction. "Shall we do the bite lesson tomorrow, then?"

"Yes."

I held my breath for a moment. I'd never been bitten. I knew what happened with the bite, and it terrified me. At that moment, no matter how angry I was with him, I wanted Hank. I wanted his reassurance and soft words. I wanted to feel safe. I didn't feel safe. My hand shook as I lifted it to my forehead.

"Breanne?" Charles's voice came from far away. Darkness fell, and I fell with it.

~

Baby, where are you? Are you okay? Please answer me.

"Huh?" I mumbled aloud.

"There she is," someone said. Fingers touched my forehead. I jerked and gasped, my eyes flying open.

"Nobody here will hurt you," Charles soothed. My thoughts were scattered at first and I blinked at his face in confusion. I found myself on the bed I'd slept on the night before, with Charles sitting beside me and Gavin standing behind Charles.

"Too much all at once," Gavin snorted. "Breanne, Charles will carry you to my vehicle, and he will follow us quickly. There is not much night left, and I wish to get you home and comfortable."

"All right," I moved to sit up. Charles took over and lifted me into a sitting position. "Feel better?" he asked.

"Yeah. I don't know what happened," I said.

"Gavin will feed you again before bed," Charles said. "I don't think you got enough the first time." He turned to Gavin, who nodded his agreement. I whimpered at the thought of drinking even more blood.

"You must learn to eat better, even if you find drinking repulsive," Gavin declared as Charles stood and lifted me off the bed. I wanted to tell him that if I had a veggie sub, I would make my way through it quite happily.

"I'll try," I replied instead.

The drive to Gavin's manor, which was built and decorated in Louis XIV splendor, didn't take long—perhaps half an hour. I was shown to a suite that included a bedroom, a sitting room, a large closet and a really nice bath. At least the bedrooms were more modern, and I was surprised the bed linens and curtains were more to my taste than the rest of the house.

"I am to your left, at the end," Gavin informed me. "Charles will be on your other side. Should you require anything, ask us. Anthony is on assignment, but will return soon. You will be introduced when he arrives. Have no fear of him—he will not harm you."

"Thank you," I said.

"No, the gratitude should come from me," he said, causing me to stare at him in shock. "You saved my life. I am grateful for that."

"You're welcome," I sighed.

"It's a church," Trajan set his cell phone in front of Winkler. A photograph was displayed of a rather large, new building, its construction almost completed.

"Are they in a hurry to save people? That thing has gone up in two and a half months."

"I wasn't aware that the area was zoned for that—it's two miles away and in the middle of a pasture," Trajan observed.

"There are laws protecting religious land use," Winkler pointed out while examining the photograph. "Did you see this?" Winkler tapped the phone screen, enlarging a portion of the photograph.

"Yeah. It has a tag, now, but it sure looks like the same car," Trajan said. "White Pontiac Grand Am. Same one, in my estimation."

"Why were they driving in front of the house?" Winkler stood and stretched. "Get Director Bill to run that plate. I want to see who owns the car."

"Already on that. Got a message from Bill's assistant—she's checking the car—says Bill is working on something else, and he's worried."

"That doesn't sound good. Probably has something to do with that building that exploded in San Francisco," Winkler said. "And Zach Tanner trying to kill Bill shortly after. Want coffee?"

"Yeah. Jimmy's in the kitchen—he'll make it for us."

"So, nobody has seen Breanne Hayworth since her impromptu appearance at Hank Bell's club," Colbi tapped a pen against her legal pad.

"Except me, and I'll never tell," Janine smiled. "I'm set up to take pics of Jayson Rome tonight, and you can splash those wherever you want tomorrow."

"What will he be doing?" Colbi was more than a little interested. "I mean, if we point in his direction and hint that he and Bell had something to do with Breanne Hayworth's disappearance, we need something juicy to make the public believe it might be possible. Damn, I always wanted to take down a big fish." Colbi scribbled notes on the pad.

"Oh, he's into flogging and fire play. I can probably get pictures of both."

"Before you came along, I'd have said this was impossible," Colbi made another note. "Too bad I can't get a camera crew in there."

"I can do video with my phone, if you want it."

"Good. We can block out other images—I just want Jayson Rome and Hank Bell. Any chance you can get photographs of Hank?"

"Not really. I've been banned from his club, and that's where he'll be."

"Right—the restraining order," Colbi said. "Too bad. Do you know any regulars at his club who might get images—for the right price?"

"Maybe," Janine sniffed. "If the price is right for me, too."

"I thought it might come to this," Colbi said, opening a drawer and pulling out folded cash. "Here. A thousand, and you'd better deliver."

"Oh, I will," Janine dimpled. "I will."

Breanne's Journal

Breanne? Please answer. Bill's mental voice woke me from a sound sleep.

Bill? I hadn't known his mindspeech might be powerful enough to reach me. Obviously it was.

Thank God. Tell me where you are, sweetheart, and I'll come for you.

Bill, you can't. I'm with the vampires. They sort of own me, right now. If I leave, some of them might die, and that will be a really, really bad thing.

You're in the UK?

Yeah. Bill, I'm okay for now, and you ought to know I can get myself out of here if I have to. There are some things I have to do, and if I leave now, they'll come hunting. You know why.

Rogue. Yeah. I get that. Look, everybody else here is worried. What do you want me to tell them?

That I'm fine at the moment, and that things got sidetracked and I have work to do. Hank won't understand that, but let's face it, he wasn't very nice the last time I saw him.

He said so, Bill confirmed. *I just can't tell you how glad I am that you're all right. Can you tell me what happened in San Francisco?*

I found Oscar Forde and Keir Arthur, I said. *I was ready to take them down when Gavin Montegue showed up and burst into the room. You know Gavin, don't you?*

I've worked with him, Bill replied.

Yeah. Anyway, the minute Gavin came riding in on his vampire high horse, thirty-five vampires—all rogues—flew in behind him. It was all I could do to take down Oscar and get Gavin the hell out of there before he died.

How did the building explode?

Well, there was the question with no easy answer. *Lissa could do it,* I said. *I can, too.*

Lissa. I see.

Bill didn't really, but he accepted the explanation anyway. *All the vampires and all the employees at KingDom's were obsessed,* I went on. *There wasn't anything we could do for them unless we found the one who obsessed them, and some of them were involved in the murders we investigated. I got everybody else out and then took the building down. I hope it hasn't caused too much trouble.*

Sweetheart, let me handle the awkward explanations. I don't know whether this had anything to do with KingDom's, but a werewolf assassin tried to take me out a few hours after the building exploded.

What? Are you okay? You're not hurt, are you?

No, Bree. I'm fine, a chuckle came through in Bill's mindspeech. *I was wearing a vest. My worry now is that the werewolf's family will be up in arms, since Jayson killed their brother.*

Jayson? If I'd been speaking, my voice would have squeaked.

Yeah. Hank has taught him well. He's pretty good with a pistol.

No doubt, I responded dryly. *I hear Henry Hank Bell is pretty darn handy with that stuff, too.*

That's what his records say, Bill agreed. *I'm offering extended temporary employment to both of them. I'm in desperate need of qualified agents, and since Hank has trained Jayson, he's good enough to add to the roster.*

Are they going for it?

Looks like it. Both are worried about you, and being employed by my department will ensure that they get better updates on this mess—and on you, too. Hank's promoted his assistant manager and found two others to fill in. Jayson hasn't had a real vacation in years, so he's taking time off.

Bill, I need a favor, I said.

Anything, sweetheart.

Can you freeze my assets? If you don't, the vamps will take them. It's what they do.

I can do that. Making calls now. Do you want me to set up another account for you, for emergencies? I can put it under an alias and give you the numbers.

Bill, I want to kiss you for that, I said.

I'll remember you said that. I'll get back with you as soon as this is done. Thanks, Bill.

I love you, Bill answered.

Honey, I love you, too.

~

Lissa's Journal

"Tell me why." I deliberately kept my arms at my sides and resisted the urge to plant fists on my hips.

"Mom, she was a distraction. At least that's what I thought at the time. And she could have cost me my warlocks."

"Is this my son standing in front of me, telling me he placed compulsion on my sheriff, a vice-director of the ASD and his warlocks, something he promised he would never do, just to cover his ass and destroy any affection anybody might have for Breanne?"

Gavril sat heavily behind his desk. He didn't understand how his mother discovered what he'd done, but she had. "Mom, I don't know how to make this right," he began. "If I remove my compulsion, they'll know I made them forget."

"And you see this as a problem because?" I snapped.

"For starters, I'll lose my warlocks. Yeah, I deserve that," he held up a hand to hold off my immediate response. I was about to tell him he deserved to lose his warlocks. He'd promised them long ago that he'd never place compulsion. Mind cloud or not, he'd broken that promise.

"Would you like me to tell Ildevar that you fucked with a vice-director of the ASD? Breanne has saved Ildevar's life twice. What reaction do you think you'll get if he learns of this? What I don't know, because your compulsion is still in place, is how much they cared about Breanne. Which of your warlocks cared about her, by the way? Gavin was too ashamed to explain any of this to me." I was getting wound up and my voice was getting louder. I'd yelled at this son more after he became an adult than I ever had when he was young.

"Stell. Stellan."

"The one who's never found anybody. The one who thinks he won't find anybody," I snapped. "His brothers have a mate or mates. Stellan, thanks to you, has nothing, and not only that, you cheated my sister, too. She won't even talk to me, because of you. And your father."

"What do you want me to do?"

"It shouldn't matter what I want. What should matter is what's right. Do you even know what that is anymore?"

"You think I cheated Stell out of a mate."

"Yes, I think you cheated Stellan out of a mate. Possibly Trevor and Kooper, too." I tossed up a hand in disbelief. "Hasn't that crossed your mind even once—that you mistreated people, or does that not matter to you?"

"I worry about that in him—that he seems to no longer feel," Dee walked into the room.

"I thought I taught you to have sympathy for all things deserving," I sighed. "I've failed." I folded away.

"Is that how you see me, now?" Teeg glanced up at his foster-father.

"Yes. It began when you mistreated Reah and kept her from the others, just to have your way and achieve your goals. You assured me then that it was temporary, and that you'd make it up to her later. She has given you a child, and still your mate is nothing but an afterthought. I know not what has happened to you, Gavril Tybus Montegue, but I dislike it greatly." Dee stalked from Teeg's office.

Hank and Jayson walked into Bill's temporary office at the local FBI headquarters. "You wanted to see us?" Jayson took a seat in front of Bill's desk. Hank slipped onto the other chair and waited for Bill's answer.

"Yeah. I spoke with Bree." Bill tapped his head. Jayson nodded his understanding; Hank's mouth pulled into a frown. "She's fine, but the vampires have her," Bill added. "She says that if she doesn't stay with them for a little while, that some of them could die. I'm not sure exactly what that means, but I trust her judgment."

"What does that mean for us, then?" Jayson asked.

"It means that I want to keep you on. Whether it's temporary or permanent, that's up to you. We're still following the money on KingDom's, and most of it leads out of the country. We have a Sirenali —according to Breanne, and she says all the employees and the vampires at KingDom's were obsessed. Some of them were responsible for the local murders. She got everybody else out and left those inside to die."

"How many vampires?" Hank asked softly.

"Including Oscar Forde and Keir Arthur, probably thirty-seven. Apparently, the Vampire Council sent an assassin in to take Oscar and Keir. Breanne had to pull him out of there before he died."

"Is that how they got their hands on her?" Jayson asked. "One of their assassins took her?"

"Looks that way. Believe me, you don't argue with Gavin. He's the Council's elite Assassin and nobody messes with him."

"Is she safe?" Hank asked.

"She says she's all right for now," Bill replied. "While I can't predict the polarities of the Head of the Council, he does recognize a good thing when he sees it."

"He thinks Breanne is a good thing?" Jayson asked.

"She's not dead, and I think she would have said something if he'd locked her up or restrained her in any way. My guess is that Gavin knows her talents, because she saved his ass. Anything Gavin knows, Wlodek knows shortly after."

"His name is Wlodek?"

"Yes, and keep that to yourself, unless you'd like your body julienned before burial."

"Not me," Jayson held up a hand.

Bill's cell rang. Bill lifted it from his desk and checked the sender. "Sheila?" he answered.

"Director, I ran the plates on that car in Dallas," Bill's assistant said.

"What did you find?"

"Plates registered to Saxom Meletius. There are no records anywhere, indicating this person exists."

Bill had gone perfectly still. "Say that name again—slowly," Bill instructed.

"Saxom Meletius. S-a-x-o-m M-e-l-e-t-i-u-s," Sheila spelled the name.

"Holy fucking Christ," Bill sputtered. "Sheila, get somebody on this. Dig deep. Find out who bought that car, what they look like, how much they paid and what they had for breakfast. Understand?"

"Yes, Director." The call was terminated.

"What's going on?" Jayson asked. The color still hadn't come back to Bill's face.

"All hell just broke loose," Bill said. "What time is it in the UK?"

"Hold for Wlodek, please," Charles said.

"Director, what do you have for me?" Wlodek spoke to Bill over the phone.

"I have disturbing news," Bill said. "We've had evidence of surveillance on William Winkler's home in the Dallas area. At first, the car had no current plates. The vehicle was recently spotted, and we ran the new plates."

"Does this concern me?" Wlodek asked impatiently.

"That's what I'd like to find out," Bill replied. "We have a name on new registration and nothing else to go on at the moment."

"The name?"

"Saxom Meletius," Bill said flatly.

Wlodek cursed fluently in Greek.

CHAPTER 10

*B*reanne's *Journal*

Something was definitely up, but since I couldn't read Charles, I had no idea what that might be. Gavin had been called into Wlodek's office and the bite lesson postponed. Was I grateful for the reprieve? You bet.

"Charles?" Wlodek's voice spoke from a walkie-talkie clipped to Charles's belt.

"Honored One?"

"Contact Merrill immediately."

"Of course, Honored One."

"Winkler?"

"Bill?"

"I'll be flying to Dallas tomorrow," Bill said right away. "I've gotten information on that car tag."

"What did you get?"

"Just a name, but it has put everybody on edge."

"What's the name?"

"Recognize Saxom Meletius?"

"Saxom. He's dead."

"So we all thought. Regardless, that's the name the vehicle is registered under. Any thoughts on why there's no other information to be had, and why anyone else would use that name?"

"None—that I know," Winkler's voice betrayed confusion. "You think it's somebody playing with us?"

"If it is, it's a really bad joke."

"Agreed. Who the hell would even know to use that name, unless it's another vamp or a were?"

"That's the current theory, but we can't say that for sure, now can we? Wlodek says he only has the word of two people that Saxom died, and he's attempting to contact them now."

"Bill, have you ever met their kind?" Winkler asked.

"I don't even know who we're talking about, so my answer is no," Bill sounded exasperated.

"You can't even talk about them without their permission. That's what I know. Lissa's father was one of them."

"You're joking. That's what we're dealing with?"

"Yeah. That's what we're dealing with, but they're not all like that."

"I hope to hell not," Bill huffed.

"Are you still going out tonight?" Hank studied Jayson with an unreadable expression in his dark eyes.

"Yeah. No reason not to," Jayson shrugged. "Belinda agreed to a play date."

"Be careful," Hank warned.

"I'm always careful."

"Yeah."

Breanne's Journal

"Honored One, Merrill says he'll have an answer in two days." Charles had left his office to make a call to Merrill, but now he was back and giving Wlodek information via walkie-talkie.

"Is that the best he could do?"

"He says that is the best he can do. He said you would ask that question, and asked me to tell you that he cannot move time, as much as he'd like to do so."

"Of course not," Wlodek sounded displeased. "I knew I should have called him myself."

Breathing a sigh, I went back to my assignment for the night—filing. Had I thought the job on Le-Ath Veronis boring? Well, I'd just been introduced to worse.

"Tell me what you're thinking," Charles almost sang the words as I stuffed another folder in a file drawer.

"That you have the patience of a saint," I said. He burst into laughter.

"What's that awful racket?" Wlodek's voice blasted over the walkie-talkie. I almost fell to the floor, I laughed so hard.

"I've never been in your Mercedes," Charles said as he climbed into the back seat of Gavin's sleek, silver vehicle. The steering wheel was on the left, like American cars, but the speedometer showed kilometers per hour instead of miles. "Did you get a better deal in Germany?"

"I did," Gavin shifted and tore out of Wlodek's driveway. I hadn't read him yet to see what he'd discussed with Wlodek. In fact, I was almost afraid to do so. I held on as Gavin raced away from Wlodek's manor.

"Will we move into your basement?" Charles asked. "Wlodek intends to sleep in his bunker."

"Yes." Gavin's voice was clipped.

"There's a basement at your house?" I asked.

"Closed off, most of the time," Gavin said. I didn't ask any more questions—Gavin wasn't in the mood to talk and I sure didn't want to push him. I'd seen enough of his temper in the future.

"Gather clothing for the next three days when we get home," Gavin instructed as he drove. "There are beds and bathrooms in the basement. We will be securely locked in while we sleep."

Whatever Gavin knew, it sounded bad. It made me think of the years I'd spent in Texas, when the threat of tornadoes came every spring. The wind would come up, rain and hail would pelt down, the television stations would issue dire warnings and everybody would troop to the cellar to wait out the storm. If they had a cellar.

"Hey," Charles's head appeared between my seat and Gavin's. "We'll be fine, you'll see." I stared into hazel eyes for a moment.

"Come here," he gestured me closer with a hand.

"Huh?" I leaned forward.

"Hold still," Charles stroked my face with a gentle hand. I frowned at him as his hand moved to the back of my neck. Careful fingers massaged my neck. It felt good—I'd spent most of the night filing a backlog of folders, and I felt tired and achy. My eyes closed as Charles continued to rub my neck.

"That's it," he murmured close to my ear. "Breanne's tired, isn't she?" his words were whispered against my collarbone. I wanted to relax against Charles and let him keep soothing me. I shrieked instead when his fangs pierced my throat, and then the intense waves of pleasure hit. I was unconscious (again) in no time.

~

"Effective, although unconventional," Gavin mused as Charles lifted Breanne from the passenger seat.

"Shhh, don't wake her," Charles whispered.

~

Breanne's Journal

"Are you going to wake, my love?"

Charles's voice. I came awake fighting.

"No, no, there's no need for that, no need," Charles's voice was almost mesmerizing as he held my wrists in his hands. "Lie back, everything's all right," he breathed before kissing my forehead. I sobbed.

"What's wrong? What's wrong with my baby?" I was in his arms quickly.

I struggled to hold back tears as I trembled against Charles.

"What happened?" Gavin settled on the bed beside us.

"Scared," Charles murmured into my hair. "Almost took my head off when I touched her."

"Understandable," Gavin sighed. "She has no guarantees that we won't hurt her—that anyone won't hurt her."

"I know. Breanne, it's all right, darling. It's all right."

The tears fell during the hours of daylight over Kent. I didn't know what to do. Charles had lulled me into believing he wanted to soothe, and then he'd bitten me. Granted it may have been a much quicker process than the one I kept imagining, but the shock of it—and the ensuing intensity of the climax, had ended up terrifying me.

Does it count as sex if there's no intimate contact? I trembled again at the thought. I didn't know what to think, either, about Charles taking care of me afterward. Calling me darling and other endearments. They'd come so readily to him, it made me wonder if those were simply common words for him to use with any woman. Since I couldn't read him, I couldn't know those things.

Hank and Bill wandered into my thoughts, and I huddled into a ball on the bed. Gavin's basement smelled like a musty, closed-in space, and with my claustrophobia, I was finding it difficult to breathe. The bedroom I had was little more than a cubicle, and the shower was tiny. No surprise, given that it had been added long after the house was built.

You can do this, I repeated my mantra. *You can do this. You can do this. You can do this.* I counted my breaths, hoping they'd even out soon.

~

"Get the pics?" Janine sounded breathless as she spoke to Colbi Wayde over her cell.

"Got 'em," Colbi crowed. "The video, too. This is going to be so good—to rip into him with this. There's no way he can deny this. No effing way."

"Hank wasn't at the club tonight," disappointment coated Janine's words. "His new assistant managers threw me out."

"You do have a restraining order, darling," Colbi laughed. "Don't worry; we'll catch up with Mr. Bell. If we can get footage of him doing something like this," Colbi played the video again of Jayson Rome lashing a woman tied to a wooden contraption, "then we can destroy both of them."

"What if somebody asks about your source," Janine said, worry creeping into her voice.

"No worries—sources are usually protected," Colbi assured her.

"But what if," Janine hesitated.

"What if what?"

"Never mind," Janine said. "Bye."

"You bet your ass never mind, I paid you a grand, you bitch," Colbi muttered after ending the call.

~

Breanne's Journal

"Remember, we have a Council meeting tonight," Charles poked his head into my cubicle. I was showered and dressed appropriately, but probably looked as if I'd been in a fight with a troll.

"Hey," he stepped inside. "What's wrong? Didn't you sleep?"

"What kind of question is that to ask a vampire?" I turned away from him and straightened the covers on my narrow bed.

"Breanne," his hands wrapped around my upper arms. "I didn't hurt you. If I did, I didn't mean it," his voice was soft. "You're my girl." He pulled me against him. I struggled in his grip.

"You say that to everybody," I accused.

"To my knowledge, Charles hasn't courted a woman in three centuries," Gavin rumbled behind us. "I sincerely believe he *does not* say that to everybody." My shoulders sagged at Gavin's words.

"I don't know what to believe anymore," I muttered.

"I didn't mean to scare you," Charles said, turning me so his eyes could meet mine. "Really. Usually the climax will mitigate the fear, so to speak."

"Yeah. It sucks to be a vampire with PTSD," I said, pulling away from Charles. "No pun intended."

"None taken," Charles nodded, holding back a smile. "But speaking of sucking, you're obligated to do that, now. It's the second part of the bite lesson. I know you have the rules and the mechanics down, you just have to commit the act."

"Yeah. Thanks for ruining breakfast," I said.

"You must eat," Gavin informed me. "How much did you take from her? She looks pale," Gavin pointed his question in Charles's direction.

"No more than a cup or so," Charles was offended, I could tell. "Don't you think I know better than that?"

"Here," Gavin handed Charles a fresh bag of blood. My stomach almost rebelled at the sight of it.

"You don't have watermelon instead?" I asked. It was meant to be a joke. It didn't sound like a joke.

"No, love," Charles clipped the top off the bag with slightly extended claws. "Drink this quickly, it'll help. As much of it as you can."

Holding my breath, I drank as much as I could and stopped before I gagged. Not even two-thirds of the bag was gone when I stopped. Charles eyed me skeptically as I handed the bag back.

"We will feed the rest of this to you later," Gavin declared. "Rinse out your mouth quickly and come—the Honored One does not like to be kept waiting."

"Have you seen the news?" Wlodek asked as I was ushered into his study. He was dressed impeccably in a dark suit, white shirt and burgundy tie. His shoes alone might buy a yacht. Thankfully, his question was for Gavin, not me.

"I have," Gavin nodded slightly.

"This will cover the holes in our story," Wlodek almost smiled. "Charles, do you have a copy of that news segment?"

"Yes, Honored One," Charles tapped the tablet in his hand with a finger.

"Good. We will proceed," Wlodek swept through the door, leaving us to bob along in his wake.

"Jayson, I can do some damage control, but too many have seen this already," Bill sighed.

Jayson blinked in shock as the video played over and over. "Janine," he growled. "She was at the Sub-Mariner."

"I've already sent someone to pick her up," Bill nodded. "And I have someone else questioning the reporter. The reporter, at least, has been set straight on Breanne's disappearance, but as we cannot produce her at the moment, many will believe the lies."

"How could they even think that Hank and I would hire someone to pretend to be Bree?" Jayson dropped his head in his hands and moaned. "My dad fired me an hour ago. I don't have a job, now," Jayson's voice was muffled.

"You have a job, but your current status as a, well, celebrity," Bill said, "will work against you in my department."

"I get that," Jayson said.

"I've been fired, that's what happened," Colbi shoved personal items into a box while Mitchell Graves and a security guard watched. "How was I to know Hayworth was working with the NSA?"

"If you'd discussed this with me beforehand, we could have researched it a little better," Mitchell snapped. "I hear Jayson Rome lost his job over this, and if he sues the station, I can kiss my job good-bye, too."

"He's the one engaging in deviant behavior," Colbi snarled.

"His privacy was invaded—at your request. Anyway that's what I'm hearing," Mitchell snapped. "Why didn't you just point a camera through his bedroom window? The club where that footage was taken may have a thing or two to say as well."

"He was whipping that woman," Colbi began.

"And she was begging him to hit her harder. It's a lifestyle, and consenting adults, Colbi. Hold on, my phone is ringing." Mitchell pulled the cell from his pocket. "Hello," he said and listened for several seconds.

"How did you get that information?" Mitchell demanded. "It's not true, I swear it." Mitchell ended the call a few seconds later. "Get in my office," he growled at Colbi.

~

"What was that about?" Colbi asked.

"I just got a call from Jayson Rome's attorney. He said that they have information regarding our affair, and that if we don't do damage control on all this, it'll go public."

"How the hell did they find out about that?" Colbi gaped at Mitchell. "Oh, my God."

"If this goes public, I'll lose my kids," Mitchell said. "And my wife. Fuck!"

~

"How is our prisoner today?" The lieutenant surveyed the shackled vampire, whose emaciated body rested on the stone floor at his feet. "Weak from a lack of blood?"

"I know who you are," the vampire lifted dark eyes to the lieutenant. "I may be weak, but my hearing is still quite strong. I know they call you Acrimus."

"And I know who you are as well, *Tybus*," Acrimus laughed. It was awkward, that laugh. Acrimus still had difficulty with human emotions of any kind. "You look exactly like your reincarnation, you know. Too bad you're sucking his soul away. That's the rule, after all. A soul can't coexist with itself in the same timeline without sufficient power, protection or permission. Only one body gets the soul in those cases, and since you came first," Acrimus attempted a shrug. "If I can't destroy a target directly, then it's only prudent to do it indirectly."

"You did this," Tybus hissed. "You should have left me dead in the past."

"Ah, but where might my satisfaction be in all of this?" Acrimus struggled to smile. "And if you're not good, I'll leave you without blood for another day. I think you can make it that long, can't you?"

Breanne's Journal

"You will not recall how to get here," Wlodek laid compulsion after we'd parked in a wooded area. I nodded, although his compulsion didn't even cause a flutter in my brain. Chislehurst Caves lay below us, consisting mostly of excavated warrens and halls carved in centuries past for chalk and flint. The Druids had begun it, followed by the Romans and then others. Parts of it had even been used as a bomb shelter during World War II.

One section, however, was a natural cave, and only the Druids had found it in the past. That cave was a holy place to them—before the vampires stumbled across it. Now, that cave housed the Vampire Council meetings and the entrance was carefully hidden and guarded zealously.

I followed obediently behind a vampire named Russell, who'd

arrived to ferry Wlodek to the meeting. Wlodek followed me, Charles came next and Gavin trailed behind, keeping watch. Russell was Chief of Wlodek's Enforcers, and Gavin Chief of Assassins. Their duty was to protect Wlodek. I felt it was my duty to protect them; they were all important to the future. I figured Charles was important, too—since I couldn't read him, I could only assume that was true.

Two vampires stood at the cave entrance, and I almost stumbled when I saw them. Trevor stood there, watching the area around us with sharp eyes.

Will, the other vampire, drew in a breath as I recovered and slipped past him. He smelled female vampire, and wasn't old enough to hide his surprise as Trevor did. Was his brain furiously working, however, attempting to determine how a female vampire might be brought to a Council meeting?

I struggled to keep my shields up so the others wouldn't hear the frantic beating of my heart. Yes, I wanted to run back to Trevor and fling my arms around him. I couldn't. This Trevor had no idea who I was. None. Sadly, the Trevor in the future had no idea who I was, either. Silently I cursed Teeg San Gerxon and kept my eyes on Russell's back as he led me through a dark, narrow tunnel.

"They're freaking," Terrence "Terry" Johnston informed Hank over the phone. "I have no idea where your information came from, but it appears to be golden."

"It came from Breanne," Hank replied. "Good job, Terry. Keep the pressure on. Bill's handling some of it, but these people need to sweat."

"Where is Breanne? Do you know?" Terry asked.

"Bill says out of the country, but I don't know exactly where."

"Probably a good thing to get her away from all this," Terry said. "I don't know if her life will ever be normal."

"It probably won't be, and that's a shame," Hank agreed. "Thanks for taking this case, Terry. We owe you."

"Oh, it was my pleasure, and you'll get the bill, trust me," Terry chuckled.

~

Breanne's Journal

Radomir stood at the end of the tunnel, just inside a wide cavern. I almost hyperventilated when I saw him. Lowering my shield for a quick reading, I swiftly raised it again. He didn't remember me, and I found that more frightening than if he'd recognized me.

I hadn't done this—made him forget. Someone else had and I was terrified, because I had no idea who that someone might be. Focusing on breath control, I kept my steps as even as possible and turned my eyes back to Russell's broad shoulders.

We were early as it turned out—Wlodek preferred it that way, so Charles could set up and he could survey the Council members as they walked inside the cave. I was shunted to the side and hidden beside Gavin; he intentionally blocked sight of me from anyone entering the cave.

Wlodek took a seat at the center of a large, horseshoe-shaped stone table, and Charles set his tablet, a laptop and several other items out beside the Head of the Council, preparing to take meeting notes.

Is the cave wired for electricity? I ventured to ask Gavin mentally. Muted lights shown around the perimeter of the cave, dimly lighting the space.

"The lighting is solar-powered, from the surface," Gavin replied softly. "No more questions, now. I will answer those later, if you ask. Charles will also answer, if you'd prefer to speak with him."

I nodded my thanks and went back to watching Charles and Wlodek prepare for the meeting.

~

"Ready to see Director Bill?" Winkler walked into the kitchen where Trajan and Trace waited.

"Yeah, boss, let's go," Trace lifted van keys off the kitchen island.

"He says he has two agents with him, and we may inadvertently recognize one of them," Winkler rolled his shoulders.

"Been working too long on that computer," Trajan grinned as Winkler worked kinks out of stiff muscles. "Meet me in the dojo later, and I'll beat that out of you."

"Maybe we can beat on Bill's agents," Trace snickered. "Show 'em what a werewolf is made of."

"Please, don't destroy the relationship we have with Bill's department," Winkler said with a grin.

"Come on, boss, you know you want to cream some of those guys."

"Maybe." Winkler's grin widened.

"I think you wanted to cream Bill in the beginning, when Hancock was still Director," Trajan teased.

"I may have, I can't recall," Winkler waved a hand, dismissing Trajan's words. "He kinda grows on you, though," he added.

"I like Director Bill," Trajan said. "Better than I like Hancock, nowadays."

"I like my dentist better than I like Hancock," Trace joked.

"Bro, you don't need a dentist, you're a wolf," Trajan slapped Trace on the back.

"I get my teeth cleaned. He always says I have perfect teeth," Trace said.

"I like my lawyer more than I like Hancock," Winkler quipped. All three werewolves burst out laughing.

"These guys are werewolves?" Jayson gazed out the jet's window at three men waiting on the ground for them to disembark. "The shortest one is over six feet."

"That's Winkler, the Dallas Packmaster. He's six-three. The tallest, Trajan, played basketball in high school. Being a werewolf brought a halt to any college ball, though," Bill explained. "He's six-eleven. His brother, Trace, there, is six-ten. Both are experts in martial arts. If you want a workout, go ahead, but tell 'em to take it easy on you. Otherwise, they'll beat you down until you're part of the floor."

"Sounds like fun," Jayson muttered.

"Come on, door's open," Bill rose from his seat and stretched. "They'll take us to dinner. Believe me, you've never seen anybody eat until you've watched werewolves devour a meal."

Breanne's Journal

The Council members filed in, one or two at a time, all of them guarded by at least one vampire. Some I recognized, some I didn't. I knew Baxter and Dmitri—they worked with Drake and Drew in the future. I'd only seen them a time or two, and they'd had nothing to do with my mistreatment.

I wanted to gasp as Nestor and Cecil walked in together, guarded by two Enforcers. Lissa had known in the past that they were bad, but so far, that hadn't come out. They were still members in good standing on the Council.

The one who'd taken Ilaisaane's seat on the Council—Marcellus—walked in last. I read him quickly—some members considered Marcellus a yes-man and deep in Wlodek's pocket, but he voted as he saw fit. His votes often aligned with those of the Head of the Council, and some resented it.

"This meeting will come to order," Charles announced. "The first item on the agenda is funding for research on blood substitute."

"We haven't seen the car again—I've had some of my wolves cruise past the place, and never in the same vehicle," Winkler said, wiping barbecue sauce off his fingers. A plate of rib bones lay on the table in front of him; they'd gone to his favorite barbecue restaurant for dinner.

"I had someone analyze the photographs you sent—it's the same car, rust spots and all," Bill said.

"If it hadn't been registered like it was, I wouldn't be half as worried," Winkler nodded. "Saxom was the mastermind behind Xenides. While we didn't have much to do with Saxom, Xenides still gives me nightmares."

"I've sent the photographs and plate numbers to local law enforcement, so they're all looking for it," Bill said. "The trouble is, these guys are overworked now, and one more car added to a long list won't get priority. Since we don't have much information, I don't really have any excuse to maximize the search."

"What the hell do you think they're up to, if somebody is posing as Saxom?" Trajan asked.

"They want to get your attention, one way or the other," Hank spoke up for the first time all evening. "You say this one was vampire, and you're not completely sure he's actually dead? It may be a trap." Hank leaned back in the leatherette booth and sighed.

"That thought has crossed my mind, too," Bill said. "We already know somebody paid to have me killed—the Grand Master says Zach Tanner wouldn't lift a finger without the promise of big money. I have no idea whether this is connected, but it sure looks suspicious."

"I figure Obediah sent Zach," Winkler observed. "That means the hit is still active. Obediah likes his money, almost as much as he likes buffalo meat. Zach's death probably pissed Obediah off, whereas before, it was just a business deal. Now it's personal."

"Nothing like a vendetta, is there?" Jayson said.

"You'd know," Trace nodded. "Dude, I can't decide what to think about that video."

"That was a violation of privacy, that's what you should think about it," Hank said.

"True, that," Trace nodded. "I don't know if anybody might pass scrutiny, if their private life was splattered across the television."

"My mother needs therapy now," Jayson slapped his napkin on the table. "She knew about my preferences, but there's nothing like shoving it in the public's face, is there?"

"Jayson, enough," Bill said. "We're here to do a job. I've got people on that, for damage control."

"Yeah." Jayson sighed.

"Want to work out your aggression in the dojo after we're done here?" Trajan asked.

"Yeah," Jayson nodded.

~

Breanne's Journal

"How did you manage to keep this from us?" Cecil demanded.

"There was no guarantee that the attempt would succeed—you know the odds," Wlodek answered, his voice turning cold. The regular meeting was over and when requested, Gavin had ushered me to the center of the Council chamber, where I faced all eight members plus Wlodek. Surprisingly enough, Gavin remained standing next to me while I was scrutinized and the questions began.

"Once she survived the turn, we waited—you know how fragile suicide attempts can often be. We did not know whether she would choose to survive."

"She was turned shortly after the book's release?" Susila asked.

"Yes."

"It was wise to wait this out, for obvious reasons," she nodded. "It would only raise hopes, just to dash them again if the turn was not fully accepted."

"Lawrence and I discussed that, when he notified me," Wlodek said. "I was made her guardian, in case anything happened to him. Fortuitous, as it turns out."

"You and Lawrence were close, as I recall," Oluwa said.

"We were. His death was a blow. Gavin tracked his killer, and dispatched the rogue before bringing Breanne to me."

"Are her lessons proceeding well?" Jarl asked.

"Her lessons are current," Wlodek said. "There is no cause for complaint or concern. However, there have been discoveries of late, and we are fortunate that Lawrence thought to test her before his demise."

"Test her?" Montrose said. "In what way?"

"Tell them, Gavin, since you have observed this firsthand," Wlodek instructed.

"She is a talented mister and mindspeaker," Gavin announced. "She traveled to San Francisco with me on a recent assignment, and assisted in taking down rogues."

"Which rogues?" Nestor's eyes narrowed.

"Keir Arthur and Oscar Forde," Gavin replied evenly.

"We've been searching for them more than two years," Flavio broke in. "Has Director Jennings been notified?"

"Yes. There are other developments on that front, however," Wlodek said. "If you have further questions about Breanne, now is the time, as important information must be disseminated before we adjourn."

"Who was the woman who appeared on that news segment in San Francisco? She looked very much like this one, here." Cecil wasn't done, yet. He suspected something, he just didn't know what.

"The news reported on that earlier, claiming the woman was an actress planted to make everyone believe that Miss Hayworth had returned," Wlodek replied smoothly. "Charles has the video, should you wish to view it."

"I wish to witness the misting," Cecil said.

"Breanne, turn to mist," Wlodek laid compulsion. Well, it was trained monkey time. I turned immediately to mist. Gasps erupted—nobody was used to anyone turning that quickly, because they didn't remember Lissa.

"Now," Wlodek continued, "lift Gavin into your mist." That was the new trick, and Wlodek was waiting to spring it on the Council. His other misters couldn't perform that trick—they could only turn themselves to mist.

"This is preposterous," Cecil stood and declared when Gavin disappeared.

"Not preposterous," Wlodek replied smugly. "Breanne, release

Gavin and reappear." I did both those things. Gavin seemed unflustered and none the worse for wear when I let him go and appeared at his side.

"Take Cecil, now," Wlodek nodded toward me.

"Of course, Honored One," I nodded to Wlodek and went to mist again, before flying toward Cecil and lifting him up. We hovered briefly over the others before I set him down again—as gently as I could. He was a dangerous asshole, and I had no desire to draw his interest. I was enough of a target as it was.

"That was—enlightening," Cecil squared his shoulders. The others stared at him while I reappeared at Gavin's side. "What about the mindspeech?"

"Breanne, send mindspeech to Cecil. Send the same message to me and the others," Wlodek barked.

I am at your service, Honored One, I sent to the entire Council. Cecil blinked in astonishment, but there was no way he could deny he'd received the message.

"Astounding," Flavio breathed. "None of the others can send to anyone except another mindspeaker."

"What is your name now, my dear?" Marcellus was the first to speak directly to me.

"Breanne Arden," I replied.

"Very good," Marcellus nodded. "A suitable name, I think. Will she be trained to assist our Enforcers and Assassins?" He turned to Wlodek.

"That is our goal," Wlodek said. "Talent such as hers will augment our existing staff admirably."

"Have you taken over her teaching?" Marcellus asked.

"No. Gavin and Charles are working in tandem to provide instruction. Breanne will be with one or the other for the remainder of her training period."

"Did you make that assignment?" Susila asked.

"No, both volunteered," Wlodek replied. "Charles will see to the bulk of her lessons, while Gavin will train her in combat techniques. She is already quite fierce, with only a minimum of instruction."

"Charles, you have never taught a vampire before," Nestor pointed out.

"I have reviewed every record of every vampire trained in the last three hundred years," Charles didn't even look up from taking notes. "I know all the rules, and have been notified of every breaking of those rules, filed the complaints and witnessed every punishment meted out. Do you think I cannot impress upon a new turn the seriousness of the laws?" Charles lifted his head and turned to Nestor, then.

"I was only concerned for the well-being of the turn," Nestor bluffed.

"Then your concern is noted," Wlodek said. "There are other, more serious matters to attend to, if there are no further questions regarding our newest female?"

"This sounds rather ominous," Cecil said.

"It is. I have communicated with Director Jennings for the past two days. It seems that William Winkler has been spied upon recently. The vehicle involved, which appeared suspicious, has been tracked and the plates identified. The car was registered to Saxom Meletius, and we can uncover no other information, except that name."

CHAPTER 11

"That was interesting," Charles placed his laptop bag in a corner of his office and blinked at me with a sigh.

I'd followed Gavin to the side of the cave again while the Vampire Council erupted in heated discussion. After reading them, I realized that they never did that—their emotions were generally tightly controlled. Saxom's name was the hottest of hot buttons for the vampires present, and I learned, both through readings and listening to the chaos, that Saxom was a very bad vampire.

"That almost gave me a headache," I muttered, dropping onto Charles's single guest chair.

"Don't let it upset you, they're just a bunch of old, fusty vampires," Charles said. "How about some blood?"

"No," I moaned and dropped my face in my hands.

"If I let you get by without drinking extra tonight, you have to make up for it tomorrow evening," Charles informed me. "It would be better to drink a little tonight."

"Fine." I lifted my head and worked to calm my gag reflex.

"Good. Go to the kitchen and pull a bag from the refrigerator. I'll drink what you don't."

161

"Okay." I rose from the chair and shuffled out of Charles's office.

~

Baby? Hank's voice came to me as I opened the door on a refrigerator the size of Rhode Island.

What? Did I miss him? Horribly. Was I still mad? Yeah. Some. A little.

What are you doing?

Getting a disgusting bag of blood out of a fridge so I can drink some of it, I replied.

You don't like that, do you?

What part of disgusting eludes you?

Hank's mental chuckle sounded heavenly. *What are you doing?* I sent back.

In Dallas with Bill. I wanted to tell you that Jayson lost his job with Rome Enterprises. Have you seen the video?

What video?

Thought so. Janine managed to record Jayson and Belinda having fun. It's all over the news stations and the Internet, now.

Oh, no, I said. *I swear I want to punch that bitch.*

You'll have to stand in line. Bill hired Jayson as a full-time temp, but everybody recognizes him, now. That's not a good thing for a special agent.

I get that. Look, maybe I can do something about that in a couple of hours. Where are you in Dallas?

Hank rattled off an address.

I'll be there as soon as the vamps go to sleep, okay?

Baby, if you can help with this, I'll give you the biggest kiss ever.

Is that what it takes? Damn. I thought you just didn't want to get your mouth dirty.

Bree, I'd like to swat you for that. You know I won't. You taste like heaven to me. If you were here right now, my mouth would be all over you.

Look, I have to get back with this blood or they'll think I've gone rogue. Around here, that's not a good thing.

I'll see you in a couple of hours, then, he said.

~

"Ready?" Charles grinned, the tips of shortened claws poised above the tube on our bag of blood.

"No." I hugged myself.

"Hey, come here," Charles said, setting the blood on the edge of his desk and motioning me forward.

"Why?" I stayed where I was and hugged my ribs tighter.

"You think I'm going to hurt you. Or scare you. I won't, I promise." He took a step toward me. I took a step back. The fact that he'd lured me in with soft words and then bitten me still stung. That didn't take into account how much it had frightened me. The climax? It wasn't worth the fear.

"I didn't want to scare you any more than I had to," Charles spoke softly. "I know I did anyway. Come here, love. Let me take care of you."

I blinked. Charles was right in front of me, taking my hands and pulling them away from my waist. "Shhh, there's no need to be afraid. I won't bite again unless you ask me to. Why don't you bite me, instead? Right here," he tapped the side of his neck. "You can smell it, can't you? The blood, right beneath the surface of my skin? You won't hurt me, I promise."

"But," I whimpered.

"No, darling. Put your hand here, at the back of my neck, to hold me still. If I move during the bite, the skin will tear." He placed my left hand on the back of his neck. "Grip firmly, so I can't move," he instructed, leaning in to kiss my forehead. "Don't let go," he added.

I gripped the back of his neck firmly with my hand. "Now, look me in the eye and tell me you won't hurt me," Charles breathed against my temple. Keeping my grip on his neck, I leaned back far enough to look into his eyes.

"I won't hurt you." My words were shaky whispers.

"I know you won't," Charles reassured me. "Now, lean in and place a kiss over the site, then bite. Be gentle."

"I will," I promised. I wanted to shiver, but this was an impromptu bite lesson and if I flunked, I'd have to do it again. And again—until I passed.

"I won't hurt you," I repeated, breathing against Charles's neck before kissing the spot over his artery. I discovered he smelled really good. Like cinnamon and sugar. "You smell wonderful." I kissed him again before forcing my fangs to descend. I sank them into the artery as gently as I could. Blood filled my mouth.

Charles's arms squeezed me against him as I fought to swallow, and I knew he was having an intense orgasm. I licked the wound clean as required after swallowing my mouthful of blood, and gently massaged the back of Charles's neck.

"That was incredible," Charles said, his voice still breathy from the climax. "The best ever," he added, lifting me in his arms and carrying me to his desk chair. "I'll have this," he pulled the bag of blood toward him while balancing me on his lap, "and you can close your eyes and rest on my lap while I drink it."

～

As promised, as soon as the sun came up for the day, I misted out of my cubicle in Gavin's basement and folded space to Dallas. I had to *Look* to determine where the address was, and landed outside a very large home between Dallas and Denton.

There, it was still the middle of the night and I fidgeted about what to do. Was I supposed to ring the doorbell? Who lived here? I figured I'd find a hotel, not somebody's house, for Pete's sake.

"Bree? Thank God," Bill swung the door open. Hank, Jayson, William Winkler and *Trajan* were right behind him.

～

"Hello, little hellion," Acrimus attempted to smile at a cringing Janine. "I just visited Miss Wayde, and while she doesn't suit my purposes, you do."

"Who are you?" Janine trembled.

"You can call me lieutenant," Acrimus' ensuing grimace terrified Janine. "You like pain. I can give you all you want. And, if you want, you can hand it out to others after I'm done with you."

～

Breanne's Journal

"Look, I shouldn't be gone long," I said, staring at Jayson. I'd never seen him look so pitiful. We'd gathered inside Winkler's enormous kitchen after Bill pulled me inside the house.

"You think you can do something about him?" Hope shone in Bill's eyes. Jayson had saved Bill's life, and Bill wanted to hire him full-time. He couldn't, with everybody recognizing Jayson.

"So, you know what it feels like now, don't you?" I said.

"Yeah." Jayson ducked his head.

"At least you weren't naked when that video was recorded," I pointed out. Jayson had worn leather pants, at least. I'd had no choice when photographs had been taken of my mangled body in the past. Belinda was the one naked this time, and thankfully they'd blocked her face (and other parts) before splashing the images everywhere.

"What do you want to look like?" I asked.

"Huh?"

"Didn't Hank tell you? I can probably change the way you look."

"He said you might help, but I didn't know what that meant." Jayson's honey-brown eyes held a well of grief and guilt. I hoped some of that was for his mother, who was surely suffering through all this.

"Breanne, can you make it so he might disappear in a crowd?" Bill asked.

"Yeah," I shrugged. "He might not like it, though."

"Just do it," Jayson begged.

"All right. Bill, what will you do about his name?"

"Temporary change, which could become permanent if he wants."

"Okay. Let's see, here," I went to Jayson and put my hands on his face. Dim light shone around my hands as I performed cosmetic surgery just like the Larentii might. No pain was involved, and when I pulled my hands away, Jayson still looked at me expectantly.

"It's done," I said.

"That's amazing." Winkler, who'd sat beside Trajan at the island, rose now and came to examine my work. "Is that for real? It's not an illusion?"

"It's real until I change it back," I said. Jayson now had brown hair, hazel eyes and was two inches shorter than he'd been seconds earlier.

"Here," Hank handed a small mirror to Jayson, so he could look.

"What the hell?" Jayson muttered, staring at his new image. "That's just—weird."

"Nobody will recognize you, now. You even have new fingerprints," I said. "Have fun with that," I added before folding back to England.

~

"Here's your new profile," Bill pulled up information on his laptop and turned it so Jayson could see.

"Matthew Michaels?" Jayson stared at the name listed.

"Matt for short?" Bill grinned. "See, you're listed as being from Los Angeles. That's close enough to the real thing, don't you think, and you won't have to spout information about an area you're unfamiliar with."

"Matt Michaels, huh?" Jayson stared at the photograph displayed—Bill and his department could move quickly when motivated. This profile had taken less than an hour to create and Jayson's new ID would be delivered quickly.

"I wish Bree had stayed. I wanted to talk to her," Bill said.

"I don't think talking was all Hank wanted to do," Jayson grinned. It was the first time he'd smiled since the debacle had begun. "What can I tell my mother?"

"I'll handle that," Bill sighed. "I think she's having enough difficulty as it is. I'll find another job for Trina, too, if you'd like. I think Jayson Rome needs to disappear, at least for a while."

"Yeah. Ask Mom to close up the house. Can you do anything about my bank accounts?"

"For the most part," Bill nodded. "Just leave that to me."

~

"I'll get her up," Charles nodded to Gavin.

"How did it go—the rest of the bite lesson?"

"Very well. She did it perfectly," Charles said. "I don't believe she needs the food lesson."

"I doubt it. She keeps asking for watermelon, so there's no doubt she'd hold onto real food as long as possible."

"My thinking as well. Regardless, we have little time. Wlodek wants to send me to Dallas, and I believe Breanne can get me into difficult locations while I'm there."

"Please take care of her," Charles muttered.

"Do you think I won't?"

"I don't know," Charles turned away. "I realize how much of an asset she is, but I'm terrified for her."

"I understand that," Gavin sighed.

~

"Merrill," Wlodek nodded as Merrill walked into his study.

"I have your answer. You're not going to like it," Merrill sat on one of Wlodek's guest chairs with a sigh.

"I seldom like the answers gathered from the Saa Thalarr. Tell me anyway."

"Saxom died when they say he did," Merrill reported. "But," he held up a hand as Wlodek began to speak, "Many can bend time. There is no guarantee that this did not happen at the moment of Saxom's death. Similar events have occurred, when a soul—or a body—has been transferred the moment before death, with another being substituted. The death is real, but the victim is not the one intended."

"This is untenable," Wlodek hissed. "You mean to tell me that this bastard could be back to torment us again?"

"It is my sincere hope that this is not true. Nevertheless, it is possible. I spoke with Kiarra myself. She, understandably, is quite upset over the news I brought to her."

"I will send Gavin to Dallas immediately. This must be researched carefully, and Gavin can be trusted. If Saxom has returned, I will mobilize everything I have to bring him down."

"That may be what he's hoping for," Merrill observed. "Tread carefully, Father. We may all be in danger."

Breanne's Journal

"Hey," Charles's fingers brushed hair back from my forehead. "Still sleepy?"

"Yeah." I wanted to turn over, but I didn't. I'd given Charles a climax, after he'd given me one first. I probably would care more for him if those things hadn't happened.

"You're embarrassed," Charles smiled gently. "There's nothing to be embarrassed about. You gave me pleasure. I liked it. I didn't even feel the touch of your fangs."

"That's not what this is about," I closed my eyes to block the vision of him.

"What is it about then?"

"I don't know." I lifted a hand and let it fall onto the bed again.

"Me calling you darling? Is that it? You're uncomfortable? I scare you? You don't understand what's going on?"

"All those things," I opened my eyes again and stared at Charles.

"Some people say that love at first sight doesn't exist," Charles murmured, leaning in to kiss my forehead. "Others swear by it."

"What are you saying?" I frowned at him.

"When the time is right, you get to choose the ending to this story," Charles whispered. "Meanwhile, Gavin wants you up and dressed. You'll be flying to Dallas in two hours."

"You really know how to make a woman's day, don't you?" I leaned forward and rested on an elbow while blinking at Charles.

"Come on, get in the shower. I'll have blood for you when you get out, and I'll help you pack."

"We're going after that Saxom guy?" I dropped my legs over the side of the bed.

"Investigating, yes. If Saxom is still alive, Wlodek will send backup."

"Wow," I pushed hair behind an ear and studied Charles, who'd stood aside to let me up. "None of this sounds good at the moment," I added. "I don't feel comfortable with any of this."

"You can easily get Gavin into places he might find difficult to breach, and we need that kind of stealth with this," Charles said. "I know you're worried. I am, too, and not least because we could lose you and Gavin both."

"It's gonna be hot in Dallas this time of year," I muttered, shuffling toward the bathroom.

"There's something you should know about Breanne," Bill said. "And I just heard from Wlodek—he's sending Gavin and another vampire to assist with this investigation. I hope to hell he's sending Breanne."

"What should I know about her, other than she seems to have abilities I've never seen before?"

"She's Lissa's sister," Bill stated flatly. "Lissa's half-sister, actually."

"What?" Winkler, who'd taken a seat at the kitchen island for a cup of coffee with Bill, stood quickly. "Don't tell me that, Bill Jennings. What the fuck?" Winkler turned his back to Bill and raked fingers through his hair in frustration.

"Breanne says they share the same sperm donor," Bill said. "I think she found out about Lissa after the fact."

"Fuck," Winkler muttered.

"I love her," Bill added softly. "Breanne, I mean."

"I thought that Hank guy was going to drool when she showed up last night," Winkler turned back to Bill.

"She loves him. Says she loves me. Jayson—Matt—wants in, too."

"Multiple mates? It's not unheard of, but it's also not accepted as the norm," Winkler observed dryly.

"Polyamory happens. Damn, that sounds like a bumper sticker," Bill grinned.

❧

Breanne's Journal

"We'll have some time when we arrive," Gavin said. "While safe houses are available in the area, Wlodek suggested they could be compromised. Therefore, we will be guests of William Winkler, the Dallas Packmaster, during our stay. I have stayed at his compound before, and his wolves will guard us during the day."

"Okay," I said with a shrug. I'd already seen part of Winkler's house. It was huge.

"Some werewolves still do not trust any vampire, so please be circumspect and do not react if one of them upsets or insults you. Werewolves can be rude or crass at times, and it is never wise to challenge them when there are many surrounding you."

"I understand," I said.

"If any of them attempts to harm you, I will consider it a challenge against me," Gavin added, sitting back in his seat. "They will not wish to see my wrath."

Yes, I stared at Gavin. Was he saying he'd protect me? Where had this Gavin gone in the future, leaving the one who'd spawned me in his place? I probably wasn't destined to get an answer to that unspoken question, so I settled back in my seat, too, determined to rest on the flight to Dallas.

❧

"I'm not joking, Weldon, that's what Bill said."

"I'm coming down there," Weldon huffed. "If she's an impostor, well."

"Weldon, I don't know what to think, but it's guaranteed she can do shit even Lissa couldn't."

"Did you ask what her father's name is? We both know nobody can mention that asshole unless they know about him and are with somebody else who also knows about him."

"No, but Bill is hoping she's coming in with Gavin."

"Wlodek's sending Gavin? That ought to be fun," Weldon muttered. "Look, I'll get a flight out this afternoon."

"I have the jet on standby," Winkler offered.

"Send it. I'll be packed and ready."

"Bad news, Jayson," Bill sat on the sofa inside Jayson's borrowed suite. "Colbi Wayde's body was found an hour ago in her home. Looked like she'd been ripped apart. San Francisco police are looking for you, now."

"Why? I wasn't even there," Jayson sputtered.

"You and I know that, but, well, let's just say things are getting complicated. We're getting death threats against you from those idiots online. When the reporter mentioned that you and Breanne may have been engaged, those people hunting Breanne are now focused on you as well. Trust me; you don't want to see what they're saying, especially since the Wayde woman was killed. Janine has also disappeared, and I have no idea where she is."

"What about Mom and Trina?" Jayson asked.

"I'm moving them to your mother's house in Tahoe, and setting up guards. Dan, your mother's driver, is on vacation so he's been instructed to stay with his family. I told your mother you were safe, but things are blowing up on the Internet."

"Like they weren't blowing up already?" Jayson asked. "Can this mess get any worse?"

"I hope not, but it's not anywhere near good at the moment."

"At least nobody recognizes me now. This is a nightmare."

"It's that, all right," Bill agreed.

~

Breanne's Journal

It's easier to come back to the U.S. than flying to the UK. We still had plenty of night left, and Bill was waiting when our plane landed.

"I know Bill—I worked as an interpreter for him before," I told Gavin, doing my best not to cringe as I did so. I was still waiting for his temper to explode, but so far, that hadn't happened.

"Did you? That may make this easier, then," Gavin's dark eyes studied me. The lights blinked on inside the jet, making me blink, too, at the sudden brightness. "We realize that you may meet people you know. If there is a problem, I will lay compulsion. Director Jennings has vampires employed in his Department, so he is a trusted associate. Many of his human agents are also aware of the vampires and werewolves working for the department, so if Bill allows them to know, then they are trustworthy."

"Thank you," I sighed.

"I will protect your identity just as fiercely as I protect my own," Gavin unbuckled his lap belt. I followed suit and rose when he did, preparing to walk down the steps and pretend (under Gavin's scrutiny) that I didn't recognize Hank, Jayson and the others standing on the tarmac with Bill.

~

"Gavin," Bill nodded to Gavin but didn't extend his hand. You don't shake with a vampire unless he offers first. Gavin didn't offer. "This is Hank Bell and Matt Michaels, two of my agents. They've been advised," Bill said.

"This is Breanne," Gavin introduced me. "I understand you two are already acquainted."

Interpreter, I sent hasty mindspeech to Bill.

"Yes. Breanne worked as an interpreter for me on a few special projects. Her Arabic is exceptional." Bill smiled at me.

"Hi, Bill," I gave him a bittersweet smile. *We can talk after sunrise*, I sent. "It's good to see you again," I added aloud and held out my hand. Bill took it and shook warmly.

"Shall we?" Bill indicated the van behind him. Thank goodness it held all of us, plus Gavin's and my luggage.

~

"What's the name of this church?" Gavin examined photographs of a new church building not far from Winkler's mansion. "You say the car was parked there?"

"We saw it there one day. It could have been a worker, a parishioner or someone stopping for directions," Winkler said. "It hasn't been back there since. We've kept careful surveillance, and Bill's agents have been watching the parking lot as well."

"No sightings by local law enforcement?" Gavin asked.

"None reported," Bill shook his head. "Not surprising, given the size of the area. They're calling it *The Church of the True God*, by the way," he added. "No idea why they felt the word true was necessary, but I've seen odder names."

~

"Opal, why is this happening?" Kathleen Rome's hand shook as they watched Jayson's home in San Rafael burn.

"I don't know," Opal soothed. "I'm just glad we got you out of there when we did."

"This is fucked up," Trina agreed. They'd moved into Kathleen's Tahoe home the day before, after leaving San Rafael behind. "Are they going to save any of it?" The television camera, mounted on a helicopter, was poised overhead as firefighters struggled to extinguish the fire.

"Probably used some sort of accelerant. What I want to know is how they got past the agents at the bottom of the hill," Opal sighed.

"People can be so evil," Kathleen wiped tears away.

"They can definitely be that," Opal agreed.

~

Breanne's Journal

Gavin had gone to bed with the sun's rising, and as soon as I knew he wouldn't find me wandering about, I misted out of my bedroom inside Winkler's mansion and went looking for Bill, Jayson and Hank. I'd found them in the kitchen, having breakfast with Winkler, Trajan and Trace.

"Please tell me you have fruit," I begged the moment I appeared at Bill's elbow.

"Bananas, cantaloupe and watermelon," Winkler grinned. "In the fridge."

"Hey, I get a hug, first," Bill pulled me against him.

"Hi, Bill." I leaned in to kiss him.

"Vamps treating you okay?" Winkler asked.

"Surprisingly, yes," I nodded after Bill let me go. "I keep waiting for Gavin to go animalistic, but so far he hasn't." I shrugged over my puzzlement on that quarter.

"Animalistic is a good word to define Gavin," Winkler agreed. "Who turned you, anyway?"

"I can't tell you that," I said.

"You're susceptible to compulsion?" Winkler asked in disbelief.

"Nope. None of that works on me, including obsessions from Sirenali. If I told you who turned me, you'd freak. Trust me; you're better off not knowing."

"The Grand Master," Ace announced as he walked in with Weldon Harper.

"This is the one claiming to be Lissa's sister?" Weldon Harper growled. He was ready to defend Lissa to anyone claiming to be related. He was ready to kill, too, if I were lying.

"We have the same sperm donor," I said, working to keep the shakiness from my voice.

"Name him," Weldon barked.

"You mean Griffin, the asshole? Or Brenten Arden, which is his birth name?" I asked as steadily as I could. "What else would you like to know? That he's the first member of the race known as Saa Thalarr? That he's retired, now? That his father is a Karathian warlock and used to be King of Karathia? That his mate's name is Amara? Anything else you'd like to know? His eating habits, maybe?"

"Are you fucking kidding me?" Weldon turned dark eyes on Winkler.

"I told you," Winkler shrugged.

"Breanne is who she says she is." Hank's fingers settled on my shoulders. "You are frightening her. Stop it now."

"Who the fuck are you?" Weldon's gaze fell on Hank, who stood behind me.

"Grand Master, that one had Trajan down and howling on the floor last night," Winkler sighed. "He's not human."

"Huh?" I turned around in time to see a slight curl of smoke drift from Hank's nostrils. Fainting is usually my last choice of things to do. Regardless, I did it anyway.

"High Demon." Weldon tossed up a hand in resignation.

"He says so. I believe him, after I got a good whiff," Winkler said. "He says he can pass for human most of the time, until you get him riled up enough to make the change. Trajan attacked last night, and you don't want to know what we saw after that."

"Yes I do," Weldon crossed arms over his chest. "Explain."

"Taller than Trajan," Winkler shook his head. "With black scales, wings and curved horns. Bill says that Hank had already shown him what he was, and Jayson long before that. The only one who didn't know—until now—is Breanne."

"And she didn't take it well. I saw that for myself. I'm convinced that she's Lissa's half-sister, now, but she's in the same position Lissa was in—under Gavin's thumb."

"You think I haven't considered that?" Winkler's words were a growl. "We have no claim on this one, Weldon. The vamps have full control, although Bill says they have no idea she can walk in daylight."

"I heard her asking for fruit, so that's not the only similarity," Weldon huffed. "Lissa got used by the vampires and killed by her father's interference."

"Let's hope Griffin stays the hell away from this one, then."

Breanne's Journal

"Wake up, baby." Hank's voice. Hank's mouth, kissing my ear and my neck. My eyes didn't want to open. My brain didn't want to consider what I'd seen earlier. What the hell was a High Demon doing on Earth? I realized I'd spoken that thought aloud when Hank chuckled against my throat.

"Someone told me recently that I've gone native."

"You know, I'm afraid to ask who that was," my eyes opened to narrow slits, testing the brightness of the light. Wherever I was, it was nicely dim. I opened my eyes wider.

"Does it bother you that I might be High Demon?" Hank asked, nuzzling my chest. When had I gotten naked?

"Does it bother you that I might be vampire?" I said. Hank nipped the skin above my breast, making me draw in a breath.

"Not at all. I recognize my baby when I see her. That's all I care about."

"You schmuck," I hissed as his mouth settled on a nipple.

"Uh-hmmmm."

"You could have moved that stupid safe by yourself. Instead, you whined about it."

"I had an audience," he lifted his head and grinned (yeah, I almost had a climax on the spot). "Just like you had an audience."

"Just because you're High Demon doesn't mean you're indestructible," I pointed out.

"And you're not indestructible, either." Hank's eyes became serious. "Now, we can use the next hour to fuck, or we can use it to argue. I know which one will make me feel better."

"I thought High Demons put their claiming marks on their mates." The memory of that trait hit me, then. "That means we're not," Hank's fingers covered my mouth to keep me from finishing.

"First off, that's a barbaric practice," he said. "Second off, they're already there." He pulled his fingers away.

"What?" I tried to sit up in bed. Hank pushed me back down.

"New rule," Hank grinned before kissing me. "When a High Demon claims his mate now, there is a natural anesthetic and healing agent in the initial kiss. It knocks his mate out, he places the bite and then heals it up again. Something like the vamps can do with their bite marks, only the marks are left behind, as they should be. Cool, huh?"

"Are you kidding me? That's not the way I understood it."

"It's the way it is, now. My marks are right here," his fingers massaged the back of my neck gently. "You think I'd terrify my baby like that, or deliberately make her sick? No fucking way."

"Does Jayson know? About the High Demon thing?"

"I went nuts when you disappeared more than two years ago. He saw the smaller Thifilathi then. Took me a week to calm him down. Bill saw it after he and Opal came to San Francisco. The others saw it last night, after Trajan thought he'd wipe the floor with me. I showed him what it was like to dust and mop."

"You did not hurt Trajan," I struggled to rise again.

"Baby, I didn't hurt Trajan. He says he enjoyed the competition. Lie back. You need some sleep. I'll make sure you get it, about forty-five minutes from now. Put your arms around my neck, Bree, and hang on. I'm gonna fuck hard the first time."

I'd just gotten out of the shower when Gavin showed up in my bedroom, a bag of blood in his hands. I'd gotten decent sleep after Hank was done with me.

"Thank you," I sighed at Gavin, while toweling my hair dry. If Gavin knew that Hank and I had fooled around after he went to sleep for the day, he'd be pitching a fit. I sure didn't want to see what a fight between Gavin and a High Demon might look like, either. At least I smelled like soap and shampoo, now, instead of Hank and sex.

"Eat and dress quickly, Director Jennings wishes to follow a lead. The car may have been sighted in Denton, and two bodies were recovered not far away."

~

"These were murdered just like those in San Francisco." Bill said the moment we gathered in Winkler's kitchen. He handed me photographs of two men.

Criminals, I sent to Bill. *Andy Schaeffer and Kevin Branch*. I handed the photographs back.

"Throats cut?" Gavin asked.

"Just the same. I was hoping you could tell me if a vampire may have been at the murder scene."

"If it hasn't been disturbed too much," Gavin nodded.

"Let's go, then," Bill said. "The scene is guarded, and the bodies are still there."

~

Obediah Tanner studied the two werewolves before him. "Jennings is in Dallas, according to my source. With Winkler, or so I hear. Take Jennings out. If you happen to get Winkler, too, I'll hand you a bonus."

CHAPTER 12

$\mathcal{B}$reanne's Journal

"Jayson, I'm sorry about your house," Bill said.

On the drive to the crime scene, Jayson, whose name was officially Matt, now, studied photographs on Bill's tablet. Opal was coordinating the arson investigation with Bill's agents on the West Coast while doing her best to guard Kathleen and Trina in Tahoe.

"We figure some type of accelerant was used, but it hasn't been determined, yet."

"Fuck." Jayson wiped his face with a hand as he stared at the images of smoking rubble that used to be his house.

How much of this is my fault? I sent to Bill.

Sweetheart, we don't know that any of it is your fault. We did find Colbi Wayde's body, though. We figure she was killed for information. The authorities are telling the news outlets that they're searching for Jayson, but I've already talked to them, and they know he's not involved. Since Jayson has disappeared, we'll let the public believe what they want for a while, so the locals can track the real killer.

"This is so messed up," I sighed. "I am so sorry about your house," I shook my head helplessly at Jayson. "And sorry about your cars, too."

"I may have to borrow your TinyCar," Jayson attempted a joke.

"You have a TinyCar?" Winkler lifted an eyebrow at me. Well, I didn't figure you'd ever find a werewolf in a TinyCar.

"Bree, a high wind could knock that thing off the Golden Gate Bridge and all the clowns would drop out," Bill smiled at me.

"Stop dissing my car," I sputtered. "Jayson, you can have my car if you want it, but I figure you'd just be too ashamed to be seen in it."

Yeah, somebody had explained to Gavin that Jayson was incognito, now, and that we knew one another. Jayson was still working on getting used to the new name, though. It didn't matter with us— everybody who was with him now would protect his identity. Still, I felt responsible for the fire at Jayson's house.

"Breanne, you must learn that things such as this are not your responsibility," Gavin broke in. I jerked my head around to stare at him. "There will always be those whose minds are warped, and at times they exert power over the weak. The truth, however, is the truth, and none can change that, no matter how much they'd prefer it otherwise."

"The truth is we need those pricks in jail," Winkler pointed out. "Along with whoever has moved into this area to make us sweat."

"Yeah," Trajan growled. He hadn't said much up to now, and I was surprised to see him sitting next to Hank in the back of the van. How did knocking each other around form a bond of friendship with men? I failed to understand any of it.

I sat between Bill and Gavin in the second row of seats, with Jayson at the end. Trace drove, with Winkler in the passenger seat. Hank, Weldon and Trajan took up the back. Jayson handed Bill's tablet back. "The house is insured," he mumbled. I knew he was upset more than he let on, though.

"We're here," Trace announced as he maneuvered the van as close as possible to the crime scene. We were just outside an alley between brick buildings, and the air smelled strange the moment I exited the van.

"This smells weird," I whispered as Bill pulled out ID to show to the officer in charge of the crime scene. The officer nodded to Winkler, who stood beside Bill, so they knew one another.

"I notice this scent as well," Gavin said softly.

"Something's not right," Trajan said. He and Hank came to stand beside us.

"Yeah," I agreed. My skin had begun to tingle and prescience kicked in. Gathering all the live bodies to me, I turned them to mist and hauled them from the scene, which exploded in a fireball behind us.

~

Gavin placed compulsion on six officers, who didn't need to remember that they'd been floating invisibly for a few moments, instead of getting blown to bits in a Dallas alley.

Fire crews were on the scene and one of the buildings was still on fire—we watched a live feed on television while Gavin did his trick with unsuspecting human officers.

"Daddy?" A little girl, clutching a stuffed toy in her arms crept into Winkler's study, where we'd gathered to discuss what had happened—and what had almost happened—to us.

"Baby, did we wake you?" Winkler held out his arms and four-year-old Wynter ran toward him.

"I had a bad dream, Daddy," she burrowed into his arms.

"Who's that?" she pointed to me. "I want to see her, Daddy."

"That's Breanne," Winkler soothed.

"Hey," I walked over to Winkler and smoothed dark hair away from Wynter's face. "You're too pretty to have bad dreams."

She smiled and hid her face against Winkler's shoulder.

"Come on, let's get you back in bed," Winkler said and walked out of his office. Wynter shyly waved at me as he carried her away.

"You said you noticed a smell when we arrived?" Bill said. He'd just gotten off the phone with the Dallas FBI office.

"Yeah, but it wasn't something I recognized," I said. I'd *Looked*, too, and the cause of the smell—and the explosion—was blocked.

"Same here," Trajan agreed. "Nothing I've ever smelled before."

"I didn't smell anything," Jayson said.

"You're human," Trace and Trajan said at the same time.

"What about you, Hank? How's your sense of smell?"

"Chimera shapeshifter," Hank growled. "Fire breather. Not native to this world, and supposedly extinct."

"What the hell?" Jayson had pulled up information on his cell and stared at an image of a chimera—according to Wikipedia.

"They don't look like that—I just said they're not native here," Hank said. "They have an ugly head that looks like a lion and a pug got friendly, and there are horns growing out of its spine, similar to those of a goat. Its tail does have a false head, to lure prey to it, looking for an easy meal."

"Does it cook before it eats?" Trace asked.

"Yes. It likes things crispy," Hank nodded.

"Do they fly?" I asked. "Do you think one of those things burned down Jayson's house?"

"Could be. Their fire continues to burn—you can't put it out with water," Hank explained. "They don't fly, though. They walk or run, like most animals. Remember, this is a shapeshifter, so he or she will appear human most of the time. Their scent may give them away, unless they're shielded."

"So we may have more than one of those things, then, unless somebody is transporting them around," I said.

"Possibly, but we have to ask how an extinct species is here to start with," Hank pointed out.

"Same thing with the Sirenali," I nodded. "They're supposed to be extinct, too."

"Where can we start looking? There aren't any witnesses, and the bodies we went to examine are nothing but ash."

"Why isn't there more information on the vehicle registration?" Gavin asked as he shouldered his way into the room. "There should be an address, at least."

"We feel the information was removed afterward, and was likely false to begin with. It was designed to worry us," Trajan said. "The clerk was interviewed, and she doesn't recall the registration."

"Security cameras?" Jayson asked.

"Went fuzzy," Winkler walked back in the room. "Same thing with the cameras on a building outside the tag agency."

"Previous owner?"

"Found dead in his garage—some kind of poisonous snake bite, but there's no information on the type of snake responsible. They only found the bite marks. He died quickly, according to the M.E." Bill was worried, I could tell. I didn't want to worry him further, but if we had a lion snake shapeshifter in addition to a chimera, a Sirenali and who knew what else, we could be in a lot of trouble.

"Have they isolated the poison yet?" Trajan asked.

"Having trouble identifying it," Bill said.

"The snake may not have been local," I sighed.

"What do you mean?" Bill and Winkler both turned to me, but Bill was the one speaking.

"She means the snake may be a shapeshifter as well, and there is one type so deadly, it will kill you in seconds," Hank said. "You don't want to tangle with a lion snake shapeshifter."

"This just gets better and better," Trajan tossed up a hand in frustration. "What the hell do they want from all this?"

"They want everything," Hank said simply.

~

Lissa's Journal

"Norian, when did I say you could come back?" I lifted my eyes to watch him as he stood in front of my desk.

"You didn't. I need your help, breah-mul."

"With what?" Too many things made me grumpy of late, and Norian showing up unannounced and asking for help made it worse.

"You know I've kept tabs on Reedy all these years."

"Your murdering asshole brother, Yaredolak?" I asked sweetly.

"That's the one," Norian said.

"What about him?" I went back to studying the comp-vid in my hand—or at least pretending to study it. "He hasn't sold any more of

183

his siblings, has he? Or his own kids, maybe?" I'd met Norian's brother once. It was once too many, in my opinion.

"He's disappeared. My parents contacted me three days ago, and said he met with two men he claimed were old friends a week before he disappeared. Everything seemed fine afterward, until he left for the fields one morning and never made it to the work site. His vehicle was found abandoned halfway there, and there's no sign of a struggle."

"And they're all missing the endearing little fucker, aren't they?" I asked.

"They are. I'm just worried his old friends are the kind who kidnaps kids to sell or exploit," Norian snapped. "I'm worried that Reedy is getting his hands dirty again. I just can't find any trace of him."

"I told you he'd never be anything other than a criminal," I said.

"Can you help me find him? What if heads of state start dropping dead? I wouldn't put anything past my brother."

"Norian, I know you suspect that power has been employed somehow in his disappearance, so stop beating about the bush and just say so."

"Beating about the bush?"

"Never mind. Stop wasting our time and say what you really mean."

"I borrowed one of Gavril's warlocks to investigate around the abandoned vehicle. Astralan said the place stinks with power, but it's nothing he's ever come in contact with before. I'm asking you as nicely as I can, and I'll even grovel if you want me to, but you have to come look, Lissa. I don't know who else to ask."

"Fine, Norian," I huffed. "Let me find Gavin or somebody else to go with us, and we'll go."

"Thank you," Norian sounded relieved.

"Nori, there's no guarantee I'll have any better information than Astralan," I said.

"But I need to know that," Norian sighed. "If you can't tell me, then we'll know it's worse than we thought."

"You think it's worse already, don't you?" I frowned at Norian.

"Like you don't? Ildevar is practically jumping at shadows, and if he's jumpy, then something big and dangerous is going on. Isn't it?"

"Norian, this is complicated, and there's no rule book for any of this," I said. "Honestly, the less most people know, the happier they'll be."

"Lissa, you frighten me at times," Norian said.

"Most people don't know when to be frightened," I snapped back.

"Bill, we have problems," Opal said, pulling back a curtain slightly with the barrel of her pistol and peering out a window of Kathleen's Tahoe home. "There are three vehicles outside; they pulled up together and they're just sitting there, now."

"What happened to the guards at the end of the drive?" Bill asked.

"I can't reach them," Opal breathed. "I know they were there earlier —we checked in." Opal held her cell in one hand, the gun in the other. Kathleen and Trina were locked in an inside bathroom near the center of the house.

"Any movement from the vehicles?" Bill asked. "Bree is next door; we may be able to get her to," Bill began.

"Bill, we have movement, a door is opening. One man is getting out. He's tall. Ugly. Wait, he's changing. He's a shifter, Bill! I've never seen anything like this."

Just before her phone went dead, Opal heard Bill shouting for Breanne.

Breanne's Journal

Images blazed through my brain and I heard Bill shouting my name in a fog. He'd stepped into another room to take a call, and I knew now that Opal, Kathleen and Trina were in trouble.

Without wasting time, I gathered everybody into my mist and folded to Tahoe. We landed in a heap, almost, right behind Opal, who had a gun drawn while watching a creature approach the house. I could see him through the narrow space Opal allowed between curtain and window. I was thankful the sun had set already in Tahoe, or Gavin would have fried on the spot.

"Who do you suppose is still in those vehicles?" Bill went to stand beside Opal.

"No idea. What the hell is that thing?" Opal breathed.

"Chimera," Hank said matter-of-factly. He, Jayson, Gavin and Winkler gathered behind Bill and Opal to get a look. "They want to burn this house the same as Jayson's in San Rafael. They're looking for him. And for Breanne, most likely."

"How the hell did you get us here?" Trajan leaned down and whispered next to my ear.

"It's called folding space," I whispered back.

"Pretty damn handy," he muttered.

"What are we going to do about that thing? It's getting close to the house," Winkler pointed out. "I'm not in any mood to get barbecued, and Gavin sure as hell wouldn't like it."

"I'll take care of the chimera. The rest of you take care of what's in those vehicles," Hank said.

I watched as guns were pulled out and checked. Jayson had a nine millimeter in the back waistband of his jeans, plus a Smith and Wesson revolver in a front pocket. Gavin released his claws and fangs. Trajan, Winkler, Weldon and Trace came out of clothing and became wolf. What the hell?

As if that weren't enough, Hank became his smaller Thifilathi. Well, no fire would burn him like that. He looked like obsidian scales and death as he prepared to go outside and deal with a chimera.

"What do you want me to do?" I asked.

"Stay here. Guard Mom and Trina," Jayson muttered.

"Jayson, you're fucking human. Those out there may not be. You could be road-kill in the next five minutes."

"They burned down my house, destroyed my cars, and they're trying to kill my mom. What do you want me to do?"

"Let him do this, Breanne," Gavin said. "This involves his honor. If he falls, then one of us will avenge him."

Hear that? You must be special, dude. Gavin doesn't avenge lightly, I sent to Jayson.

"I can skip us outside, but after that, you're on your own." Hank's Thifilathi spoke. Like that, his voice was lower. Almost guttural. *Breanne,* he sent, *keep yourself safe. These do not need to see you. Understand?*

I drew in a breath. Hank suspected something. Might someone else be watching if I came out of the house? I was beginning to worry, and fear made me tremble. *Then make sure you stay safe,* I said. *The others, too.*

Didn't he know that I was much better off doing something, instead of hiding and worrying? I watched as Hank skipped the others outside the house and all hell broke loose.

≈

Lissa's Journal

"Norian, Astralan understated the problem," I huffed. "This doesn't just stink of power, it reeks. If evil has a smell, it might smell like this."

Drew, Norian and I stood on a narrow track shaped from years of vehicles driving through to waiting wheat fields. Tree branches hung over our heads as we examined the abandoned vehicle, last driven by Norian's brother.

I'd sniffed inside it and detected Reedy's scent, but that's all there was of him. He'd been taken straight from the solar-truck and transported elsewhere by power so foul I wanted a bath, and it had been days since Reedy's disappearance.

"Nori, maybe we should have hauled your brother out of here all those years ago. He might have caused less trouble that way."

"I agree with you," Norian replied grimly.

≈

187

Breanne's Journal

If I hadn't done as Jayson asked, and gone to guard Trina and Kathleen, they'd have died.

The gunshots, howling, snarling and fighting outside was just a distraction to the real danger to those inside the house. I misted inside the locked bathroom, only to catch sight of the huge snake threatening Trina, who stood in front of a terrified Kathleen.

I recognized the type of snake immediately—its pattern was similar to the friendly snake on Le-Ath Veronis. This wasn't my friendly snake, though. His pattern wasn't as nice, and he was a few feet shorter. It didn't matter, I relieved him of his head the moment he coiled to strike at Trina.

"Fuck that was close," I stared at the snake's body, which still writhed on the bathroom floor. I watched in horror as the eyes glazed over, and without thinking, I dropped my shields to read him.

Gerilat Berandiff, lion snake shapeshifter that he'd been, lay in two pieces at my feet. He'd done murder too many times to count and he'd assassinated kings, queens, heads of state and anybody else he'd been paid or ordered to kill.

"Where's Jayson?" Kathleen's hand shook as she reached out to me.

"Probably in the middle of the fight out front," I said, drawing her and Trina close. "They played the testosterone card and sent me to guard you."

"I'd rather have you in here," Trina stated flatly. "Those claws came in pretty handy."

"What kind of snake was that?" Kathleen's voice trembled. I rubbed her back gently and shook my head.

"No ordinary snake. Lion snake shapeshifter. From a long way off. I hope he's the only one they brought with them."

"You all right in there?" A knock sounded on the door. Jayson's voice.

"Baby?" Kathleen rushed for the door.

"Mom?" Kathleen was in Jayson's arms the moment the door opened.

"Honey, they said you looked different, but I don't know what to think," Kathleen drew back and stared at Jayson. "I guess I'll get used to it," she sighed. "Are you hurt?"

"Nah. I couldn't get close enough to get hurt. Hank, Gavin, Opal and those werewolves ripped the others apart. I think they were expecting a chimera to protect them."

"They were expecting a big-ass snake to kill your mother, Mister," Trina's fists went to her hips.

"Snake?"

"On the floor," I jerked my head toward the tile behind me. "I took care of him."

"Hank got the chimera," Jayson lifted an eyebrow as he studied the snake's body. "You got the snake. The others were human."

"Was that all they were?" I asked.

"Why do you want to know?" Hank was back in human form, his arms crossed over his chest as he asked the question.

"Well, because there are some—uh—beings, that take over human bodies so they can—uh—avoid some of the rules," I quavered. How the hell could I explain to him that half a million rogue godlings had inhabited bodies from Evensun and then chased me through space and time, trying to kill me?

"Breanne," Hank took a step forward and wrapped me in his arms. "It's all right, baby. Damn, did you kill that snake?"

"Well, I'm outed, now," Opal had dressed again and she, Trina and Kathleen packed bags before I transported everybody back to Dallas. Bill didn't feel comfortable leaving them behind, and I felt the same way.

"We'll move you into the house next door. I own it," Winkler informed Kathleen, once we landed inside his kitchen. Bill, Hank, Gavin and I were to stay in Winkler's house while Jayson, Kathleen, Trina and Opal took the house next door.

"It's good to see you again," I hugged Opal before she left Winkler's kitchen for the house next door. Bill had finally seen the velociraptor, and I think the werewolves were more than impressed.

"Oh, I'll be back and forth," Opal eyed Hank suspiciously, as if she expected him to misbehave in the next five seconds.

"I've been good," Hank held up his hands, proclaiming innocence.

"Yeah, but your ex and that stupid reporter weren't. How the hell did you not know she was following you around? Now Jayson looks like God knows who, his house is charred wreckage, his cars are toast and all because your ex wanted to get back at you—and hurt Breanne —through him."

"I hear the reporter didn't live over it," Weldon Harper held a cup of coffee in his hand. I was learning he was addicted to the brew.

"I think those conspiracy theorists are behind this," Opal huffed. "We can't prove it yet, but this stinks of them. We have no idea who they may have allied with, either, because that pretty blonde bitch was strung all over her bedroom. Like spaghetti."

"Why would they kill her? She'd spewed everything she knew already." I felt ill at Opal's description of Colbi Wayde's remains.

"They may have wanted her for something else," Hank suggested. "And she may not have fit into their plans. I worry that Janine has disappeared, however."

"You don't think she's dead, just like the Wayde woman?" Winkler asked.

"I'm concerned that she may not be, and that doesn't bode well for me or for Breanne." Smoke curled from Hank's nostrils. How had he contained that all this time? With the way things were going, we might have to fight our way through clouds of smoke daily from now on.

"Honey, does that hurt when you do that?" I asked.

"Do what?"

"Blow smoke."

"Oh. No. I'm just allowing my feelings free rein, now, instead of holding them back, as I was before."

"Look, I gotta go. I'll see you tomorrow," Opal waved and headed for Winkler's door.

"Breanne, I wish to see you in private," Gavin's hand landed on my shoulder. *Oh, shit.* I'd just called Hank honey in front of my surrogate sire. Well, my actual sire—he just didn't know it yet.

"All right," I turned and followed Gavin as he shouldered his way past Hank, Bill, Winkler, Weldon and Trajan. Trajan winked at me when I walked past. What was I supposed to do with that? What?

"Breanne, I know you were involved with Hank. And that Bill and Jayson are interested. I will not prevent you from going to them, if you want. Bear in mind, however, that Wlodek will likely entertain offers from vampires when your training is complete. You will have to deal with that when the time comes. I know Charles is very interested, and perhaps he will accept all of this if Wlodek approves his offer. I warn you, however, that the Aristocracy will complain, as Charles has not been admitted to that body, as yet."

"You won't keep me from Hank or Bill?" I asked, blinking at Gavin in surprise.

"Hank informed me earlier that you walk in daylight. I know you were afraid to tell me this. Do not be afraid to say things in the future. These talents only enhance your value to the race."

"I didn't think you'd understand," I stared at the floor.

"It may be difficult to comprehend, but I will not harm you for telling the truth."

"If I eat watermelon, it won't come back up," I said, still not looking at him. Gavin sighed, then lifted my chin with a finger.

"Then eat as much watermelon as you want. If human food sustains you, then I will not force you to take blood. Bear in mind that you should keep this from most vampires—I do not know how Wlodek or the others might react to this information."

"Okay," I said, staring uncomfortably into Gavin's dark eyes. Was I surprised? Yes. This Gavin even Lissa didn't know. This one was gentle and considerate. Even now, he was autocratic with her. I realized he was terrified he might lose her, but there were ways to convey that message that didn't involve bullying. I went back to what I'd seen in him in Wlodek's office.

Gavin had considered suicide by sunlight. He'd felt his life was empty. I'd also seen someone I didn't recognize in Gavin's reading, but the image had been cut off. What had that man looked like in my brief vision of him? As tall as Gavin. Dark hair. Gray eyes. And then the image had stopped, as if Gavin couldn't recall meeting the man. I didn't know what to think about that, or what to think about a nicer sire.

"Thank you," I added. "For understanding."

V'ili, once high in the aristocracy on Sirena, pulled himself from the water of the heated pool. The pool occupied most of the northwest corner of the new building, and had been built to his specifications. The water was salt and held no chemicals. In his true form, he could breathe it easily. Oxygen was pumped into the water, too, to keep it viable.

"Master," Janine handed a towel to V'ili.

"Kneel when you serve me," he demanded.

"Yes, Master," Janine went to her knees in adoration. It didn't matter that V'ili was covered in scales and his mouth filled with sharp teeth. Her back bore the marks of his teeth from the night before.

"You're so adorable—for a worthless human," V'ili smiled, showing his teeth. "Now rise and beg me to allow you to dry my scales."

Lissa's Journal

It wasn't Conner who stood before me. She was the Guardian, and that was someone we all knew to hear out.

"I am receiving reports that some who have crossed over are being pulled back," she informed me.

"But that's impossible, unless those from the highest levels do it," I whispered.

"We do not know the full extent of the rogue treachery. Rogues can come from any level, and not just those at lower ranks."

"How many? Do you know?" I was terrified that the worst of the worst would be pulled away from the other side, to continue their paths of destruction.

"Not many, and few of those might cause problems in the expected sense. There are other difficulties associated with this, and not least is that we cannot find some of these doppelgangers unless we have specific information on which souls to search for, and in which timeline. Some may have been pulled away to distract us, too, from those who might cause greater destruction in the long term."

"They're being shielded?"

"In some ways, yes. Just as information is now shielded from us concerning the enemy. I would like to speak with one of the Mighty, but even I cannot approach the Mighty Hand without invitation or intervention."

"And he's the only one we know how to find," I nodded. "He's not pleased with me right now, because I didn't call him immediately when my sister was still here."

"Because he wants to meet her?" The Guardian was gone and Conner took her place.

"Partly. The other part was that she might be able to help him with his M'Fiyah."

"He wants to use her?"

"Well," I hedged.

"At least somebody looked after his butt for the most part. Who looked after your sister?" Conner sounded a bit huffy.

"You seem invested in this, somehow," I pointed out. "What's in it for you?"

"Graegar's happiness," she snapped and folded away.

I stared at the space previously occupied by Conner, wondering what she'd meant. Did this mean that Graegar had a M'Fiyah with my sister? Were she and Conner destined to be co-mates? Something else struck me, then. Whenever a Wise One had a M'Fiyah, their Protectors generally had one with the same person. That meant that Barrigar might have a M'Fiyah with Breanne as well.

I hadn't seen Barrigar often, but he was very tall, quite powerful in his own right and generally quiet. He would probably be a perfect match for Breanne, but she'd likely never met him. She'd only mentioned Graegar before.

"Interesting," I sighed.

~

"What is the target?" Saxom accepted the folder from Calhoun. Saxom thought Calhoun to be human. He was wrong. Calhoun was powerful enough to disguise his scent and did so, casually and constantly.

"Are you sure? I mean I have no trouble with it, but some of the others," Saxom handed the folder back.

"After V'ili gets done with them, there will be no problem," Calhoun chuckled.

~

Breanne's Journal

"Real food," I muttered blissfully and dipped into the eggs Trina and Jimmy cooked for me.

"You need to lie down after you eat," Hank pointed his fork in my direction.

"You haven't slept, either," I said. Few of us had—Bill had already eaten and went to bed, planning to get four hours of sleep before rising again. He'd been on the phone most of the time after we'd gotten back from Tahoe—he'd had to explain to his boss what the ruckus was about.

Human bodies were at the local coroner's office in Tahoe, but they were having trouble identifying any of them. My guess was that they might not be local either—just like the lion snake shapeshifter and the chimera. Those bodies had been picked up by local werewolves at

Weldon's command, and they would be shipped to a special lab in D.C. Bill was waiting on results from the snake especially, to see if the poison matched that responsible for the death of the vehicle's previous owner.

"Still no word on the car," Winkler said, sipping a cup of coffee.

"I don't think you'll see it again," Jayson huffed. He, Kathleen, Trina and Opal had shown up for breakfast with us, as the kitchen at the other house wasn't stocked.

Trina intended to go to the grocery store later, to pick up a few things. Regular meals were still planned in Winkler's kitchen, but coffee, sodas, snacks and fruit were needed. Winkler assigned one of his wolves to drive Trina, and she'd given Winkler a look that said the werewolf had better mind his manners with her.

"Come on, shorty," Hank pulled me off my barstool the moment I finished eating. Hank gripped my hand and I was led, almost at a trot, toward his bedroom. Well, Gavin said he didn't care. We were about to test that theory, I guess.

"Baby, if you want to go to bed with somebody else, just let me know." Hank was kissing my neck the second he shut the bedroom door.

"Huh," I muttered as Hank's mouth settled on mine.

"I'm taking you somewhere else," Hank's voice was breathy as his hands moved beneath my T-shirt.

"Whuh?" I blinked as our venue changed. We were in another room, where a leather sling hung on chains from the ceiling. No other furniture was in the room.

"Special room in the club," Hank went back to kissing.

"But," I shivered.

"This is fun," Hank murmured, lifting my T over my head. My bra was unhooked and dropped to the floor.

"Jeans, baby," Hank's hands were on my waist, tickling my ribs gently as his mouth settled on a nipple.

I fumbled with the button on my jeans, and almost lost a nail getting the zipper down while Hank launched an assault that left me gasping for breath.

"Yeah," he shoved my jeans and underwear down, and then stepped on them when they hit the floor. "Step out of your shoes, baby," Hank commanded. He steadied me while I toed off my athletic shoes, then lifted me up, leaving the jeans and underwear in a puddle on the floor.

"This is a swing, and it makes sex real easy," he settled me on the leather contraption. "I can adjust the height, so we fit perfectly together," he pressed a button hanging on a cord nearby. "See—just right." He came out of his clothes quickly.

I stared at his erection. Did I feel shameless, admitting that it fascinated me? Yeah. That didn't stop me from looking—and liking what I saw.

"You like that, don't you," Hank grinned. He'd followed my gaze, which was fastened on his penis like sonar on a submarine.

"And what if I do?" I attempted to cross my arms over my breasts, but that caused the swing to twist.

"You don't get to move. I control this," Hank sounded smug. "Just hang onto the handholds at the front," he tapped stirrup-like leather handles. "This'll be the best swinging you ever did," he promised.

"What do you get out of this?" I asked, gripping the handles as requested.

"I get to watch my body and yours play together," he murmured. "Kiss me before little Hank slides home. After that, close your eyes and let the sensation take over."

"Little Hank?" I lifted an eyebrow.

"Well, maybe not so little," he said. "Now, watch this," Hank pushed against me. My body accepted his readily. "See? We belong together. Close your eyes, baby. You're gonna like this."

CHAPTER 13

Breanne's Journal

"Baby, wake up. Bill has some news."

"Huh?" I wanted my eyes to open. Really. They were glued shut. Hank had shown me earlier that the sex swing could be used for alternative positions, and then he'd demonstrated effectively. Was I willing to admit that some sex furniture was fun? Oh, yeah. There hadn't been a single place to tie anybody up on his swing, and I liked that even better.

"Come on, I'm taking you to the shower." Hank hauled me out of bed, but my eyes didn't open until I got hit in the face with shower spray.

He even soaped me up and rinsed me off, then washed my hair. That was nice, actually. He nuzzled my neck while drying me off, and told me I had to do the same for him next time. *Okayyy*.

We walked into Winkler's kitchen in record time, to find Bill, Winkler, Trajan, Jayson and Weldon sitting around the island. It was still daylight outside, but it was waning fast—it wouldn't be long before Gavin was up and around.

"We found the car," Bill sighed, tossing a photograph onto the island. It slid toward Hank and me, which meant the others had already seen it.

"But that's what's left of," I stared at the burned and flattened metal of a white Pontiac Grand Am, sitting in the remains of Jayson's garage in San Rafael. It was recognizable, at least. The rest of his cars weren't.

"Right where I parked my Mercedes," Jayson muttered. "They took my McLaren and left this piece of shit behind. To taunt me."

"Still trying to get our attention?" Hank lifted an eyebrow and handed the photograph back to Bill.

"They're not trying—they *have* our attention," Winkler growled low. "How the hell did the car get into that garage?" he asked.

"We're likely dealing with a few power wielders," Hank said. "It would only take a low level of ability to switch objects like that."

"Bree, you mentioned that your grandfather was a warlock?" Bill said. He had a good memory—I'd been rattling off crap about Griffin and wasn't even paying attention to what I'd said.

"Yeah. There are warlocks and wizards. Hank's right—a kid with either talent could switch those cars."

"Let's hope it isn't a kid," Weldon said. "We have enough trouble dealing with adults."

"We definitely don't need that," Trajan agreed.

"I've sent information across the country, asking for reports of any unusual activity. So far, they're limiting it to this—where they know we'll see it," Bill explained.

"So they park the car at that new church, knowing we're not far away?" Winkler stood. He was worried, and I was right behind him in that worry.

"You need to get your kids away from here," I said. "Someplace safe."

"I'll send them to Boise," Winkler muttered, pulling his cellphone from a pocket of tight-fitting, black jeans. I read Winkler as he placed a call to Davis Stone, Packmaster for the Boise Pack. Davis was married to Wayne and Wynter's grandmother.

"Winkler?" Davis answered the phone on the second ring.

"Davis, we've got a situation here, and I need a safe place for the twins," Winkler said.

"Send 'em," Davis said right away. "I'll make sure they're guarded," he added.

"Good. I'll have them on the plane tonight."

"We'll be waiting. Let me know what time."

"Will do," Winkler ended the call. "Fuck," he said and rubbed his forehead. "Do we need to relocate as well?"

Bill stared at Hank and me. Well, we could be transportation if required. Hank had skipped me to San Francisco without blinking, and then back again, carrying me because I was boneless after several climaxes.

"Look, relocating sounds like a good idea, but we have a couple of things to take care of before we leave town. We have to get the twins on a plane with their nanny and a couple of guards, and that means we have to pack." Winkler jerked his head at Trajan.

"Need help?" I offered.

"We got it," Trajan waved a hand. "Their nanny knows what they need."

"We're moving tonight, so get packed," Bill ordered as soon as Winkler and Trajan left the kitchen. "Jayson, get your mother and Trina ready; they'll have to go with us. Send Opal over here, so we can figure this out."

"Will do," Jayson strode angrily out of Winkler's kitchen, heading for the front door. He was still upset about the house, the cars and the fact that we were all in danger. I didn't blame him a bit.

"Come on, baby, we'll pack and let Gavin know we're moving," Hank pulled me away.

"Where are we going?" I asked. Well, I probably ought to know, since I'd be taking everybody there.

"Port Aransas," Bill sighed. "Got any beach clothes?"

Gavin didn't look or sound surprised when Hank informed him of the intended move. Winkler, the twins, Trajan, their nanny and another werewolf had hurried out the door seconds before Gavin walked out of his room for the evening. Hank and I were waiting for him.

"I've been to the area before," Gavin agreed. "It's better than I originally expected."

I'd only walked a beach on the Gulf Coast before, and at the time, I'd flung my cellphone into the water before hauling ass back to Austin to save Opal. That had started a chain of events I was lucky to have survived.

I wondered (again) just who had slapped me out of the tunnel connecting two timelines. Whether they'd intended to hurt me or save me from foolishness, the result had cracked my skull. That sort of pissed me off.

"Breanne, child, are you packed?" Gavin turned dark eyes to me.

"Yeah," I shrugged. I'd packed in record time, actually, so I could stand with Hank and wait for Gavin to emerge from his room.

"I will be ready shortly," he nodded to Hank and went back inside his suite.

"I'm worried," I said, turning away.

"Baby, we'll get through this," Hank pulled me back and into a warm hug.

"I hope so," I mumbled against his chest.

"Honored One, Gavin says they're moving to Winkler's home in Port Aransas," Charles stood in the doorway of Wlodek's study. "He says that their targets may be aware of their location."

"If the targets know of the Dallas location, won't they know of the Port Aransas home as well?" Wlodek asked.

"Good point, but what else might we do?"

"Hold on." Wlodek tapped a number on his cellphone to make a call.

"Wlodek?" Merrill's voice was easily discernible to Charles.

"I have a request," Wlodek said. "I know your contacts have a large beach home in Port Aransas. Might it be loaned out—for a worthy cause?"

"Does this have to do with evading those connected to the vehicle?"

"Yes."

"I think it won't be a problem. Give me a few minutes; I'll get back to you."

"Thank you," Wlodek said. "I'll be waiting."

～

Breanne's Journal

"We're going to this address," Gavin handed a slip of paper to Winkler. "It was pointed out to me that the ones we wish to avoid may know of your home there. This one they will not suspect."

"I know this place—I've tried to buy it a couple of times. Realtor says they don't want to sell. Ever."

"Here's your chance to see it, then," Trajan grinned as he studied the address over Winkler's shoulder. "It's huge."

"Are we ready?" I watched as Opal herded Kathleen and Trina into the kitchen. I could tell Kathleen wasn't keen on moving again, and she looked tired to me.

"Hank, will you check on Kathleen when we get to the coast?" I asked softly, touching his sleeve. "She looks tired to me."

"I'll check her," he agreed quietly. "This hasn't done her any good, that's easy enough to see."

"I hope this house is big enough for all of us," Jayson said.

"Trina and I can share," Kathleen said. "If that's all right with Trina."

"Ms. Rome, you know it is," Trina said.

"Trace and I can bunk together," Trajan offered. Hank pulled me against him, so I knew where I'd be sleeping. Gavin didn't seem to care either way, I think, as long as he could block sunlight completely.

"Can you take all of us plus the luggage?" Winkler asked me.

"Yeah. No trouble," I shrugged. Hank let me go, and I studied those around me. Winkler, Trajan, Trace, Weldon and Jimmy made up the werewolf contingent. Gavin and I represented the vampires. Bill, Jayson, Kathleen and Trina were the humans making the trek, while Opal represented the shapeshifters. Hank, as a High Demon, was likely the first of his race ever to set foot on the Gulf of Mexico.

"Let's go, then," I squared my shoulders. I should have seen it coming. I should have. I have no idea what blocked it from me. Bullets sprayed through Winkler's kitchen windows as I folded everybody away.

"I've had a lot worse," Winkler attempted to wave Hank away, but Hank insisted on treating the graze on Winkler's arm. He was the only one who'd gotten hit, and I figured he'd been the target. I felt shaky, but didn't want to point that out—Kathleen was as white as cotton, and shaking harder than I was. Jayson was doing his best to calm her down while Hank tended Winkler.

"Mom, just breathe slow, okay?" Jayson soothed.

"Ms. Rome, we're not about to let you go," Trina said. "You do not want to see what might happen if you dare to have another heart attack."

"Hear that? Trina will yell at you," Jayson smiled gently at his mother.

"We can't have that," Kathleen's voice trembled.

"Good. Breathe with me," Jayson said. "We'll be all right, I promise. Nobody knows we're here."

"Honored One, I'm asking your permission to travel to Texas." Charles was back inside Wlodek's office.

"Charles?" Wlodek lifted an eyebrow in surprise. Charles never asked or volunteered for any assignment. Wlodek had considered sending Radomir or Russell, but Charles was offering instead.

"Rad or Will can cover for me while I'm gone, and I can work with Breanne while I'm there," Charles pointed out.

"I am willing to allow this, as you seldom ask for anything," Wlodek nodded. "Pack and call for the jet."

"Thank you, Honored One."

~

Breanne's Journal

"Charles will arrive tomorrow evening," Gavin said, pocketing his cellphone.

"What?" I blinked at Gavin in confusion.

"Wlodek wanted to send another vampire, and Charles asked to come."

"But," I said.

"Baby, it'll be all right," Hank soothed. I hadn't told him about Charles, but then Hank and Gavin may have had conversations I didn't know about.

"Charles is just as capable as any Enforcer," Gavin said, misinterpreting my worry. I didn't want a showdown between a vampire and a High Demon. That's what I worried about.

"Bree, we'll be asking you to shuttle us between Dallas and here," Bill interrupted my side trip. "We may ask to be taken other places as well. Hank says he can help, so we don't wear both of you out carrying us around. I need to be in D.C. the day after tomorrow, for a meeting. Think you can handle that?"

I turned to Gavin. "That is fine, as long as she has a guard," he said.

"I'll make sure of it," Bill said, sounding as if he were offended that Gavin might think he'd leave me unguarded.

"You're having a meeting on Saturday?" I asked. Honestly, I thought the government shut down on Friday afternoons.

"This is a meeting with the President and the Joint Chiefs, and this was the time when we could all get together," Bill said.

"Then I'll be happy to take you on Saturday," I nodded at Bill.

"Can I get a kiss with that?" Bill asked.

"I, uh, guess," I said.

"Yeah. I've missed that," Bill stepped forward and took my face in his hands. "We've had too many things going on lately. I haven't thanked you for getting us to Tahoe in time." He leaned in and gave me a tongue-scorcher. *I love the way your eyes look after I kiss you like that*, Bill sent.

Bill, I replied, and then went silent. Is it possible to be tongue-tied in mindspeech? I was. There wasn't an ounce of fat anywhere on Bill, and for a forty-something guy, he looked damn good. *You're not still worried that you're too old, are you?* I asked. *Because you're sure as hell not.*

I don't give a damn, anymore. I just want you, sweetheart. That's all.

That's what I wanted to hear, I leaned in and kissed him, this time.

Get a room, Jayson complained. Well, could I mist or what? I misted Bill into the bedroom he'd selected.

"Is this real?" Bill's hands clutched my waist and pulled me against him once we were corporeal.

"If you want it to be," I said.

"You think I don't? An old guy like me shouldn't have a constant hard-on," he mumbled against my mouth. "It's probably bad for me or something."

"Bill, I've only had one lover," I said, pulling away from him.

"Hank explained that," Bill said. "And don't be upset that he told me —we didn't discuss details—and we won't unless you want it."

"Well, I guess that's not exactly true. Does having a climax with the vampire bite count?" I asked. I might as well tell Bill all of it.

"I hear the bite lesson is mandatory," Bill leaned in for another kiss while his hands wandered beneath my top. "I just want to touch this," a hand covered one of my breasts. "I want to take that bra off and taste it, too. Then, I want to put my mouth on you and make you scream."

"Where?" I asked.

"Right. Back. Here." He walked me backward toward his bed, then coaxed my body to relax and sit on the end of it. "Lean back on the bed, sweetheart, I'm gonna undress you. Let me know if I hurt or scare you, okay?"

"All right." While I wasn't completely scared, I was nervous. I worried that Hank would be upset. I worried that Charles would be upset—with either or both. Poor Jayson, I had no idea what to do about him. No idea at all. And lately, too, I'd been having unexpected visions of Graegar in my dreams. Sometimes he was alone—sometimes he was with another Larentii I hadn't met. I had no idea what any of it meant, and Bill was pulling off my jeans anyway.

"This is beautiful." He touched bare flesh. At that moment I couldn't say for sure whether I felt good or bad about the wax job. Bill went to his knees, lifted my legs over his shoulder and dipped his head. Did some guys get lessons in this stuff? I ended up pulling a pillow against my mouth to muffle the screams.

Reah's Journal

"Tory, I don't want her anywhere near Kifirin. The god or the planet," I said. "I know you told Jayd and Glinda they could see Lexsi, but I don't want them too close. Taking her to them is too close, in my opinion."

"Her older sisters want to see her, too," Tory pointed out.

"Look, I don't want to argue, but there's nothing preventing them from coming here. Ashe said he'd allow it." I gazed down at my sleeping daughter—she was barely two months old and had the shortest white fuzz atop her head. I hoped she'd have the signature white hair that Belarok had passed to Glinda and to me.

"Baby, bring Aurelius and Edward with us. Hell, bring Zendeval, if you want. Jayd says he hasn't seen a Greater Demon in fifty thousand years."

"Zen might punch Jayd," I sniffed. "He knows what they've done to me."

"Zen isn't completely pure," Tory grumped, releasing a curl of smoke from his nostrils.

"Zen hasn't stolen my children, either," I snapped.

"Re, don't be upset," Tory soothed. "I'm sorry I told Jayd we'd come."

"Look, I'll do it, but only for a little while. They can ooh and ahh and then we go, all right?"

"All right."

Breanne's Journal

"This wine is exceptional. I wonder where it came from." Jayson poured another glass. He, Hank, Bill and I sat on the deck at the back of the house, watching a half moon hover over the waters of the gulf. Bill and I, well, Bill now wore a very satisfied (and maybe a little smug) smile, and we were relaxing with the others before going to bed.

"Let me see the bottle," I reached for it—he'd emptied the last of it into his glass. It was a red wine, and not too dry. I didn't usually drink red wine, but this was very good, just as he said it was.

"Here." Jayson handed the bottle over. To him, the label seemed printed with gibberish.

"It's Refizani and worth a lot," I handed the bottle back. "Refizan has some of the best vineyards in the Reth Alliance."

"Refizan? Reth Alliance?" Jayson stared.

"Rather bland, as a society," Hank pointed out.

"I'll have you know my favorite healer is Refizani," I said, wrinkling my nose at Hank. "And he's married to my sister," I added.

"What?" Bill sputtered, nearly choking on his wine.

"Uh-oh," I slapped a hand over my mouth.

"Lissa's alive?" Bill's voice was scratchy from the cough.

"In the future," I sighed. "I shouldn't have said that."

"In the future? What the hell are you talking about?" Jayson demanded.

"Keep your voice down, you want Gavin to hear?" I hissed. "You want to know why I can't tell anybody who turned me?"

"Why?" Jayson leaned back on his patio chair, his body stiff with disbelief.

"Because Gavin did it, around four hundred years from now," I whispered.

"Breanne," Hank held up a hand in warning. Yeah, I was telling too much.

"How did you get here, then?" Bill asked softly.

"Because Breanne is more special than most suspect." I stared. Here was the man from Gavin's memory—the one I'd only glimpsed for a moment. While Hank might be more beautiful than this one, he didn't radiate with the power this one did. He raised a hand and my head jerked—Hank, Jayson and Bill seemed frozen in time.

"It is a trick some know," he said indifferently. His voice was low. Almost gentle. "I am removing the memory of what you said from these," he gestured toward Bill and Jayson. "They do not need to recall. They are human, and humans have weaknesses." He was chastising me, albeit not harshly.

"You're the third one, then," I shivered.

"Yes. You would do well to be as circumspect as possible in the coming days. We are in enough danger without releasing all our secrets, even to the most trusted of our allies."

"Yeah. You're right," I ducked my head. I'd just gotten so comfortable with Bill, Jayson and Hank that I let my mouth get the better of me.

"Love, we all make mistakes," his fingers lifted my chin so I could stare into his eyes. They were a clear gray, and I felt I could drown in them if I looked too long. "Don't make any more," he said and disappeared.

"Breanne, tread carefully from now on," Hank said softly, as Bill and Jayson blinked. I could see that neither recalled what I'd said or that Wisdom had just made his presence known.

～

"Hank, what do you think is going on? Really?" I asked. He lay beside me, and pulled me close to rest my head on his shoulder. Bill may have wanted me in his bed to sleep, but after my faux pas, I didn't feel comfortable doing that. I'd given him a kiss instead and allowed Hank to herd me toward our shared bedroom.

"Baby, I don't know, but none of it looks good, does it?"

"No. It doesn't look good. Will you slap a hand over my mouth in the future, if I get out of hand again?"

"I can try," he said, kissing my forehead. "While a ball gag might work better, people tend to drool a lot with those."

"You wouldn't," I leaned back to stare at his chin. I watched as the corner of his mouth curled in a grin.

"Nah, I'm not into drool," he teased. "I just tell 'em to stay quiet or the hand descends."

"Huh?"

"I can spank. I don't mind doing it."

"I bruise easy," I pointed out. I didn't add that he and Jayson had already tried that tactic, with bad results.

"I know. If I spanked you, I'd ruin it by kissing your little ass afterward."

"Too bad Jayson didn't feel the same way," I muttered, huddling against Hank. It wouldn't do to go too far down that road; I was already trembling slightly.

"Hey," Hank tightened his arms around me. "This is just pillow talk. Nobody's gonna hit you, I promise."

"Yeah?" Jayson stuck his head inside the door. Hank had obviously sent mindspeech.

"Come here, Rome." Hank said. "You need to kiss Bree's ass for spanking it," Hank said.

"What?" I struggled in Hank's grip.

"Baby, he owes you more than that. Lie still, now."

"No," I thrashed against Hank.

"Hey, I'm not gonna hurt you," Jayson settled on the edge of the bed and leaned over to tug on the waistband of my short pajamas.

"See," Hank said as Jayson slowly pulled the fabric down, revealing bare skin. "Now," Jayson breathed against me, "I get to kiss this." He did. Several times. And then the pajamas came down more. Hank took my hands and kissed them before sucking on my fingers. Jayson pushed me over on my back, pulled the pajamas off and buried his head between my legs.

"Hank," I whimpered.

"It's okay, baby. It's okay. Jayson's gonna take care of you."

"God, you taste good," Jayson murmured against me.

"Bree, there's nothing to worry about. No need to feel embarrassed. This is natural. Normal, with multiple mates," Hank still held onto my hands, kissing them between words.

"Move aside, bro," Jayson pulled himself over me. Hank scooted out of the way. "Yeah. I get a kiss. Finally," Jayson locked his mouth onto mine, and his body joined mine at the same moment. "See? I can treat my girl good. Yeah. So good. So tight. Like heaven."

Did I say I felt like a shameless hussy before? That was like the snowball that started the avalanche. I'd been in bed with Hank and Jayson, all night. We may have gotten four hours' sleep. Maybe.

Hank and Jayson didn't seem to think anything of what we'd done the night before. I couldn't believe I had so little willpower. I told Hank that.

"Bree, willpower has nothing to do with it," Hank said, running fingers through my wet hair after we'd gotten out of the shower. Yeah, Jayson was there, too, and showing off the tattoo of a black rose on his left hip. The rose looked like leather. Who knew?

"It has everything to do with love, caring and affection," Hank added.

"And embarrassment," I huffed.

"You're not embarrassed are you? Bree, I want to fuck you all day long," Jayson settled beside me on the dressing bench. "I had no idea anybody could clench that hard in a climax. That pussy is like magic."

"Jayson, please shut up." I covered my face with both hands.

"Bree, bite him," Hank said.

"What?" I dropped my hands and stared at Hank's image in the mirror.

"Go on, give him that."

"Will it hurt?" Jayson asked.

"Says the man who likes to swing a whip," I huffed.

"I've never been bitten before," he pointed out.

"Fine. Jayson, I won't hurt you," I cupped the back of his neck in my hand. "I'll be gentle," I added, leaning in to kiss the skin covering the artery. Jayson moaned. "Shhh," I soothed, before sinking my fangs in his throat.

"Breanne, please bite me every day. Please," Jayson begged after coming back from the most intense climax (according to him) he'd ever experienced. I'd swallowed a mouthful of blood with difficulty, but I'd done it.

"Hon, you don't need to give up the blood. Every three or four weeks is acceptable."

"Not to me," he pouted. "I can't believe we wasted so much time, when you could have bitten me at the start."

"I've created a monster," I sighed and went to find something to wear.

"I knew I wanted this house before, but this is amazing," Winkler hopped out of the indoor pool when Jayson, Hank and I walked in. He was right—the house was huge and had everything, including ten bedrooms, a game room, the indoor pool and spa, plus a kitchen that most people could never hope to afford.

Bill sat on a lounge chair nearby, reading reports on a tablet. "Hey," I walked over to him and leaned down for a kiss.

"Sweetheart, sit here with me," Bill pulled me down beside him while Hank and Jayson dropped into the pool for laps. "Have a good night?" he asked before kissing me again.

"Yeah. I think so."

"Did you enjoy yourself?"

"I think so."

"Breanne, stop thinking in outmoded terms," Bill said, setting the tablet aside and pulling me against him. "This is how multiple mates works. Everybody knows each other and gets along. That's how it is."

"How many conversations have you and Hank had about this?" I asked.

"Several. You can't expect us not to communicate about how to make this work, Bree. We want you happy. We want to be happy, too, and if we don't get along or talk to each other, there could be problems."

"Great."

"Look, talk to us. We'll listen. It's not like we're ganging up on you or something."

"Really?" I leaned back to watch his face. "It seems to me that you all make the decisions now, and I get left out of it."

"Bree, what are you saying?" Hank stood at the edge of the pool, his black hair wet from jumping in and swimming a few laps. His elbows rested on the slate tiles as he studied me, his dark eyes unreadable.

"She's saying that you're men, and you're going to do what you're going to do, no matter what. She can talk all she wants, and you'll pretend to listen, but at the end of the day, you'll always believe you're right." Opal's bare feet pattered on the tile as she walked toward the pool. "Even if you're not right," she added, "you'll only say you're sorry afterward, instead of considering that you ought to pay better attention next time."

"Opal, I hope you're not right about that," Bill said. I pulled away from him and stood up.

"I'm going to read for a while. Feel free to argue amongst yourselves," I said and walked out.

～

"Dee, I don't feel right," Gavril complained.

"What? Do you need a healer?" Dee jerked his head up to stare at Gavril. "I thought you weren't susceptible to disease." Gavril had wandered into Dee's office after ignoring a report on dwindling resources on Campiaa.

"No. It's not that. I just feel—empty. I think I'll go for a walk."

"Take one of the warlocks with you," Dee said and watched as Gavril strode out the door.

"It's the Founder, Teeg San Gerxon." Yes, he heard the whispers clearly. He had vampire hearing, and it worked perfectly. His mind, however, could no longer be trusted. It wandered. Blanked out at times. He had no idea what might be happening to him. In fact, he'd forgotten for a moment that Dee had said to take a warlock with him before he'd misted away from San Gerxon Palace and landed in one of the casinos.

Gavril didn't even know which casino he walked through. His thoughts were almost empty. Bare. There was no joy in anything. No sorrow, either. Or guilt. Nothing. A fleeting moment of clarity informed him that this had started years earlier, but it had been so gradual, he'd barely noticed. The tipping point had passed long ago, however, and he'd only realized it recently.

"May I get you anything, Master San Gerxon?" someone asked.

"What?" Gavril turned to blink at the man. "Do I know you?" he asked.

"We've met," the man smiled and plunged a knife into Gavril's heart.

CHAPTER 14

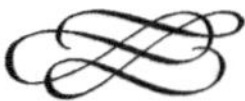

Lissa's Journal

"He's dying, despite our best efforts," Karzac's eyes held worry. Larentii were inside the bedroom with Gavril—they were the best healers, and even Karzac couldn't compete with their ability.

"Karzac, you have to save him," I wept. Gavin stood nearby, completely silent. He'd been mostly silent lately anyway, and I couldn't explain that. Didn't want to think about it, even, while our son was dying.

"What about the Wise Ones? Can't they do something?" I was about to unravel, and I needed to keep my sanity.

"Let me see if I can do something about this," Conner appeared, flanked by Graegar and Barrigar, her Larentii mates.

"What?" I blinked at her.

"We need to see him—Gavril. There's something we suspect, and if it's true, even the Wise Ones can't save him."

"What do you suspect?" I wiped tears away to clear my vision.

"That Gavril's soul has been leeched away by a former self."

"What?"

"I told you before that some were being pulled away from the other side. This is something else that can happen," Conner said grimly. "If someone with sufficient power goes back in time and pulls your former self into the future, where you also exist, only one body will get the soul. Without power of your own, or permission or protection from the powerful, both of you can't exist at the same time."

"Are you saying that Gavril in a former life was brought forward, and now he's losing his soul to the other one?"

"Because the first one gets priority," Conner nodded. "And he's not losing his soul. If I'm right, it's already gone."

"But how long?" I blinked at her in confusion.

"If the person is strong, it can take years. At times it will be so gradual it can appear natural, unless someone powerful enough to see the soul notices, anyway. Gavril hasn't been what I'd term himself, in a long time," she added.

"If we find the other one," I began.

"You'd have to kill him, and that would be the same as murder—he likely hasn't done anything wrong. I suspect he's a prisoner, wherever he is. If you carried him back in time, he'd still retain the soul. And if you did kill him, there's a good chance they'd both die anyway."

"Lissa," Graegar spoke gently, "It is my hope that we can salvage the other. He will hold the soul—and the memories—of your son, in addition to those memories he had before. It may weary him at times, but the soul will be the same one—it will merely have grown since he held it before."

"You're saying I have to let my son die?"

"Lissa, he's dying. There's nothing we can do about it. What we can do is search for the other one, because he'll die too, the moment they learn that Gavril is gone." The Guardian had appeared in Conner's eyes and blinked at me with god-like sternness.

"What happened?" Reah had arrived, with Tory, Ry, Aurelius and Edward. Edward cradled Lexsi in his arms; it was easy to see that Reah was trembling.

"Too much," I whispered and let darkness take me.

Breanne's Journal

I'd started three books and stopped reading all of them after only a few pages. Something was wrong—I could feel it. Of late, my prescience seemed to be unreliable, too, and I didn't know what to think about that. The thick, padded headboard of the bed was at my back as I sighed and tossed my e-reader onto the bed in frustration.

Breanne, the voice came. Graegar.

What is it, honey? I asked.

Breanne, I feel we need your help. Gavril is dying, and there is nothing we can do to stop it, even if we Change What Was. His soul has been pulled away, and we need your help to find it.

Where are you? I sent, crawling off the bed and preparing to leave. Hank would be pissed, as would everyone else, but this was what bothered me, and I hadn't even gotten any signal from it.

At Lissa's palace, he explained and sent me the date. Bless Graegar; he knew I wasn't in the same time period.

On my way, I sent and bent time.

I didn't need an explanation—I read it in Graegar the minute I set foot inside Lissa's palace.

"How in hell is that even possible?" I breathed and shook my head.

"We have to save the one from the past, because he holds Gavril's memories as well as his soul." I stared at Conner as she spoke.

Yes, she'd been a Shining One once—a messenger for the One. She still ferried souls to the other side—if they couldn't find their way or refused to go. Now, she appeared human, with long, blonde hair, blue eyes and a faint resemblance to Kiarra. They were half-sisters as humanoids.

"Any idea where to look?" I asked.

"I can locate the soul," Conner sounded determined, "Now that I know which one to search for. But I'll need your help to get him away, more than likely."

"I can't tell you how much it scares me that they can do this," I pointed out.

"Usually they can't, because only a few have the talent to discern who somebody was in a former life. Lissa named Gavril appropriately. He was Tybus in his former life."

"The architect? Who designed this behemoth?" I tossed out a hand, indicating Lissa's palace.

"And the one on Kifirin, yes," Graegar agreed. "We feel that they may have been guessing when they stole Tybus away from his previous death, but they guessed correctly."

"Well, let's hope they stop guessing correctly in the future," I muttered.

"We can't guarantee that," the Shining One stared through Conner's eyes.

"Wow. Thanks. Where do we need to go and how should we go about this rescue mission?" I asked.

"It will take finesse, and the assistance of the Mighty Hand," the Shining One announced before leaving Conner behind.

"Great. The mighty asshole," I muttered angrily.

"I have contacted Renegar. He is close to Ashe," Graegar said and opened up his mindspeech to me. I heard Renegar contacting Ashe, and Ashe's reply. Both arrived in seconds.

"Breanne," Ashe nodded to me. The sight of him—tall, with light-brown, unruly hair and blue eyes—squeezed my heart. I ignored it.

"Ashe," I acknowledged, my voice as frosty as I could make it.

"We need your strength to get past a barrier," Conner informed Ashe. "I can locate Tybus through the soul, but you two will have to get him out of there."

"What do you need me for?" I asked, confused. If Ashe could get them in and out, why did they need me?

"You have to heal him—with Love," Conner said simply. "He has likely been tortured and mistreated for years, while he leeched

Gavril's soul away. He's damaged. You can fix that if you send him Love."

"Well, that explains a few things," I muttered.

"I will gather all of you inside my mist," Ashe announced. "Conner, guide us." I almost shrieked as I disappeared. I'd never been carried like this before—I'd always been the carrier. The experience was slightly unbalancing at first.

I won't hurt you, Ashe assured me as we folded space.

~

Lissa's Journal

"Lissa, they didn't say where they were going." Reemagar settled on a barstool next to me in the kitchen. A cup of tea, gone cold, lay on the counter in front of me; I hadn't touched it. Cheedas busied himself at the sink opposite the island—he was terrified. As was I.

Gavin had disappeared the moment he learned Conner, Ashe, Graegar, Barrigar and my sister had left to search for Tybus. Connegar, Lenigar, Pheligar and Renegar remained in the bedroom with Gavril, keeping his body in stasis.

That's all it was, now—a body. Nothing of my son was left inside it. Whatever remained of Gavril was held inside an ancient vampire, who was likely insane after years of torture.

"Honey, do you remember much of who you were before?" I blinked up at Reemagar—he'd been my husband Don, once.

"No. What little I know, I know through Connegar and Conner. They provided vague memories. It is just as well, I do not wish to remember pain."

"I think that's why people usually don't recall past lives. It would frighten them too much at times, to remember how they'd suffered."

"I agree. I know some might bear it, if they only remember a few things. I realize you could tell me much, but those memories are for you, and not for me." He smiled gently at me and rubbed my shoulders with large, blue fingers.

"Yeah." I brushed a tear away.

"We will get through this," Reemagar pulled me onto his lap and began trilling. I closed my eyes and huddled against him as he soothed me with Larentii song.

~

Breanne's Journal

If Ashe hadn't been with us, we'd never have made it through the shield. Somehow, he was able to bore the tiniest hole into what seemed an impenetrable barrier, and ferry us through. If I'd been corporeal, it would have felt as if I'd been spun as thin as a silk thread to flow through the opening.

Once past that, Ashe had to keep the tightest shield around us—because power radiated through the place. They were looking for anything to set off their alarm, and Ashe was determined not to do that.

Could I explain how he did what he did? No. I was the Mighty Heart, not the Mighty Hand. Perhaps the Mighty Mind could explain it, but I didn't want to dwell on that too long.

Should I tell Ashe I'd seen Wisdom? I decided I still hadn't forgiven Ashe enough to have a conversation with him.

We found Tybus in the lowest level of a dungeon inside a massive castle, perched upon a planet made of nothing but iron. It hit me, then. He was still vampire. He couldn't walk in daylight. Well, something would have to be done about that.

Do this, dearest. Send him Love and wake him, Graegar sent mindspeech.

Tybus was shackled with power cuffs. Ashe would have to mist him away, but that shouldn't be a problem. Taking a mental breath, I sent *Love* to Tybus.

~

"Did you feel something?" Acrimus asked Calhoun.

"No. Why?"

"Nothing. I imagined a brush of something against my shield, that's all. I can't feel it, now."

"Your imagination, perhaps?" Calhoun was smooth in humanoid guise. Much smoother and more polished than Acrimus might ever be. He was from a lower level of the Hierarchy, and had dealt with humanoids in the past. He knew them and their emotions. He could duplicate anything a humanoid might do.

"How goes it with the quarter-blood whelp on Earth?" Acrimus asked.

"He will do anything I say. He has his own agenda, and as long as it aligns with mine, I will allow him his secrets."

"Even their powerful are pathetic," Acrimus grimaced.

"Was that a smile or a frown?" Calhoun lifted an eyebrow.

"Contempt," Acrimus replied.

"Ah," Calhoun nodded.

~

"What do you mean, you missed?" Obediah growled at one of his werewolf assassins over the phone. "What the hell do I pay you for? I didn't want you to send flowers and a note. I want him dead, and that fucker Winkler, too. I hear you only managed to graze Winkler, and missed Jennings completely."

"They left Dallas," Obediah could smell the wince as his assassin told him of that development. "We figure they went to Port Aransas so we flew down, but the house here is empty. We're looking around, though, to make sure Winkler isn't someplace else down here with Jennings. Winkler knows the local Packmaster, and she may be hiding his worthless skin."

"See if you can get information through that channel, then," Obediah snapped. "And call me with better news, next time." Obediah ended the call with a snarl.

"Problems?" Wildrif asked innocently, running a hand along the curved horn of one of Obediah's prized possessions—the stuffed body of a white buffalo.

"They'd better get this done," Obediah said. "Or I'll take care of them myself."

"I have information you may wish to hear," Wildrif almost smiled.

"What's that?"

"A unicorn shapeshifter has been born," Wildrif announced.

"Well, ain't that a kick to the head," Obediah was suddenly in a better mood. "How long do you reckon we ought to wait to get our hands on that?"

"Maybe fifteen or sixteen years. Never hurts to plan ahead, does it?" Wildrif asked.

"Not at all," Obediah agreed.

Breanne's Journal

Tybus blinked dark eyes open. I marveled that he looked exactly like Gavril.

Don't speak, I sent to him. *We will take you out of here*, I added. *Don't worry that you can't see us, we're mist*, I explained.

He nodded, then tapped the cuffs on his wrists.

We'll take care of that, I said. *Are you ready?*

He nodded again. Ashe drew him inside his mist, being careful to lower the cuffs to the stone floor and leave them behind. Did we know that would set off the alarm? We did now.

"Do you have the list?" Jimmy asked.

"Right here," Trina pulled it out of her purse and waved it at Jimmy. He grinned at her. He liked Trina—a lot. He'd even convinced her to get in bed with him the night before, and neither had been disappointed.

"Don't grin at me now, we have stuff to buy," Trina smiled back.

"You are gorgeous, you know that?" Jimmy leaned in to whisper as they walked down an aisle in the only grocery store Port Aransas had.

"You know, maybe you ought to say that again. I'm not sure I heard you right the first time," Trina said.

"That you're gorgeous? That you give me a rock-hard," Trina slapped a hand over Jimmy's mouth.

"Someday maybe I'll learn," she said, taking her hand away.

"Wait till I get you in the car," Jimmy laughed. Trina leaned in suddenly for a kiss. A shot rang out. Jimmy stared as blood sprayed against his temple and Trina fell. After that, the werewolf took over and death became his mission.

"Mr. Jennings, I had no idea this would end up being connected to your department," the local sheriff pushed a paper toward Bill. Bill signed it and nodded brusquely. "I got no problem letting him go—I just wanted to get him calmed down enough to allow him out. I hear he took out the shooter with his bare hands. We got the other one in a cell back there, and you can question him whenever you're ready."

"Thank you," Bill said. "I'll come back later tonight, and bring one of my agents with me. We'll get the truth, one way or another."

"Good. I'd like to close this case quick."

"Where's Trina's body?"

"County picked her up half an hour ago. I can take you to the crime scene if you want."

"I don't think I'll find anything more than you did. Our answers are with that prick in your jail cell."

"I think you're right."

"Calhoun, we have problems," Wildrif left a message on Calhoun's cellphone. "Obediah's assassins got caught. One's dead—he's not the problem. The other is in jail in Corpus Christi, and I think they're waiting for nightfall so a vamp can question him. We don't need this to come back on Obediah. At least not yet." Wildrif ended the voicemail with a sigh.

"What the fucking hell did they think they were doing, trying to take down Jimmy Tyler?" Obediah growled. "Instead, they shoot a woman; one of 'em ends up dead and the other's in jail, ready to spill his guts."

"I have a message out to someone who might help," Wildrif ventured. Obediah's temper couldn't be calculated, especially if the evidence was stacking up against him. He didn't want the Feds or the Grand Master sniffing around his compound, and he sure as hell didn't want to spend the rest of his life in a jail somewhere.

"Good. You handle it. Meanwhile, I'm heading to Juarez. I haven't seen my oldest brother in a while." Obediah lifted his hat off the white buffalo's head and slapped it on. "Don't call unless you have good news." Obediah stalked from his study.

Breanne's Journal

The hole Ashe blew in the shield so we could escape was a lot larger than the one he'd created in the beginning. We had to get the hell away, because we had no idea whether we'd be able to take down what had been inside that castle.

All I'd known was that it pulsed with a violet light. Maybe the others couldn't see it, but I figured Ashe and I both did. It scared me. A lot.

Ashe folded space the moment we breached the shield, yet I still held my mental breath. Would they be able to track us? I sure hoped not. There wasn't any way I wanted whatever was behind us to follow. And, if we managed to get away, they'd relocate, just so we couldn't find them again. Our priority, however, was getting away now with our precious cargo intact.

I shouldn't have been concerned. Ashe jumped from here to there and then back again, as if he were intent on losing any tail. Eventually I was dizzy with all the location hops, and that's when he took us back to Lissa's palace.

Graegar was the one to settle Tybus on his feet while Ashe stood in a corner, breathing hard. *We need water or juice or both*, I sent to anyone listening.

"Breanne?" Lissa arrived, Cheedas in tow. Cheedas held a tall glass of water in one hand, and orange juice in the other.

"Ashe needs that," I snapped at Cheedas. His eyes seemed dead as he blinked at me. What was I supposed to do with that? What? I was glad when Cheedas walked toward Ashe and handed the water to him first.

"Bree, what am I going to do?" Lissa's face crumpled. Well, this wasn't going to be easy for me. I did it anyway. I opened my arms. Lissa came to me. I sent her *Love*, just as I'd done for Tybus, and let her cry on my shoulder.

~

"Come," Conner motioned for Tybus to follow her. He was dressed in rags, covered in filth and had been starved for many years. Nevertheless, he followed Conner into an adjoining bedroom.

"You're Gavril Tybus Montegue, from now on," she informed him. "But you'll be known to most as Teeg San Gerxon." Tybus stared at the body on the bed, surrounded by tall, blue men. He recognized them with Gavril's memories. "Larentii," he said, his voice rough.

"Yes. You have all of Gavril's memories now, as well as your own. You know that, don't you?"

"Yes. Some of them I dislike greatly, however."

"I understand that. This is your chance to make him a better man," Conner said. "Treat his mother with respect. She's losing her child," Conner whispered.

Tybus watched as the woman who'd birthed Gavril walked into the room, supported by another, dark-haired woman. Lissa's eyes turned to him and she sobbed.

"Lissa, it'll be all right," the other woman soothed. "He's still here. Really. All of him is inside Tybus. I saw it. I read him."

"But," Lissa wept.

"I know," the dark-haired one said. "Someone said once that what we lose, we will find again. I hope that means something to you, someday."

"Lissa, it is time to say good-bye to the body on the bed," a Larentii spoke.

"Yes. Oh, God, where is Gavin?"

"I am here, cara." A vampire rushed inside. Glancing briefly at Tybus, Gavin went to Lissa's side.

"We will release the stasis when you say," the Larentii said.

Tybus watched as Lissa and Gavin knelt beside the bed and put their hands on their son.

~

Breanne's Journal

It didn't matter at that moment how Teeg had treated me. Lissa and Gavin had loved him, and now they had to let him go. Lissa wept openly, her face pressed against the covers. Gavin, his face rigid with pain, stared at his son. I felt numb.

"Do it again," Conner whispered next to me. "Send *Love* to both of them. They need it." I nodded and steeled myself before sending *Love* to my sire for the first time, and to my sister for the second.

Gavin dropped his head in his hands and wept at that moment. People react differently, I suppose, and I had no idea when Gavin had last released his sorrow by weeping. Lissa, tears still streaming down her face, lifted her gaze to Gavril's face.

"I love you so much, honey," she sobbed. "I remember when Karzac handed you to me when you were born. You were so tiny, and we were so proud."

"My child," Gavin sobbed and gripped Gavril's hand in his. I wept for him at that moment. For the time he'd missed with his son because of Kifirin's interference. For the hard man that Gavril had become, because of other interference. He'd been star-crossed, almost from the beginning, and his parents grieved for him now.

"Breanne?" Corent touched my hand.

"Corent?" I turned to him, only then realizing I was crying.

"Don't be afraid to weep," he said. I sobbed against his chest.

Tybus' Journal

I was led away by one of the Larentii—Gavril knew him as Renegar. "Come," he'd said, and pulled me gently from the room. I was given a bottle of something a servant called blood substitute. I drank it all and asked for another. It was provided quickly.

Then I was led to a bedchamber, and shown to a bath. "Clothes will be waiting when you come out," Renegar explained. I washed myself—several times—after I was left alone. I pondered, too, what my role might be in the future. If the dark-haired woman—her name was Breanne, I'd learned—hadn't done what she had for me, I might have been a fragmented wreck. As it was, I now felt something I hadn't felt in a very long time—*hope.*

Reah's Journal

I wasn't sure what to do. What to feel, even. Teeg had continued to pull farther away from me, and I'd allowed it. I hadn't gone looking for a reason, and now I learned that there was one. Oh, he'd been different, but that was to be expected. What none of us had realized was that he'd slowly been disappearing before our eyes, his soul sucked away by a prisoner from the past.

"Reah, you are not expected to," Aurelius began.

"We will talk with him. We will work this out," I said. "Even if we disagree, I won't dissolve the marriage. At least not right away. Auri, what are we going to tell Garwin Wyatt?"

"Let us wait on that," Aurelius pulled me against him. "Let us see how things proceed. Lissa, too, must be consulted. After all, this one will be forced to step into Gavril's shoes and run an Alliance. Any indication that things have changed may destroy a delicate balance."

"I know," I whispered. "Auri, what are we going to do? All those people saw Teeg get stabbed in a casino. The guards killed the assassin, but they know it happened. It's all over the news."

"Then there will be a recovery," Aurelius sounded determined. I nodded and huddled against him.

~

Breanne's Journal

"Breanne, I see nothing," Corent announced. I'd explained what happened whenever someone touched my tears, but they didn't appear to affect Corent at all. I blinked at him in surprise. He'd stared at everybody inside Lissa's kitchen, and couldn't read them.

"Let me read you again, then, and see if I can figure this out," I said, lowering my shield. Drawing in a breath, I stared. I couldn't read Corent, now. Yes, I could read everybody else in the kitchen so I quickly slammed the shield up again, but I was still confused.

"What happened?" Corent leaned in to kiss me gently.

"Honey, I can't read you now," I whispered.

"That's not a bad thing," Corent replied softly. "Is it?"

"I sure hope not," I said. Corent's hair turned a serene, royal blue as he kissed me again.

~

Lissa's Journal

Renegar released the particles of my son's body. I grieved over that as well, but there wasn't anything else we could do. Tybus would have to take his place, or the Campiaan Alliance would crumble. I just hoped a damaged former architect had enough strength to do what needed to be done.

Dee had to be contacted, too, as well as thousands of news outlets, thirsty for a story. The Campiaan Alliance was holding its breath, and we needed to present a living, breathing replica of my son to them or things would go bad in a hurry.

Gavin had disappeared once Gavril's body was gone, and I had no idea where he was. It didn't matter—I had to dry my tears and keep my back straight to get through the next few hours.

"Rigo?" I said. He, Drake and Drew had been beside me ever since I'd left the bedroom.

"Tiessa?"

"We need to get to Campiaa. Go get Tybus, and tell him everything he needs to know for a short news conference. We'll put him in a hospital bed in Campiaa City, and he can do it from there. At least it's night in Campiaa City. After the conference, I'll give Tybus blood and let him sleep it off."

"I will do this for you," Rigo nodded. If anybody knew etiquette and protocol, Rigo did. If Tybus had any kind of memory, Rigo would see this done right.

"We'll do transport," Drake offered.

"Thanks, honey," I said.

Breanne's Journal

Corent stayed with me, and we watched the newsfeed as Tybus, looking like someone who'd been through an ordeal (although not the one everybody thought) gave a short interview from a hospital bed in Campiaa City.

"I just wanted to take a walk," Tybus said, smiling slightly. "It was interrupted."

The journalist laughed before asking how long he might be away from his office.

"Not long," Tybus claimed. "The physicians tell me the wound wasn't deep, so I may be up and around in an eight-day. I can work from my bed, too, so that's not a concern. The appointments are the only things that will have to be rescheduled."

"Well, that's my cue," I rose and stretched.

"Are you going?" Corent rose with me, looking as if he were prepared to beg me to stay.

"I have to. Some things might turn out badly if I don't." I didn't add that if Hank, Bill, Jayson and Gavin found out I'd been missing, there would be hell to pay. Something was making my skin crawl, too, and I hadn't figured that out, yet.

"Breanne, you should go back six hours after you left." Wisdom appeared in front of me. "I realize you did what needed to be done here, but things haven't gone well in your absence," he added. "You can't change any of it, so don't try."

I stared at him in shock—I know I did. "What?" I began.

"Go back, like I said. The news will be waiting. I hope they are not too harsh with you."

"Harsh?" I was shaking, now.

"Breanne," Wisdom shook his head. "You know you cannot tell them where you have been or what you have done."

"You know, you may be smart and all," I gave him my best Texas accent, "But so far, your ass has been kind of useless." I bent time to get away from him.

~

"Breanne can fix Kay. I'm convinced of it, now," Ashe settled on a barstool next to Trajan.

"You saw Breanne?" Trajan growled.

"Yeah. We, ah, did something that needed to be done. She fixed what I thought would be unfixable. We have to get her here, Traje. For Kay."

"I don't count?" Trajan tapped his chest and stood, his body stiff with anger.

"I didn't say that," Ashe sighed. "We'll get her here for you and for Kay."

~

Breanne's Journal

I did as Wisdom dictated, and got back six hours after I left. I knew it when I landed. Kathleen was shut up in her room, Bill was handling the case and the rest of them were grieving and pissed at the same time. Trina was dead, and there wasn't a damn thing I could do about it.

CHAPTER 15

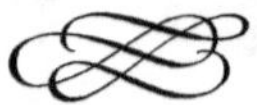

*B*reanne's *Journal*

Did I feel guilty? Yeah. Not only did I feel guilty, I *was* guilty. If I'd been here instead of haring after Tybus, then Trina might still be alive. I couldn't bring her back now—the memory of what had happened the last time I *Changed What Was* still burned in my brain. Wisdom had known it too—somehow.

Nobody was speaking to me, that was certain. Night would fall in two hours, and I was waiting for the sire to wake and the surrogate sire to arrive so Hank and Jayson could tell them what a bad girl I'd been. And Trina was still dead.

"Where were you?" Opal settled beside me as I sat morosely on a deck chair, staring at the water behind the house.

"Opal, I can't explain that right now. All I can say is that I needed to be where I was. I needed to be here, too, but I can't be in two places at once."

"I sure hope the other thing was important."

How could I tell her that I'd had to sacrifice one life for millions of others? The Campiaan Alliance wouldn't survive without Teeg—or at least the image of Teeg—at the helm. Trina had been an innocent victim of violence, and I intended to find out why that was. I knew

Bill wanted to take Gavin with him after nightfall to question the remaining prisoner. Well, I was going now. "Want to go with me while I question that asshole?" I asked.

"Yeah." Opal pulled a gun from the waistband of her jeans and checked the clip. "I'm ready."

"Good. Be ready for them to not speak to you, too, when we get back."

"I got this," Opal shoved the gun into the back of her waistband.

"You know, that gun might become an option," I said and folded Opal away.

"Hello, asshole," I said the moment we landed in Jeremy Brill's cell. I read him, too. It's a good thing I did—prescience kicked in and I turned Opal to mist as another chimera appeared, burning Jeremy to a crisp before devouring the body in three gulps.

"Bill, we didn't stick around after the chimera disappeared again," Opal said. "It happened so fast, and Bree was afraid I'd die. Otherwise, I think she would have taken that thing on." I watched as Bill and Opal had a staring and growling contest. Bill was pissed (even more than he was earlier) because we hadn't taken him with us.

Hank, Jayson, Winkler, Weldon and Trajan were happy enough just being pissed and settled for glaring at me from time to time while they listened. Did they think I didn't feel bad enough as it was?

"They were looking for you, Bill," I said. Bill jerked his head around at my admission. "I read Jeremy Brill before he was cooked and served for dinner," I added.

"Jeremy Brill. Werewolf rogue," Weldon growled low.

"Working for Obediah Tanner," I said. Well, somebody didn't want that cat out of the bag—that was easy enough to see. Too bad the chimera got there after I did. "They wanted Winkler, too, because they were offered a bonus for him," I said. "But the other one, James Brill, Jeremy's brother, saw Jimmy and started shooting. Trina was in the way."

"We couldn't get Jimmy to talk after he came home," Winkler sighed. "James Brill always had it in for Jimmy."

"So he had a feud with your cook and decided to end it in a grocery store," Bill tossed up a hand. "Instead, Trina dies and the second shooter gets cooked. I already heard from the sheriff—he says the cameras didn't record anything and they don't know how Jeremy escaped."

"What's worse is we have another chimera to deal with," Weldon pointed out.

"I didn't know they could fold space," I said.

"They can't. Somebody else got that thing in and out," Hank said, snorting a curl of smoke. Yeah, he was really pissed. "You could have exposed yourself, Breanne," he said. More smoke ensued.

"And we'd be left wondering what the hell was going on," Opal snapped at Hank. "Bree was smart to go when she did. The rest of you," she flung out a hand. "I have no words."

"Look, we need to talk to Bree for a minute. Hank, Jayson and I," Bill said, dismissing everybody else. Well, here it came. Time to pay the piper.

"I'm staying." Trajan crossed arms over his chest and dared anybody to remove him. Bill had chosen the media room to do his grilling, and I watched as Opal shot him a dark look before leaving with Winkler and Weldon.

"Now," Bill said, rounding on me, "I don't know where you went, but you didn't tell us. I don't care how important it was, you could have sent mindspeech." He was right—I could have. They'd have argued, too, and that would have taken time I didn't have.

"I made a choice, instead of taking time to fight with all of you about it," I said. "You have no idea how tiring that is."

"Here's what we decided," Hank began. Well, they'd decided. *Yay.*

"You can take five swats from each of us, on your bare behind, or we won't have anything to do with you for a week. Your choice."

Hank's eyes were completely dark, and more smoke poured from his nostrils. Well, that was lovely. They wanted to hit me or hurt me another way.

"Fuck all of you," I snapped. "You have no idea that this day has been crap, from one end to the other, and all you want to do is punish me for it. Fuck you, and in the worst and most painful way possible." I was wiping tears away as I stalked out of the room.

"That went well," Trajan drawled.

"Trina died. What the fuck do you expect?" Jayson hissed.

"You don't think Breanne would have saved her if she could? I don't think you know her very well. I've been watching her for three days, and that's not how she is."

"She didn't tell us she was leaving," Bill pointed out. "I want to stop that behavior, if possible. Do you have any idea what that does to us?" Bill indicated Hank, Jayson and himself.

"I'm beginning to understand," Trajan said. "But sometimes, you need to pick your battles. Breanne is right—you don't know where she was or what she was doing. I'll wait until I have more information before I threaten her with punishment."

"I am incensed," Acrimus declared. Calhoun cringed—Acrimus was grimacing again. "Our prisoner has disappeared. We are forced to relocate and our assassin failed to destroy Teeg San Gerxon."

"We followed, but the twists and turns through time and space," the Hound whined as he knelt before Acrimus.

"It was one of the Three," Acrimus waved the hound away. "I don't expect you to keep up with them. It was a noble effort. You may go." The Hound rose gratefully and turned to walk from Acrimus' presence. Acrimus leveled a blast at the Hound's back, relieving him of his corporeal body. "Do better next time," he shouted.

Breanne's Journal

Close to midnight, there was a knock on my door. Hank had moved his things out of the bedroom earlier—he'd known which choice I'd make. The trouble was, the fact that they'd offered swats was just as bad as handing them out.

"Breanne?" Charles's voice came through the door. Well, another country heard from.

"Come in," I said. No, Gavin hadn't weighed in, yet, and that worried me. I wanted to huddle into myself and wish the world away. One Gavin I'd seen today had been grieving. The one here refused to speak to me, now. And Charles was here. Joy.

"Breanne, I heard you disappeared for a few hours earlier," Charles walked in, shut the door behind him and came to sit on the side of my bed.

"I did." There wasn't any reason to lie.

"Was there a good reason?"

"Yes."

"I understand that your friend was killed while you were gone."

"She was." I'd spent the past three hours mourning that fact.

"Want to talk about that?"

"No."

"Have you been crying?"

"Yes."

"Here." Charles scooted closer and reached for me. "Now," he pulled me against him and settled my head on his shoulder, "This wasn't your fault. A criminal killed your friend. We will mourn her passing and keep her memory strong. Close your eyes. You look exhausted, my love."

I woke Saturday morning and realized I was expected to ferry Bill to D.C. Except that I didn't—they were keeping their word and not having anything to do with me. Hank was going to take Bill instead. Well, he could damn well skip to hell with the rest of them, too.

Charles had disappeared sometime during the night, but he'd left me comfortable and covered up in bed before he left. He was right—I had been exhausted. I wandered toward the kitchen, knowing that Trina would never be there, waiting for any of us again. Forcing more tears back, I went looking for something to eat. Nobody had pointed it out, but I hadn't eaten anything the day before, and my body wasn't reacting well to that fact.

Bill didn't say anything when he walked in—he merely went to the coffeepot and poured a cup of coffee. Winkler, Weldon and Trajan were out on the deck having their coffee, and as I didn't want to disturb them by walking away from Bill, I stayed where I was and kept eating my bowl of cereal.

Bill fixed eggs and bacon for a small army (I sure wasn't about to offer) and ate in silence. Kathleen shuffled in. He served her, then took his seat again. Hank and Jayson arrived, and I could tell they'd been beating on one another in the exercise room. They put plates together and sat down to eat.

My bowl went into the dishwasher; I found a notepad hanging on the refrigerator door, found a pen in a drawer, wrote out a note, slapped it in front of Bill and disappeared.

"Where the fuck did she go?" Jayson snarled, coming off his seat.

"Grocery shopping," Hank held up the note.

"Fuck," Bill grumbled.

"We told her she had to tell us. We didn't tell her we had to approve it," Hank sighed.

"You think she went to that store in Port A?" Bill asked.

"Probably not. She's pissed enough to go to China," Hank moaned. "And since she can speak the language, we'll probably have squid in the fridge when she gets back."

~

Breanne's Journal

I'd had to mist to my house in San Rafael and dig through my sock drawer for the cash I kept there, but I had money. No, I'd never asked Bill for the numbers to the accounts he'd set up, and I sure wasn't going to ask him now. I had several thousand dollars in my pockets, and I could buy wherever I wanted. I went shopping in France, because I hadn't had good cheese in a while.

I bought enough fruit for an army, too, along with vegetables, canned goods, prosciutto, all cuts of meat for the carnivores, cookies, bread, and anything else I thought we might need. I'd had to stop at a bank to get Euro, but everything was easy after that.

Thankfully, I was able to get help carrying bags out of the market, then placed compulsion before gathering everything in my mist and folding back to Texas. Yes, I'd bent time, so only ten minutes had passed for those still eating at the kitchen island. I busied myself, putting everything away.

"All of this is in French," Opal observed. She'd walked in halfway through my restocking episode and started reading labels.

"I went to Paris," I informed her.

"No squid," Jayson high-fived Hank. I had no idea why.

"Have a seat, I'll make an omelette for you," I told Opal.

"If you'll eat half," Opal offered.

"Sure." I made an omelette, put prosciutto in Opal's half and served it up a few minutes later.

"This is really good," Opal said around a mouthful.

"Prosciutto. I understand it's really good. I've never had any," I said, cutting into my veggie half of the meal. "It's Italian, but the market I went to seemed liberal enough."

"Cheese in this is awesome," Opal sipped her coffee.

"Yeah. I like French cheeses. Swiss cheese. Some Irish cheese. Stilton. Gruyere, if it's made with vegetable rennet. All of that with fruit. And crackers."

"Are you sure you're getting enough protein?" Kathleen asked.

"I got some protein drinks and bars," I said. "I'm not fond of them, but they serve their purpose. I didn't get to eat yesterday, so I'm hungry today."

Hank cleared his throat but didn't say anything. *Score.*

"How about some milk with that omelette, then?" Charles walked in, making my eyes almost pop from my head.

"What the hell?" I stared at him.

"I learned from Hank, there, that your blood may have interesting properties," Charles grinned. "I woke the day after I took from you, and didn't fry when I peeked outside. Two days later, I went to London during the day and ate two baskets of fish and chips at a pub. You have no idea how good it tasted."

"You've been talking to Hank?" I frowned at Charles.

"I got tired of listening to Gavin's phone ring so I answered," Hank shrugged.

"Oh, we're talking now?" I stared at him.

"I'm talking to Charles," Hank said.

"Go on," Charles nodded.

"Anyway, you asked me what the hell was going on with Breanne, so I told you."

"Oh, like Wlodek won't get his underwear in a knot if he finds out," I snapped.

"Wlodek won't ever know unless you tell him," Charles soothed. "He never asks me questions like that. I'm completely safe with the information."

"I don't believe this," I slapped a hand over my eyes. "All I need is for every vampire on Earth to think I ought to be killed."

"They'll have to kill me, too," Charles declared. "Because I'll stand beside you."

"Honey, that's sweet, but there's no way I'll let you do that." I went to the fridge to get eggs and prosciutto to make an omelette for him. He got his food fifteen minutes later.

"This is so good," Charles sighed after eating half the omelette in record time. "I didn't remember what real food tasted like before."

"Charles, please pace yourself. I don't want you to get a stomach ache," I said.

"Come here, sweetheart," Charles motioned me toward him. I went. "Here," he leaned in to kiss me. "That's for this, and making it so I can eat it," he grinned.

"What are we going to do about Trina's funeral?" Jayson asked.

"I've already sent her family a note, offering to pay," Kathleen said. "They said they'd let me know when the service will be held."

"This is all so wrong, it reeks," I muttered, stuffing dirty dishes in the dishwasher. I started cursing in French, then moved to Italian. Went to German after that, and then Russian. I ended up with the High Demon language, which made Hank raise his eyebrows in alarm. "Stupid, fucking difiks," I ended my diatribe and slammed the dishwasher door shut.

"All right, I call a truce," Bill muttered. "I can't handle this, sweetheart. Not talking to you when you're right in front of me. Refusing to comfort you, when I know you're upset. Telling you how grateful I am that you care about me at all."

"Bill, I love you. I don't care who knows it. Anybody who sees something wrong with that can kiss my posterior. Charles, I'm sorry you walked into the middle of all this. Has Hank given you the multiple mate speech? Because he seems really good at doing that behind my back. Jayson, on the other hand, just wants to hit me."

"Hey," Jayson protested.

"It's like this—if both parties want it, it's all fine and hunky-dory. If one doesn't want it, it's abuse. Right?" I stalked out of the kitchen, leaving them behind to discuss my snit.

"Yesterday was a test," Hank sat heavily beside me. I'd chosen a covered swing on the deck and tucked my legs under me to continue staring at the gulf.

"Some women seem to like the spanking," he said. "If you offer it often enough, and they learn they're really not getting hurt. Usually the swats are filled with a whole lot of fondling in between. Maybe some kissing, too."

"Sure." I refused to look at him.

"Look, we were mad. And upset. Still are, actually. Bree, why should we expect you to do something about Trina? None of us are helpless. We should have gone to the store with her and Jimmy. We didn't. We weren't doing our job, yesterday, and since you left us behind, we grabbed a convenient scapegoat when you got back."

"And nobody won," I muttered.

"Yeah. Nobody won. You're right about that."

"Is Charles recovering after the multiple mate thing was served up with breakfast?" I asked.

"He was completely cool with that when I told him three days ago."

"No surprise," I said.

"Bill wants you to come with us to D.C."

"Fine."

"You need to get cleaned up and dress nicer," Hank said.

"I'll go do that right now." I let my feet fall to the deck.

"Breanne?" Hank's hand brushed mine as I stood.

"What?" I didn't turn to look at him.

"I love you. I've never loved anyone so much."

"You have a strange way of showing it at times," I said and walked away from him.

"I've never been here," Charles grinned. Well, he was in D.C. now. And not only was he in D.C., he was sitting in a room just outside a meeting with Bill, the President and the Joint Chiefs. Hank, Jayson and Opal were with us, too, and all three were armed to the eyebrows.

Charles and I were armed to the fangs, I guess, with claws and enhanced strength. The Secret Service guys were in the room with the President, and they were loaded for whatever might come their way, too.

"How long will this take?" Jayson asked Opal.

"They could be in there for hours, it just depends," she shrugged.

"Aren't you tired?" I asked Charles.

"Nah. I'll sleep better tonight," he grinned. Charles smiled more than any vampire I'd ever met.

"Bill may want dinner afterward," Opal said. "A couple of restaurants he likes are nearby. He may want to drop by his house, too."

"I can do that," I said. I could take Bill anywhere he wanted to go, even if it was off-planet. Jeez, why hadn't I thought of that sooner? I could have taken Trina and Kathleen to Le-Ath Veronis. Nobody would bother them at the palace, as long as Lissa was there.

It was too late for that—at least for Trina. I wanted to cry again, and couldn't. That took me back to Corent, and why he hadn't been affected by my tears. It made absolutely no sense at all. I also wondered about Tybus, and how he was getting along. He wouldn't have a moment to himself, to attempt a recovery after what he'd been through. With a sigh, I sent *Love* to him again.

Lissa's Journal

"How are you feeling?" I asked. It was so hard for me to see his face —he looked exactly like Gavril. I'd had Drake and Drew check, and somehow, my sister had even changed his fingerprints to match my son's.

My son was dead. I had to keep reminding myself. And there could be no funeral or public mourning for his passing. Reah had come the night before—after I'd given Tybus my blood—and we'd had a long talk.

There was no need to let anyone think Tybus was anything other than Teeg San Gerxon, she'd said. She was waiting, too, to speak with him and offer to keep up appearances. The problem, however, would be Garwin Wyatt. Granted he was at school, but what would happen when he came home in two months for his holiday?

"I feel good. Very good." Tybus blinked dark eyes at me. "I received another infusion of whatever it was that Breanne provided yesterday. I can't begin to explain how healing and invigorating that is."

"I think you're one of the few who's gotten that from her," I said. Honestly, she probably didn't realize how much that simple act might accomplish. She'd done it for me, too, and for Gavin. Somehow, it made Gavril's death easier for us to bear.

"Are you ready to move to San Gerxon Palace?" I asked. "Dee will be here shortly, with all four warlocks. How strong are my son's memories?"

"Very strong. I recognize those he knew easily. I believe what love he had left in him was reserved for his son, and I feel that residual emotion."

"Thank goodness," I muttered. "Look, I checked earlier, and whether you were before, you're a King Vampire now."

"I was before," he inclined his head.

"You also have misting ability," I said. "Plus mindspeech."

"That will be most helpful," he said. "Thank you."

"Don't thank me. Breanne did that for you. All you needed was my blood, and I think she knew that in some way. You have my blood now. Just as Gavril had it before." I wiped tears from my face before folding away.

Breanne's Journal

The meeting lasted more than four hours and darkness was falling outside. Charles had already left a message for Gavin, telling him he was with us. Obviously, he'd told Gavin he could now walk in daylight.

That concerned me. Wlodek might learn of this, and I didn't want to guess what his reaction might be. Worse, vampires who learned of my "special blood," might line up to get it, and let's face it—humans needed daylight to put distance between themselves and a lot of vamps.

Regardless, I sort of liked my blood where it was—inside my body.

The thought of a strange vampire sucking on my neck terrified me in ways I couldn't begin to describe.

"Sweetheart, you just went pale." Bill's arm folded me against him for a tight hug. We sat in a round booth in a corner of one of his favorite twenty-four-hour restaurants. We'd been served drinks and waited for our meals to arrive. I'd been lost in thought once I ordered and the others talked.

"Yeah." I leaned my head on his shoulder.

What's wrong with my girl? Shockingly enough, that came from Jayson. Sure, he'd been introduced to the President earlier as Matt Michaels, Bill's newest agent, but to me he would always be Jayson Rome, occasional asshat. Yeah, he knew how to deliver on what he considered vanilla sex, but I could never deliver on what he really liked.

I know what you're thinking, and you need to stop, Jayson informed me. *Hell, not all subs are alike, either. Some want to be beaten. Others want light taps. I understand now that you don't need any of that. Bree, most of what I do I do because they beg for it. You saw that fucking video. That's what Belinda likes. If you came over and asked me to kiss your ass again, I'd do it. Although I'll admit I like the begging. A lot.*

His last statement came through with a cheeky, mental grin. I knew he was teasing me. I also felt he was doing his best not to grieve in public for Trina. I felt we were all trying to do the same.

"Bill, are we going to Trina's funeral?" I asked.

"Sweetheart, someone may be looking to trap us there. They know she was Jayson's employee, and the notice has already been put in the newspapers and has been reported on a couple of news stations. I managed to get the place of death listed as Dallas since that's where her family thought she was, but that's the best I could do."

"This sucks so bad," I sighed before lifting my head. Well, was I who I was or what? I already knew somebody who could help.

"Bill, do you have to be anywhere for the next two hours?" I asked.

"No, sweetheart."

"Good. There's a place I want to go after dinner."

"Anywhere you want."

"Great. Remember you said that," I said.

"Breanne left nothing to chance, as I understand it," Dee sighed. "You even smell the same."

Tybus nodded at Dee, whose given name was Dormas. "I've only met a few vampires close to my age," Tybus said. He knew by scent that Dee was more than ten thousand years old.

"Your age from before?" Dee queried.

"Yes. I suppose I must refrain from thinking in those terms."

"Definitely. You were from the Le-Ath Veronis of old, before the fall?" Dee was aware of the history—he'd heard it from Lissa.

"Yes. I was comesula before I was vampire, too, just as all the vampires were from that age. The Queen offered me a place on Kifirin —she felt that the High Demons would accept me when they refused all others, because I'd designed their palace. I wouldn't allow her to ask, and fought by her side at the end."

"Why did you refuse? Were you mated to her?" Dee's dark eyes studied Tybus carefully.

"No. She was my child—my only child, before I was made vampire."

"Would it interest you to know, then, that Lissa is the former Queen—reincarnated?"

Tybus' hands shook suddenly. "Yes," he whispered. "That interests me very much."

Breanne's Journal

"Graegar, thank you for doing this for me." I smiled up at him. Jayson stared (as did Opal) at the tall, blue Larentii Wise One, and at his taller (and bluer) Larentii Protector, Barrigar.

"My mate will be most happy to see you," Graegar smiled back.

"She said you might make a request. I am happy to provide transportation."

"Where are we going?" Bill asked.

"As well you should ask," Graegar replied. "We will pay a visit to your friend—you can say your farewells," he said and ferried us away from Bill's house.

"Hello," Conner said the moment we were settled inside a spacious, private library. A large painting of Conner graced one wall, and it had been beautifully executed.

"This is my mate, Conner," Graegar introduced her. "She is known as the Guardian, and holds a key to the curtain separating this world from the next."

"What?" Jayson mouthed at me.

"We're here to see Trina," I said.

"What?" Jayson repeated. He was the one to turn pale, this time.

"There is nothing to fear," Conner said. "Come."

It felt as if we didn't move, but our surroundings changed and we stood in a beautiful meadow, filled with the brightest and most fragrant roses. "She is coming," Conner's eyes went bright as she spoke.

"Bree," Hank's hands settled on my shoulders as a figure, hazy at first, walked toward us.

"It's Trina," Opal wept.

"There is one more who should be here," Conner said, her eyes going brighter. Jimmy appeared at her side. Conner took his hand to keep him from turning werewolf after he was drawn from one place to another.

"Trina's coming," Bill told Jimmy. "This is our chance to say good-bye." At least Bill grasped our reason for being where we were. Bill Jennings was a very smart man.

"Look who's here," Trina flashed us a smile as the last of the haze dropped away from her and we could see her clearly.

"Trina," Jimmy reached a hand toward her.

"Jimmy, someday we'll be together," Trina said, reaching out to touch his fingers. "I promise. They already told me that. They just said we have to be patient."

"Baby, I'll look forward to that day," Jimmy's voice trembled with emotion. "You don't blame me, do you?" I could see that this worry troubled Jimmy a lot.

"No. Don't ever take the blame for this. Not your fault. Never your fault," Trina said gently. "It won't be long before we're together," she added.

"Jayson?" Trina went on, turning to him.

"Trina?" I thought Jayson was going to lose it as he wiped tears away.

"You were the best boss I ever had," she said.

"Trina, I never thought of you as an employee. I always thought of you as family," Jayson mumbled.

"We are family, Jayson Rome," Trina said. "And don't you forget it."

"I won't," he nodded.

"Opal, you are something, you know that?" Trina turned to her. "I get good friends—the best friends ever—just before I die. That's poor planning on somebody's part," Trina huffed. "Hank, you're included in that," Trina lifted an eyebrow at him. "I don't care how you like to make whoopee; anybody would be glad you had their back. You, too, Bill."

"Thanks, Trina," Bill said.

"Oh, you're welcome, hon. Tell Ms. Rome that I'll be keeping an eye on her now and then," Trina added.

"I will."

"Bree," Trina came to me last. "I wish I'd recognized you from the beginning. Probably a lot of people wish that, too. All I'm allowed to say to you now is, stay alive, and kick some ass for me."

"Trina, I will kick major ass for you. And keep kicking ass until there's none left to kick," I said.

"You do that," she said, determination in her voice. "You know what depends on it."

"Yeah. I know that, all right," I agreed.

"Trina, it is time," Conner's voice echoed.

"Yeah. I get that," Trina said. "Look, thank you. For this," she swept out a hand, encompassing all of us. "Jimmy, I love you. Don't forget," she said and faded away.

"Oh, my God," Jayson sighed and rolled his shoulders. Graegar and Barrigar, who'd remained silent during the exchange, folded us away.

CHAPTER 16

"This seemed like the best place," Torevik Rath stood amid knee-high grasses next to a wide pond on the light half of Le-Ath Veronis.

"Yeah." Rylend Morphis didn't get to dress casually very often, since he'd taken the throne of Karathia. He'd dressed in comfortable jeans and a soft, collarless shirt.

"Is Reah coming?"

"She said yes," Ry shrugged. "The baby may need something before she leaves."

"I'm here," Reah appeared between Tory and Ry.

"Of all of us, Gav was the one I'd think would be least likely," Tory began.

"Tory, don't talk. Let's skip rocks and remember Chash."

"Yeah." Tory knelt to scoop up a handful of stones. "This is for you, bro," he tossed the first rock into the pond.

Breanne's Journal

Gavin seemed perfectly fine with Charles's new state. Apparently they'd already held a lengthy conversation, and the world hadn't ended over it. I had no idea why that was, and still found myself wondering if the Gavin I'd known would ever show up.

I'd leaned against Charles after returning to the beach house in Port Aransas, while he and Gavin talked quietly and the others went to bed. Charles's voice eventually soothed me to sleep—he and Gavin were discussing rogues in South America.

Sunday morning dawned clear and hot, with only a thin line of clouds far to the east, turning the early-morning sunlight pink and red. Insects were already singing in the dunes when I wandered onto the deck with a cup of coffee in my hands.

My dreams had been unsettled the night before, but I couldn't recall any of them when I slipped out of bed. Charles, who'd taken me to bed the night before, had loved me, nipped my neck to intensify the climax and then soothed me whenever I jerked awake throughout the night.

"You're up early," Weldon Harper commented as he chose a deck chair near mine.

"Not a choice. Couldn't sleep," I said, sipping coffee.

"I'm old enough now that the wolf wants up before I do," Weldon grinned. "I don't argue with the wolf, much."

"Probably a wise decision," I smiled into my cup.

"Want to argue with this wolf?" Trajan pulled a deck chair alongside mine and settled his tall frame onto it.

"Why would I want to argue with you? You are kind of awesome," I said.

"Hear that? I'm awesome," Trajan grinned at Weldon over my head. He had perfect, white teeth, just as most werewolves I'd met did.

"Don't let it go to your head," Weldon grunted. "It'll have to climb too far," he added with a snicker.

"Always the height jokes," Trajan growled.

"They have to compete with your awesomeness, Trajan, so of course they'll settle for the least imaginative slights," I said.

"I think I just got insulted," Weldon sipped his coffee. Trajan laughed.

"Why wasn't I invited to this meeting?" Winkler pulled up a chair beside Weldon's. He held a huge cup of coffee in his hand, which meant that somebody might have to make more soon.

"I sent you an email about this meeting," Trajan teased.

"I don't read my email until after I've had coffee," Winkler pointed his cup at Trajan.

"I know that," Trajan said with a grin.

"Hey, stop hogging all the chairs," Trace walked out of the house, holding a cup of steaming coffee.

"I can fix that, bro," Trajan lifted me out of my seat with one arm and settled me onto his lap. "See? All done."

"Seriously?" I blinked into Trajan's dark eyes. He was still as unreadable to me as the day I'd met him in the future.

"Yeah. Seriously." Trajan's mouth curled into a smile as he leaned in and took my lips with his. Well, he wasn't wasting any time, looked like. He was just as attracted now as he was in the future. With a sigh, I slipped my arms around his neck.

"Hey now, I haven't had breakfast yet," Trace chuckled.

"I'm having mine now," Trajan kissed me again.

"Boss, I know where Breanne is. More than that, I know *when* she is," Trajan settled beside Ashe on the back deck of Ashe's huge house. "But my mind goes blank after that," Trajan growled. "Like I can't remember what happens afterward."

"What?" Ashe stared at Trajan in alarm.

"Should I go over these reports with you?" Dee handed a comp-vid to

Tybus. Tybus had settled on the patio surrounding the pool behind San Gerxon Palace, to reflect on the recent events in his life. Sunlight filtered through the trees overhead, and Tybus breathed in the warmth it provided. So many years had passed since he'd been able to withstand sunlight, and now he quietly reveled in it.

"There's no need, I have sufficient memories to get me through, I believe," Tybus replied, shaking off his thoughts and accepting the comp-vid from Dee. He sighed as he entered the passcode.

"You do have the memories. Only Teeg had that passcode," Dee nodded before leaning back in the chair he'd taken beside Tybus.

"I am vampire, just as you are. I recall all that has happened and all that has been given me," Tybus said absently, already scrolling through figures and notes. "I believe we ought to eliminate this chemical—it appears to be affecting the atmosphere," he pointed to the one in question.

"Yes. I agree completely. I'll add this to the agenda for the next conclave."

"Thank you," Tybus said and went to the next page.

~

Breanne's Journal

The day would have been perfect, except the unsettled feeling didn't go away as the day progressed. I even mentioned it to Hank, but he didn't seem to notice anything amiss.

The hours passed and it seemed as if Hank was correct—the unsettled feeling had no foundation. Until it did.

~

Lissa's Journal

"Mom, this is the worst, isn't it?" Nissa twined her fingers together anxiously.

"Yes. I wanted you to know, because your older brothers know. Travis and Trent, well, that can wait until a better time."

"There's something you should know, Mom," Nissa sighed.

"What's that?"

"I heard it from Kyler and Cleo," Nissa sighed. "Everything is so messed up," she added.

"I agree about it being messed up. What did you hear from Kyler and Cleo?"

"That Amara's getting married. To Edan Desh. I hear the Saa Thalarr will offer him blood when they marry."

"Oh, Lord." My fingers shook as I raised them to my forehead. Amara was leaving my father behind—for good. She'd found someone else—a healer, this time. I'd heard she and Edan worked well together, and had a common cause of helping needy children by providing health care at no cost, but Griffin—I had no idea how he might react to this.

"Does Reah know about this?" I asked.

"I don't know. You didn't," Nissa pointed out. "Mom, we can have a memorial service on Grey Planet if you want. Nobody from the outside will ever know."

"I wonder if Griffin will ever know he lost his grandson," I muttered.

"I don't know him at all, so I can't say. Toff just sighs and looks sad whenever his name comes up."

"I understand that," I said. "I feel exactly the same."

Breanne's Journal

When the church exploded in a fireball in Maine, it made the news and everybody in the media was speculating about the cause. Bodies were hauled out, charred beyond recognition after the flames were extinguished.

That was the beginning.

Before the news crews could settle in comfortably, three more churches exploded in New York, New Hampshire and Vermont. With people beginning to reel from those reports, another ten blew up in other states. Bill got notification after the ten blew up, and then, before word could get out across the nation to evacuate churches everywhere, a church exploded in every remaining state, simultaneously. That included Alaska and Hawaii.

The news outlets were almost numb from too many disasters to report on completely. Estimates of the dead nationwide blew out of proportion. I watched in horror, my hands clutched by Hank and Charles, as we watched the reports on television. In every case, no evidence could be located as to the cause of the explosions and ensuing conflagrations. There were no survivors. Anywhere. I *Looked* for the cause, and just like many other things, it was blocked. The Sirenali had a hand in this, there was no doubt. Or an obsession, at least.

Bill had been on the phone almost constantly after the first call, and then on his laptop and Winkler's laptop, too.

"Bree," Bill came to me an hour later, looking disheveled and in shock, "Can you get me to D.C.? The President wants a meeting."

"Yeah," I rose from my spot between Hank and Charles.

"I will come." Gavin had sat silently nearby, as had Jayson, Opal and the werewolves. Hank had given Kathleen a sedative earlier; she was weeping after scenes of the carnage were televised.

"We're not getting left behind," Weldon and Winkler rose from their chairs.

"We need somebody to stay with Kathleen," Bill sighed.

"I'll stay," Jimmy said. "I'll keep her safe."

"Good," Winkler nodded to his cook. "Everybody else, let's ride with Bill."

Surprisingly enough, we were allowed into the meeting this time. I think the President wanted as many opinions as possible, and he trusted Bill's judgment on who to bring in. Bill pulled all of us in.

"We have a theory," Bill said when the President came to him after talking to the FBI Director, the CIA Director and a few generals and admirals.

"Let's hear it," the President sighed.

"You'll think it's outrageous at first, but hear us out," Bill said.

"All right, tell us."

"Bree?" Bill turned to me. I swallowed hard.

"I'm having trouble with this," Dan Kelsey, the FBI Director, said as a three-dimensional image of a Sirenali hovered over the center of the meeting table.

"I'm not sure this is all that's responsible, either," Bill said. "It's just that Breanne can't seem to see past these obsessions to get to the underlying causes or find any other participants."

"You're telling me that any one of us could fall victim to one of these things?" A general from South Carolina said, his Southern accent drawing out his words.

"Yes. But there isn't anyone inside this room that has been victimized," I said.

"How the hell can she tell that?" the general turned to the admiral on his left.

"It's a special talent, and shouldn't be taken lightly," Bill said. Poor Bill—this could cost him his job if nobody supported him in this.

"Frankly, anybody who can put up three-dimensional images and tell me what I had for lunch today gets my vote," another general remarked. "That's beside the fact that she survived what should have killed her years ago."

Yeah, they all knew who I was. Recognized me immediately, in fact. I was waiting for the meeting to be over so I could hyperventilate in a seemingly proper fashion somewhere else.

"How do we track this thing?" someone else asked.

"That's the trouble—it's difficult without some kind of information to go on," I said. "The last time I killed one, I just happened across her —almost by accident."

"We're fucked," Dan Kelsey slapped a hand on the table.

~

"There has to be at least twenty or thirty chimeras," Hank and Jayson had worked out the logistics with Bill after the meeting adjourned. Nobody had a clear picture as to what to do—all they could say was that everybody needed to stay away from church. Well, that wouldn't sit well with a bunch of people, for obvious reasons.

The President asked to schedule another meeting the following day, but without new evidence, I didn't see that it would do any good at all.

"Bree," Bill sighed, "If we go to some of those churches tomorrow morning, can you, Charles and Hank sniff around with the wolves?"

"I'll go," I nodded. "I just don't want to be photographed or recorded."

"I'll make sure you're not," he nodded. "I figure at this point the conspiracy crazies are in with your Sirenali, and they're all going nuts."

"Why would they hit churches? I thought the conspiracy crazies were all conservative or fundamental," I blinked at Bill without finishing my question. "Never mind. With a Sirenali involved, that's a really stupid question."

~

"You can't let this destroy your good sense," Wylend cautioned. "Brenten, you have no jealousy, remember?"

"She is doing this to hurt me," Griffin muttered angrily. "Like I hurt her."

"You're saying she doesn't love him? That this is revenge?" Wylend sounded skeptical. "That doesn't sound like the Amara I know."

"Our child died, Wylend, because I refused to see what was in front of me. Why wouldn't she want revenge for that?"

"Griffin?" Renegar appeared in Griffin's kitchen.

"Ren?" Griffin studied the Larentii Nameless One, his gaze troubled.

"I have received a message. You must travel with me to Avendor. Someone there has a confession to make."

"What the hell?" Griffin rose from his seat.

"I wish to come," Wylend stood.

"Then come," Renegar said sternly and folded Wylend and Griffin away.

~

The Shining One known as The Ear stood nearby, watching Thurlow carefully. This involved Thurlow's previous existence as Thorsten, and Thurlow was ashamed. Nevertheless, he'd been commanded to reveal the truth and he would do so.

~

"I should have known," Griffin snarled at Thurlow the moment Renegar appeared with him and Wylend.

"Do you think that our long feud does not make me ashamed now?" Thurlow's face bore lines of sorrow, something unusual for even the lowest in the Hierarchy of gods.

"Nothing has changed for me," Griffin hissed.

"Tell me you did not flout the rules," Thurlow said. "Even now, you do not admit it. It makes that fact no less true."

"Tell me you did not interfere," Griffin retorted.

"I did. I say this freely. I am still paying for my interference. It is why I am a prisoner here and also why they have brought you to hear my confession."

"What confession? That you admit to harming me whenever possible? That you admit you left Lissa in an untenable situation and almost let her die? That you allowed her mother to die in a horrible way? Is that what you're going to admit?"

"I admit those things. I wanted to retaliate against your willfulness, and the secrecy you employed to do as you wanted. But that is not what I must confess now, nor the reason I have been placed here, under the watchful eye of the Mighty Hand."

"Then say it and be done. I'd rather take a beating than stay here and listen to you prattle," Griffin snarled.

"You will never let this go, I see that now," Thurlow said sadly. "I am sorry—for all those things. Very sorry. Do you think I do not feel guilt whenever Lissa looks at me with love in her eyes? I do. I am responsible for so many things that should have been done better—or not done at all."

"Then tell me."

"Very well. I knew you were planning something, so I followed you when you traveled into the future on a particular day. You walked into a bar and chose your target." Thurlow shook his head. "I should have left you to your tryst. I thought that's all it was at the time."

Thurlow drew a painful breath. "I was wrong," he said. "I watched you buy a drink for your target, and talk to her. You waited patiently for her to visit the toilet. That is when I interfered. I appeared to her and told her to leave. I chose another woman to go back to you. Changed her scent and appearance so she'd seem the same, and sent her out to find you."

"You interfered with that. No wonder a child came of that coupling," Griffin muttered angrily.

"I sincerely regret my actions on that day. Had I not interfered as I did, Breanne would have had a much better life. She would have been raised as a strong, competent woman who could easily accept the role she was born to have."

"You screwed both of us, then," Griffin accused, his hazel eyes flashing red. The vampire remained in him, it was merely kept hidden most of the time.

"You did not intend that she live," Thurlow pointed out. "You *Looked* to see that the woman you'd chosen would have the child aborted. You did not know that other powers were at work that would change that history. None of us did."

"Why are you telling me this? The Larentii have their Vhanaraszh now. Let them heal her."

"You still do not understand," Thurlow said. "Breanne is the Mighty Heart."

"You're joking," Griffin accused.

"No, he's not," Ashe strode into the room. "I've worked with her recently. There's no doubt of what she is. Between the two of you, however, you've managed to cripple her. Make her fragile. She should be strong and confident, yet I see that she isn't. Have you not read that worthless book?"

"What worthless book?" Griffin turned to Ashe.

"This worthless book." Ashe *Pulled* a copy of *Torture in Texas* into his hand and tossed it to Griffin. "That's your daughter on the cover— at age fourteen. Thanks to Thurlow, there, she was tortured when she was a child."

"That is not all I have to say, nor the real reason I am a prisoner, now," Thurlow hung his head. "Once I learned the woman was pregnant, I placed a mark upon the child in her belly."

"Not the first time you've done that, either," Griffin pointed out maliciously.

"No. But you know that a power mark cannot be removed, once placed. I can find the Mighty Heart, no matter where she is, because of that. I place her in danger, by merely existing. The one who should be hidden from all is visible to me."

"We believe the power mark enabled Breanne to stay alive when she was younger," The Ear spoke. "That does not mitigate the harm done by the interference. We are not pleased."

"I understand," Thurlow bowed respectfully to The Ear before turning back to Griffin.

"I am sorry for my part in all of this. For my interference. For the retaliation, as I wished to punish you in subtle ways. As you see, I managed to harm the innocent more than I ever harmed you. That is my failing. Perhaps I will be given a task in the future, to atone for these wrongs."

"You think a task will make me forgive you?" Griffin exploded. "No. I will never forgive this."

"It's not about you anymore," Ashe pointed out. "So don't try to make this about you. This is about keeping everything safe from now on. Neither you nor your father will ever be able to release the information given to you this day. I command it." Ashe's eyes went a deep blue and stars fell through their depths.

"It would be wise to remember that you are not one of the truly powerful," The Ear glared at Griffin. "Except for your father, you are the weakest one here." The Ear disappeared swiftly.

"Ren, take them home," Ashe sighed. "I doubt he'll ever be sorry for his part in this," he jerked his head at Griffin.

~

Breanne's Journal

What metal there'd been in the church had been reduced to a twisted, melted ruin. The rest was ash, most of it fine and stirring in the early-morning breeze.

None of us had slept, although Hank had pulled me into bed and settled my head on his shoulder. For two hours we'd lain together like that, neither of us speaking, his hand gently stroking my face and hair.

We'd gone to the church destroyed in Abilene, Texas, because it was the closest one. It didn't matter, really, which one we visited—they all looked much the same. A pile of rubble lay in each of the fifty states and the nation was in mourning.

Many were calling this an elaborate terrorist attack, and in a way, they were right. These acts were meant to instill terror, worldwide. I worried that churches in other countries might be hit as well, but kept those thoughts to myself. Bill was probably ahead of me on that, and I didn't want to ramp up his concern.

"All I can smell is burning and death," Hank sighed and shook his head at Bill, who looked exhausted. I couldn't see that things would improve for him soon, either, since nobody had any idea where to start looking for the perpetrators, or how they might be taken down, considering how many we might be dealing with.

"I think they were transported in and out," I said, hunching my shoulders. "I've been around the perimeter twice, and can't smell anything other than humans."

"I've gotten reports that some of the bodies were decapitated before the church was burned," Bill held up his cell. He was getting constant messages, keeping him in the loop, but it was overwhelming him. I figured there were plenty of others feeling just the same.

"That spells vampires to me," Charles said.

"Yeah," I nodded to him. "Bill, did they say the slices were smooth?" Yes, that was a morbid thing to say, but a vampire's claws will deliver the cleanest of cuts in a beheading.

"As nearly as they can tell with charred flesh, yes," Bill nodded.

"So that's why they waited for the evening services," I said.

"You're probably right about that," Hank agreed.

"We may be dealing with Saxom and his brood again," Charles suggested.

"Oh, dear God," Bill's shoulders drooped. "We don't need Xenides again. Or any of the others. They can mist. Mindspeak. Some of them are shapeshifters."

"This is so wrong," I muttered.

"There's something else, too," Bill said, shaking his head after reading another message on his cellphone.

"What's that?" Winkler asked. He, Weldon and Trajan had come with us; they'd sniffed farther afield than I had, and hadn't found anything either.

"Hank, your club was destroyed last night," Bill showed Hank an image on his cell. "With everything else going on, it was shoved to the side. Fire Chief in San Francisco thought to send it to me this morning."

"How many dead?" Hank lifted the cellphone from Bill's hand and stared at the photograph.

"Nineteen—it was a slow night," Bill sighed.

"It's my guess Janine saw you go into KingDom's just before it blew," I told Hank. "Nobody's found her, have they?"

"No," Bill said.

"She's with them. The ones who did this," I swept out a hand, indicating piles of black ash and twisted metal. "She's still getting back at us—at you," I pointed at Hank. "She took Jayson down, now she's treating you to the same. The trouble with this, however, is that innocent people are now dying because of her."

Hank blew a smoky breath before hauling out his cell and calling Terry. Did I know he'd hired my attorney? Not until then.

"Terry, I need you to handle the insurance and anything else for the club," Hank said.

"Already on it," Terry replied—I could hear his voice clearly. "I contacted the insurance company this morning, and I'll coordinate with the police as your representative. I already have the information from Director Jennings, saying you were with him and had nothing to do with this."

"Damn straight I had nothing to do with it," more smoke ensued. "Was Trey at work when this happened?"

"No. The two new hires were—Trey had the night off. I talked to him—he's pretty upset."

"Tell Trey we'll work this out. Tell him not to worry about his paycheck, all right?"

"I already did," Terry said. "Want me to arrange for cleanup after the investigators are done with it?"

"Yeah. Sell the property, too, afterward. I'll move the club somewhere else. It never had enough parking, anyway."

"I'll need Breanne's signature on some of the paperwork."

"I'll get that for you. Thanks, Terry. Let me know if you need anything else." Hank ended the call, his eyes dark pools of anger. Well, he wasn't alone in the anger department. Janine had signed her own death warrant, as far as I was concerned.

∼

Lissa's Journal

"Cara, I don't know what to do." I blinked at Gavin, who settled on a chair beside my desk and blinked dark, troubled eyes at me.

"He's gone, Gavin," I said. "There's nothing we can do about it."

"No, my love. It's not just our son. I have memories that I did not have before. They keep filtering into my mind, as if they are being written into the past. There is no conclusion as yet, and it worries me greatly."

"Oh, no." I chewed my lower lip as I studied Gavin's face. Normally, he didn't display so much emotion. He looked gray. Worn. More than troubled. Sadness overlaid all those things, and my heart bled for him. "What are you remembering, honey?"

"I met Breanne in the past. Acted, in part, as her surrogate sire. How foolish I was, back then," Gavin shook his head.

"What?" I was on my feet immediately. "You didn't mistreat her again, did you?"

"No." He almost shouted the word. "No," he said again, more quietly. "I gave her free rein, as much as I could, and I cannot explain that at this time. I have no explanation for it, actually. Back then, I was just as strict at following protocol as I ever was."

"You think she had anything to do with that?" I asked, doing my best to regulate my heart rate and breathing.

"I do not feel this is true, but I cannot fathom how it might have been otherwise."

"Gavin, I don't know what to say. Maybe you ought to tell me what has happened so far."

"It began like this," Gavin said. "A vehicle drove past Winkler's home in the Dallas area. The tag was eventually tracked, and we learned it was registered to Saxom Meletius."

My breath stopped.

CHAPTER 17

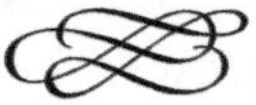

"Yeah, we're getting the same thing." Kiarra stood beside the kitchen island Adam built for her inside their NorthStar home. "It's like a television series, where you get bits and pieces as they happen in the past. Nobody knows what's really going on or what the outcome might be."

I watched as she nervously pushed long, white-blonde hair over a shoulder. "You mean you're getting the changes to your memories, like an updated script?" I asked. "That's not fucked up or anything."

"It means the enemy is fucking with the timeline," Merrill walked in and went straight to the coffee machine. That's what he did when he was worried. Actually, it's what he did anyway. He was addicted to coffee. Loved it. Drank several cups a day, and being what he was, it never bothered him a bit.

"Of all the people to pull away from death," Kiarra muttered, her arms hugging her waist. She meant Saxom. I knew that without asking.

"Darling, none of that," Merrill pulled her against him while the brewer worked on his fresh coffee.

"I worried about the memory of a report that inserted itself into my head this morning, of churches blowing up in all fifty states in the past," I said. "So when Gavin came and told me what was happening with him at that time, I just about freaked."

"Breanne is there, isn't she?" Adam walked in and nodded to me—he'd heard our conversation from down the hall.

"Gavin says she is."

"I thought it was bad enough when the army of rogue gods was destroyed," Kiarra sighed. Merrill pulled a barstool out for her and lifted her onto it gently. "All of us were holding our breaths, and at the time, we didn't even know why."

"Belen talked to you, didn't he?" I asked.

"Yes. We know about Breanne now, but we, Dragon, Grace, Devin and Conner are the only ones who know, besides some of the Larentii."

"I think the rogues are still trying to kill her, or maybe some others, to alter things in their favor," I said. "And that's terrifying."

"Lissa, we know about Gavril. Conner told us." Merrill came to me, now, while Adam moved to Kiarra's side.

"Merrill," I moaned. "How did things come to this? How?"

"Hush, my darling," he soothed as he pulled me against him.

Breanne's Journal

Just as I suspected, people across the country rose up in anger, saying they weren't going to allow anyone to steal their religion. Even the ones who hadn't been terribly religious before were up in arms. Flowers were appearing at churches everywhere, and not just at the ones destroyed.

Television talk shows were filled, not just with stories of the destruction and names of lives lost, but with declarations from those willing to "go to war," as they put it, to take down any and all responsible.

Yes, foreign countries and foreign terrorists were blamed, when they had nothing to do with it. Unless a Sirenali told them to, that is. As for going to war, the people spouting those words didn't have a chance. This Sirenali had vampires, chimeras, possibly more lion snake shapeshifters and who knew what else to fight his or her battles. Short of destroying Earth and making it uninhabitable for our unwelcome visitors, there might not be any way to get rid of all of them.

That's where I came in, I suppose. Sure, I'd gotten rid of half a million rogue gods, give or take a few, but I'd tricked them. I hadn't stood my ground to fight them, and this looked like a pitched battle. If more rogue gods were ultimately behind this mess (and let's face it, attacking the religious base would be right up their alley), then things might turn out badly for me.

"We have to find them," I said, startling everybody inside the media room. We'd gathered there to watch the televised reports, but I'd remained silent while the others pointed out flaws and ridiculed this pundit or that, for devising outrageous plans to defeat an enemy they knew nothing about.

"Bree, they're as insubstantial as smoke. If you can't find them, what do you think we mortals might do?" Opal asked.

"No idea." My neck and shoulders ached from the buildup of tension. I hadn't felt like eating anything, and lunch had come and gone long ago. Jimmy kept Kathleen consoled and fed everybody else —he was keeping busy and still grieving his loss, just not as much as before. A last conversation with Trina had done wonders for him.

"Let's go look at Hank's club," Bill stood and stretched. "I don't have to be at that meeting for another four hours."

"All right," I agreed. "Do the locals have it blocked off?"

"Yes. And we can grab something to eat there if you want."

"Maybe. Everybody ready to go, or do you want to grab a jacket? It'll be cool," I said. "I know I want one."

A flurry of movement occurred as everybody (except Gavin) rushed toward bedrooms to grab something to wear over shirts, jeans and slacks. In ten minutes, I folded them to San Francisco, leaving Trace behind to help Jimmy and to guard my sleeping sire.

~

"Is that him?" V'ili asked Janine. He gave her a sharp-toothed grin—he'd estimated that the missing owner would show up. He'd been so sure of it, in fact, that he'd set up hidden cameras across the street. He and Janine watched a live feed from those cameras now.

"Yes," Janine's head bobbed, much like that of a dashboard dog. She bore cuts and bruises from V'ili's attention the night before. He'd shown her a bit of what he was capable of doing. Today, she was barely able to walk and still stared at her master as if he were everything to her.

She hadn't understood what he might do to her—that her will would be eliminated completely and that he would demand things from her that she was too timid to do in her normal, human state.

None had ever defied V'ili. He held strong obsession, and even other Sirenali bowed to him. Last prince of a royal house before the fall of Sirena, he was determined to restore his race. He cursed the Larentii, too, who'd destroyed his world to begin with.

It didn't matter that the Sirenali had invaded the Larentii homeworld and attempted to destroy it. While they might breach the shields around the planet, they couldn't lay an obsession on even the youngest Larentii. They hadn't fully realized that until after the attack.

In the only known episode of Larentii violence, the Larentii Wise Ones, with the aid of many other Larentii, had gathered their power and destroyed not only the Sirenali attacking their world, but the entire planet of Sirena.

For whatever reason, a few with power had bent time to collect many of the strongest from V'ili's race before their deaths, and now they served those who'd rescued them, but were given a free rein and a promise that their world would live again. After the others had been destroyed, of course. V'ili looked forward to the destruction.

"My cousin is there," V'ili's grin became toothier. "He will make sure that Mr. Bell and his friends never trouble us again."

Breanne's Journal

The club was a wreck. It had burned, as had the businesses on both sides of it. The chimera hadn't cared about what might be destroyed past that, so anything farther away was damaged but not harmed beyond repair.

Just like the churches, it bore little evidence, and that had already been collected. I doubted anyone would get anything useful from any of it. The safe, however, had somehow survived, as Hank had installed it below the floor. The police had already removed it and taken it away after Terry told them where to look.

"Unbelievable," Jayson shook his head as we stared at the wreckage.

"Can you spare some change?" A man dressed in patched clothing approached. I watched him warily, but Hank was the one to go Thifilathi and grasp the Sirenali by the throat. Bill shouted for everybody to get back as the man turned into a scaled monster who struggled to bite the hand gripping his throat. We all watched as the Sirenali kicked and flailed before going still.

Hank had crushed his throat. Yes, I read him before he died. I couldn't get to his obsessions—those were always blocked. I saw he had Sirenali friends, however, and that definitely wasn't a good thing.

Janine was terrified. She'd seen Hank become something she didn't recognize. If she could get her mind to work on its own (she couldn't) she might have guessed that he was a demon. Instead, she turned a blank gaze to V'ili.

"High Demon," V'ili said, before cursing in his native language. This was the one other race the Sirenali feared. They couldn't place obsession and they couldn't defeat them. Had the High Demons policed the dark realm as intended, the Sirenali would never have approached the Larentii homeworld. They'd fallen lax after Kifirin's disappearance, and the Sirenali did as they pleased. They'd paid for their greed, however, and their desire to control Larentii. "I will see that this one dies," V'ili hissed and sent mindspeech to Acrimus.

~

"He wanted to place obsession on all of us," I said. Hank pushed a plate of cheese, grapes and melon in my direction. I'd hauled everybody to my house in San Rafael after Bill's locals came to collect the Sirenali's body for study. "And there are four more here," I said. Hank, Opal and Trajan set about making sandwiches for the others after a quick trip to the nearest grocery store.

"So there were five," Bill shook his head. "Instead of just one."

"They could all have different assignments, and be screwing all of us," Jayson said.

"Jayson, you just gave me a headache," Weldon growled.

"Regardless, he's right," Bill agreed. "We have four more targets to worry about, and that doesn't include all the fire-breathing things and the poisonous things."

"What are we going to do?" I moaned. If Hank hadn't jumped the Sirenali, he might have placed obsession before I bothered to lower my shield and read him. I'd have to lower my shields and go back to reading everybody, as much as I hated doing that. I shuddered at the thought of it.

"Baby?" Hank set a sandwich in front of Winkler and walked around the kitchen island to get to me.

"I'll have to read everybody from now on," I hid my face in shaking hands.

"No," he pulled my head against his chest and rubbed my back gently. "Just for a little while, I think. We'll get through this."

"I sure hope you're right," I said.

~

Hank took Bill to his meeting, with Jayson, Winkler and Opal going along as bodyguards. At least I knew Hank would recognize a Sirenali if he saw one, and knew what to do to keep him from talking to lay an obsession.

Charles and Trajan stayed to guard me, Kathleen and Weldon, so Trace and Jimmy could get some sleep. They'd have to rise during the night and take over guard duty for the rest of us.

"You need to sleep," Charles said. He'd herded me into the bedroom I shared with Hank, and settled in beside me so I could lean against him.

"Yeah. I feel tired and wound up at the same time."

"I hate that," he leaned in to kiss me. "Close your eyes. I'm right here."

~

"Asleep?" Gavin asked as Charles closed the bedroom door softly behind him.

"Yes. Finally."

"Shall we discuss what happened today while I slept?"

"Of course."

~

"Thorsten?" Kiarra looked up from her tablet—she'd been keeping up with current news on the church bombings that way. Fresno was hot this time of year and she really wasn't in the mood for an unannounced visit from Thorsten.

"What is this I hear about Saxom's return? I thought Adam killed him. Yet you did not see fit to inform me of this?"

"Thorsten, we think it may be a prank, but I'll admit, I can't find anything by *Looking*, and you understand how unusual that is."

"Where did you get this information?"

"From the Vampire Council. It came from a U.S. security agency before that. They found a suspicious vehicle, with the license plate registered to Saxom Meletius."

"Then it likely is a prank," Thorsten muttered. "Although it does seem suspicious that the name was available. Was other information gathered?"

"They found nothing. The records have been wiped, if they ever existed at all."

"Highly irregular. Perhaps I will investigate this myself."

"Go ahead," Kiarra shrugged.

"You merely tolerate me, don't you?" Thorsten's voice was cold.

"I think you are a little too involved with some things," Kiarra said.

"By that you mean?"

"That it's your job to supervise," she said. "You are to report to your superior if you find wrongdoing."

"It is not my job, as you describe it, to hand out punishment?"

"That's what I was told. That you would monitor our work and report to those above you. A decision would be made at that level."

"You're accusing me of interfering?"

"I never said that," Kiarra closed the cover on her tablet with a sigh. "I'm sorry. I'm just upset that all these murders have happened, and we can't do anything about it."

"It would be interference," Thorsten replied haughtily.

"Exactly," Kiarra replied. She watched as Thorsten disappeared. "Exactly," she repeated to the empty space he'd occupied.

Breanne's Journal

"Now what?" I stared at the television in disgust. The new church built near Winkler's house between Dallas and Denton was advertising.

"You're safe here," the paid actor announced. The commercial had been filmed in the church's parking lot, as the actor waved a hand grandly toward the huge, modern building. "We built this to be fireproof, and we'll have armed guards stationed everywhere, to protect you while you pray to the true God."

The commercial cut to the huge, LED sign that flashed *The Church of the True God*, interspersed with images of people singing and a Christian rock band playing. "Come on in Wednesday night for our grand opening, and get treated to great music. Bring your friends, too! We guarantee you'll be safe while you worship with us."

"Well, that's timely," Winkler said sarcastically. "No time like the present to take advantage of frightened people and pull them away from their regular churches."

"How many do you think that place might hold?" Bill frowned at the screen.

"Probably several thousand, easy," Weldon observed.

"There's a new development, too," Bill announced.

"What's that?"

"There have been disappearances in the homeless population around Dallas," he said. "No idea if those disappearances are connected with the ones we're hunting, but there it is. I just got this through the Dallas office. It's not our problem—locals are supposed to take care of it, but it finally got severe enough that they asked us if we knew anything."

"Any bodies?" Winkler asked, walking over to read the message Bill received on his cellphone.

"None yet," Bill said. "But we know there are chimeras out there that might be hungry after a long night of work, destroying churches."

"So there wouldn't be any bodies," I said, shaking my head. "Is there a particular place they're disappearing? How many are missing?"

"There's no good way to tell," Bill said, tapping a message on his cell. "I'm asking the department to search for more people missing across the country. It may not be exclusive to the Dallas area."

"There's a scary thought," Winkler said.

"It makes sense—we already know they've been transported from one place to another—quickly and easily," Hank pointed out.

"Yep," Bill nodded after getting an answer to his question. "They're disappearing in New York, San Francisco, Chicago and Atlanta, and that's just a preliminary report."

"So the major metropolitan areas are getting hit," Winkler frowned. "Where the homeless populations are larger."

"Like a buffet," Charles said. "I've heard of rogue vamps hitting the same areas in the past—nobody notices if a homeless person comes up missing now and then."

"And we know they have vampires, too," Gavin said. Well, he and Charles had discussed this. They would—vampire rogues were Gavin's business, after all.

"Want to go take a look at some of the hangouts?" Bill asked.

"As long as they don't blow up around us," I agreed.

"Locals have taken to patrolling the area—haven't seen anything like that yet," Bill said. "If you're ready?"

"Yeah. Let's go."

Thorsten settled on the driveway of a burned house in San Rafael. This was the last known location for the vehicle registered to Saxom Meletius. Why it had traveled from the Dallas area to the San Francisco area puzzled him, but there were many things that puzzled him about this.

Kiarra had *Looked*, she'd said. He merely believed this beneath her abilities. He couldn't reach the underlying cause or any other information associated with this. That angered him greatly. Griffin was the most adept of the Saa Thalarr at *Looking*, although he was now retired. It didn't matter—Thorsten wouldn't ask Griffin for assistance if he were the last possible resort. They'd been enemies too long for that to happen.

The day he'd convinced Belen to demote Griffin to Third and place Kiarra as First was the finest day in his tenure as supervisor for the Saa Thalarr. He'd gone looking for other ways to make Griffin suffer throughout their long association, too. He'd found a few things that he'd never carried to his supervisor.

"It doesn't matter, this is a dead end," Thorsten muttered, gazing at the burned ruin before him. He prepared to fold away when something powerful sucked him into a vortex from which he couldn't escape. He screamed a mental plea for help before his voice was shielded and silenced in mid-shout.

$$\backsim$$

Lissa's Journal

Time is an ephemeral thing to the most powerful. They see it as a road that leads in both directions, and they stand at the center, looking at it both ways. That's how the news came to Belen, from those far above him. They'd seen Thorsten being taken, because someone was watching.

"They didn't know of my abduction before, because I didn't have time to call out," Belen said. "Thorsten did call out, and he was heard. He has been taken in the past, Lissa, and this could prove more dangerous than anyone might imagine."

"How's that?" I blinked at him. Thorsten was a low-level member of the Powers That Be. When he'd been taken, he'd still been supervisor for the Saa Thalarr. He'd screwed up my life, that was certain, but he was Thurlow, now, and one of my mates.

Of course I was worried, but things would turn out, right? I mean, he had other things to do and then would be sent back to the beginning, to learn his lessons and start over—with me.

"At the time he was taken, he was still missing vital information. If they strip him of what he knows, however, he could become very dangerous—to your sister."

"What are you talking about?" I stared at Belen in alarm.

"We must visit Thurlow where he is now. Let us hope he does not disappear."

"But," my word was whispered. If he disappeared, that would mean, "Oh, no," I said. "No, no, no, Belen. No."

"If he is turned rogue or tormented enough to do the unthinkable," Belen muttered grimly. "Come. We will speak with your mate."

～

Breanne's Journal

Reading the homeless in Dallas was heartbreaking. None of them recalled seeing anything, however, so the ones taken had been abducted by stealth. "There is vampire scent here," Gavin stated, standing next to a pitiful pile of clothing that the others hadn't thought to take as yet.

"Fresh?" Winkler came to sniff, too.

"No. I'd say two days, perhaps."

"I agree," Winkler's nose was as good as Gavin's.

"At least there's no scent of a chimera," I said, rubbing Bill's back absently.

"Breanne, I'll give you exactly one hour to stop that," Bill grinned.

"I can do your shoulders when we get back," I offered. Bill's muscles were tight, and I knew they had to ache from stress and tension.

"I'll take you up on that," he said.

～

Lissa's Journal

"Thurlow?" I stared at him in shock. He'd known that Breanne was my sister, and he'd purposely stayed away from her when she'd been brought to Le-Ath Veronis. He'd allowed her to be abused, when he knew it was happening. All because he didn't want to be found out or called to task or be what he was now—a prisoner at SouthStar.

"I have new memories, Lissa," he wept. "They're torturing me."

"Where the hell did they take you?" I demanded.

"No!" he cried out. "No! Griffin. Griffin," he fell to his knees. They were tearing at his corporeal body; I could feel it. Belen had never developed corporeality, and only took on the similarity of it from time to time. That's why torture would have been worthless with him. With Thorsten, it was a different story.

"They've gotten a name," Belen snapped. "Where, Thurlow? Where are you?"

"Earth," he began to disappear. Images filtered into Belen's and my mind as he faded away completely.

"Fuck," I yelled before bending time and folding space.

~

Griffin lounged on the patio of Merrill's home in Kent, sipping tea and studying the lists of vintage wines offered at an auction. He and Merrill would go together, and he would begin the bidding on the best bottles, after which Merrill would take over and eventually make the purchase.

Griffin couldn't come out and tell Merrill which wines to buy, or which stocks to purchase, but he could buy for himself and leave information out for Merrill to find. Merrill had benefited greatly from his friendship with Griffin. It assuaged Griffin's guilt over other things.

"Griffin?" Amara walked out of the house. "Merrill's here."

"Good," Griffin smiled at his mate and rose. Amara screamed when Griffin was torn away with a shout.

~

Breanne's Journal

I knew. Yes, I knew. Would I have done what I did, if I didn't know it would change so much? I don't have an answer for that. Might never have an answer for that. Hank, Bill, Trajan and Jayson shouted my name the moment I disappeared.

By the time I folded to The Church of the True God, Acrimus had already broken Thorsten and killed my father.

"Here's the daughter," Acrimus observed maliciously. Could I read him? Oh, yes. He thought I was a powerful child of the first member of the Saa Thalarr. How thankful was I for that—that this was all he thought he knew? He intended to kill me for it, regardless.

"You shouldn't have come—I'd have let you live," Acrimus meant to smile—it was the most awkward grimace instead. "I like twisted victims," he added. Someday, I intended to slap James Rome, Sr. and Ross Gideon into a wall for that stupid fucking book. If I survived the next few minutes, that is.

I couldn't waste time—Acrimus was prepared for a throw-down, and I had to change a few things, first. Giving Acrimus, who'd once been one of the Ko'Ahmari, a real smile, I turned on the brightest light I could and *Changed What Was*.

CHAPTER 18

reanne's Journal

Griffin coughed and struggled to his feet while I stood guard over his body. Thorsten, surprised to be whole and free again, wasted no time folding space to get away. Well, a lot of people wouldn't have stayed, either. I wasn't sure I could blame him—I'd been tortured enough in the past to know that I'd have escaped if given the chance.

"Who?" Griffin was on his feet now.

"No time for that," I said through gritted teeth. Acrimus knew, now. Knew not only who I was, but what I was. I'd done the impossible and brought two powerful beings back to life.

I wasn't sure all the Larentii Wise Ones could have done one of those things, let alone two. Without explanation, I pulled Griffin into a slingshot of power and flung him as far away as I could.

Acrimus was beneath me in power, although he was more than powerful. So many things I understood about him as he sized me up. Too bad the Mighty Mind wasn't with me at that moment; he'd have advised me to do away with Acrimus immediately. Instead, I waited for him to make the first move.

Big mistake.

Yes, all sorts of information bubbled into my brain. Acrimus was aptly named. He was bitter. Angry that he wasn't better known or loved by all. He it was who'd breathed the beginnings of Solar Red and many other, angry, abusive and destructive religions into so many mortal minds. He'd nurtured them. Fed them until they'd turned as harmful as it was possible to turn.

Perhaps it was a good thing that I didn't have enough time, then, to set up a gate to the proper timeline and attempt to shove Acrimus through it, because *HE* came.

Glowing with a malevolent purple light, he appeared between me and Acrimus. Was he interested in saving Acrimus from me?

No.

He had no care for Acrimus, which was completely ironic.

What did he want?

Everything.

Just as Hank said.

"Well, well," he said, and the floor rumbled and shook with his voice. Acrimus cringed. Ironic, indeed.

Here was the one who directed rogue gods. Who accepted their worship and controlled their deeds. He'd promised them everything, if they gained it first and then handed it to him.

He was called many things. The General was the least offensive of his titles. To me, anyway. I certainly wasn't going to say any of the titles he preferred. He'd done nothing to earn any of them.

"Acrimus, you unfathomable difik," I hissed as the General struck his first blow.

~

Lissa's Journal

"Where is she?" I shouted at so many people, some of whom I recognized, some I didn't.

"What the hell?" Weldon Harper was the one to find his voice first. They all thought me dead. They were learning differently, at least for the moment.

I didn't have time to dwell on the lack of recognition in Gavin's eyes. Somebody else would have to fix this after the fact—I had to find my sister.

"Griffin and Thorsten have escaped," Belen appeared at my side, shining so brightly those around me covered their eyes. Except for one.

Dark-haired, black-eyed and wearing the beauty of a god, he stood, unblinking, and took us in. Something strange happened, then. Belen went to a knee and bowed his head. "Command me," he said.

"There's no time for that—what do you know?" the dark-haired man shouted.

"Wait," I held up a hand and sent mindspeech to Thurlow. Like a miracle, he answered.

The Church of the True God, he replied, urgency in his mental voice. Directions were given as well, which were passed to Belen. Somehow, the dark-haired man pulled those words and images straight from me as they flowed between my mind and Belen's.

Come, he said and hurled us toward our target. I heard the call he sent out, too. To the Mighty Hand and the Mighty Mind. Would we arrive in time? There wasn't any way I could fight what we might face. Belen, too, held insufficient power. My sister could be dying, and none of us might stop it.

Breanne's Journal

Did he think I hadn't been beaten before? That I hadn't stood again every time, my body refusing to die when it should have—for so many years?

Blood blurred my vision as he landed another powerful punch to my chest. No, he didn't touch my body directly—he settled for sending power in my direction, which manifested in blows I couldn't return.

I'd tried to walk forward at first, and was knocked back too many times.

Then I attempted to hold my ground. Foolish, I know. I was thrown back, time and again.

After that, I struggled to stand, and the blows landed until I was knocked to my knees. He laughed exultantly when that happened. "Where are the others?" he crowed. "Did they send you to challenge me? This is so easy," he carelessly landed another blow to my head. I felt my jaw break as he prepared another strike.

"Avilepha!" Hank's voice—from nearby. What was he doing here? He needed to be far, far away from this. I wasn't sure all of us together —the Three—could take down this monster. He'd grown too powerful and continued to gain power. Hank had no chance against this.

My arms wrapped around myself as another blow landed, breaking ribs and my collarbone. When the next blow landed against my face, I dreamt that the stars I saw fell around me instead of behind my eyes, and the scream that sounded came from my attacker instead of my own throat.

There. I stood over my humanoid body, staring at it. It looked so frail, huddled as it was on the floor. Bruised. Bloody. *Dead*. I felt nothing as stars continued to fall.

The End